The Radio

M. JONATHAN LEE

Matador
9 Priory Business Park
Kibworth Beauchamp
Leicestershire LE8 0RX, UK
Tel: (+44) 116 279 2299
Fax: (+44) 116 279 2277
Email: books@troubador.co.uk
Web: www.troubador.co.uk/matador

ISBN 978 1780885 315

British Library Cataloguing in Publication Data.
A catalogue record for this book is available from the British Library.

Typeset in Aldine401 BT Roman by Troubador Publishing Ltd
Printed and bound in the UK by TJ International, Padstow, Cornwall

Matador is an imprint of Troubador Publishing Ltd

For Simon

Wish you were here to see this, bro

and

For Alexandra, James and Annabel

Who make me feel amounts of love that I didn't
think possible

Acknowledgements

Thanks to the following people who have either inspired me, helped me become a better person or simply made me laugh 'til I cried: Mum and Dad, Lucy Nunns, Nikky (like Fred Astaire) Evans, Arry Balachandran, Jonathan Kirby, Scott Griffiths, Matthew Nunns, Andrew McMahon, Paul Woodward, Ryan Woodward, Craig Wassell, Janet Chappell, Graham Skinner, Brian Wilson, Ali Shankland, Chris Simmons, Mark Tighe, Richard Pierce, Aaron Powell, Craig Finn, Ian Millthorpe, Danny McNamara, Dave (Mr) Gibson, Laurence O'Bryan, Adam Duritz, Benjamin Scott Folds, Frank Turner, Stephen Lee, Stephen King, Damien Echols, Peter Allen and Paul Carter. There will be some who I have missed, you already know who you are.

I am eternally grateful for the advice and input from: My editor, Charlie Wilson who never once got irritated by my constant amendments. Sarah Taylor, Jennifer Liptrot and everyone at my publishers, Troubador. The judges of The Novel Prize for New Authors 2012. Stephen Lee and Matt Niblock for their artistic flair. Chris Hemingway at littleblackbox. My distributors at Orca.

You all own a tiny part of this book.

And if all you ever do with your life
is just photosynthesize
then you'll deserve every hour
of your sleepless nights
that you waste wondering when
you're gonna die.

– Frank Turner

Get up
get down
and
get outside
        – *Frank Turner*

one

Foraging, George had called it, foraging. Sheila suspected that George had come up with the idea following their regular lunchtime appointment with *Cash in the Attic*. She had definitely noticed some kind of glint in his eyes as he bit slowly into his egg and cress sandwich. His brain had almost audibly whirred, then he had risen quickly and with intent and announced he was going to forage.

Sheila had found this most unusual for a number of reasons.

Firstly, since his retirement a few months earlier, George had loved tuning into the programme where hopeful participants, seeking to raise some much needed money, clear out their lofts and auction off what they find, and usually he wouldn't miss a second. She recalled he had held his bladder on several occasions so as not to miss the television presenter announce the final amount raised.

Secondly, she couldn't remember the last time George had done anything quickly. Actually, this wasn't quite true, she *could* remember a time; but since George had lost interest altogether, quickness had been replaced by flaccidity. Come to think of it, she couldn't ever remember George doing anything with intent either.

Thirdly, they didn't have an attic. The room that used to be an attic had been converted into a bedroom for Mollie about six years ago. The likelihood of finding some rare heirloom in a room that had been in existence for less than a decade was more than remote.

She sighed quietly to herself and wondered whether he was feeling all right.

George slowly reached the top of the staircase and sat on the end of Mollie's bed. He had noticed that it was getting more and more difficult to make the climb to the top of the house nowadays. He stared down and clasped his hands around his waistline and sighed. The button which fastened his bottle green cords together seemed to be having its own difficulty in staying attached. He paused for a

1

moment and decided to lie down to gather his thoughts. The room was decorated in a garish pink and gold colour scheme, which made George wonder how Mollie slept. Actually, it wasn't pink, he remembered, it was raspberry. Yes, raspberry; both Sam and Sheila had been quick to point that out to him whilst he decorated. He wondered why paint colours nowadays were named after foods: raspberry, clotted cream, biscuit, melon sorbet, lemon pie – it was all much too confusing. It was also much too bright. Perhaps a nice cream with light brown woodwork would have been more suitable and would help Mollie to sleep better. With this colour scheme, it was no wonder that a few years earlier she had cried whenever she stayed over.

With foods and colours spinning round his head George closed his eyes, just for a second.

Sheila busied herself in the kitchen clearing away the lunchtime dishes. Glancing at her watch, she was startled to find that she only had three quarters of an hour before Sam would be arriving to go shopping. She rummaged around in the bottom of her handbag, retrieving and then hurriedly applying all manner of concealers, eyeliner, foundation, lipstick and mascara. Carefully eyeing the lines on her face, she agreed with the mirror that without the products she would look every one of her sixty-two years. She quickly pulled a brush through her faux black hair before forcing it into position (and submission) with half a can of hairspray. The kitchen clock gave her permission to hurry upstairs to change her blouse. It would be the tight black D&G one today, she decided.

George had no idea how long he had been asleep. Slowly, he opened his eyes, allowing them to adjust to the bright gold coving immediately above his head, and checked his watch. It appeared he had been asleep for close to an hour. He couldn't be absolutely precise, because he was unsure whether he had left *Cash in the Attic* before or after the auction took place.

Adjusting his glasses (which had somehow remained over his left eye but meandered down to his right cheek), he rose and made his way to the small cupboard door that led into the eaves. He flicked on the light and crawled on his hands and knees into the smallness. He wasn't entirely sure what he was doing there, but it was quiet and pleasantly warm.

After a few seconds George began to slowly lift lids off the neatly labelled boxes he had placed there a few years earlier. Most of the boxes contained family photographs and pictures from times gone by. There were pictures of Sheila and Sam beaming by the pool or on the beach. Adam winning his first football medal. Mollie asleep in a Moses basket. There weren't so many of George, and the ones he did find were always, well, "doing" pictures. It seemed he had spent a large proportion of his life smiling inanely with a paintbrush in his hand or up a ladder or fixing a fence or mowing the lawn.

He continued through the boxes, wondering why he was bothering to open them. Each box was clearly labelled on the outside as to its cargo and the boxes had not been moved, to the best of his knowledge, since he put them there, so there was no real need to look inside.

The following box was simply labelled "Oddments". Hmm, George thought, now this one sounds intriguing.

Removing the lid, George delved inside the box. Staring directly at him was a plastic doll adorned in full Flamenco dress, complete with maracas and a convenient display stand. He couldn't place this, but suspected that it must have been from one of their many trips to Majorca when the children were small. Delving deeper he unearthed the remains of an old doorbell system, a wooden mug tree and a pair of binoculars. George removed the binoculars and held them to his eyes as if to survey the scene. But the scene, being the inside of a slightly enlarged cupboard, didn't really require binoculars and so he placed them on the floor next to the rest of the aptly named oddments. A bag of masonry nails (why weren't they in the tool shed in the jar marked "outdoor nails"?) and a chipped plate featuring a Staffordshire Willow pattern were amongst the rest of his bounty.

Towards the bottom of the box, under a faded and slightly yellowed lace doily, George happened upon an old radio which he did remember. The radio was part of the personal stereo revolution, George recalled. Yes, that was the first time that everyone had entertainment on the move. He had marvelled at the time that

3

something the size of a box of Cook's matches could deliver radio directly to his ears. Aah, now this brought back memories. And as luck would have it, it still had the original headphones complete with orange sponge ear things. He smiled to himself as he read the red lettering on the front of the radio, whispering "Saisho" wistfully as if recalling a long-forgotten love.

After repacking the oddments and restacking the boxes, George made his way out of Mollie's room and downstairs, holding the radio in one hand and the nails in the other; the latter, of course, in preparation for their later transportation to the tool shed.

At the bottom of the stairs George heard voices which he quickly recognised as belonging to his daughter and granddaughter. As he entered the kitchen he opened his mouth, ready to greet his daughter.

"You can babysit our Mollie tonight, can't you, Dad?"

"You can, can't you, love?" said Sheila. "It's just our Sam's already arranged to go out with her friends tonight…"

"And I can't miss it, Dad…"

"She hasn't been out with her mates since last week, love, and it'd be a shame for her not to be able to go, don't you think?"

"Well…" George had managed a word but was acutely aware that it hadn't been heard and had really only served as an opportunity for Sam and Sheila to breathe.

"If you're worried about your bridge night at Norman's, it's okay," continued Sheila helpfully. "I telephoned him for you and let him know you won't be coming. You know, to save you a job."

"Oh, er…" said George.

"So that's fine then, isn't it, Dad? I'll drop our Mollie off around seven. She loves staying here, don't you, Mollie?"

Mollie shrugged. Sam didn't notice.

"See, Dad?" she said triumphantly, flicking her long blonde hair over her shoulder. "Right, I'm off then, cheers."

Sam, Mollie and Sheila headed through the lounge to the front door, leaving George in the kitchen staring though the window at a robin which appeared to have a ring pull in its mouth.

4

two

It was a wonderful, warm, sunny afternoon. When George had woken that morning he hadn't been aware that Sheila's plan was for him to spend the day alone with his three-year-old son. This had disappointed George a little, not least because he had dreamed of family time with *both* his young wife and son during the extremely long and tiring working week that had just ended. As George rolled over in bed Sheila had announced that she had things to do before promptly leaving the house at around eleven. George had been pondering for the last half hour what he was going to do to entertain Adam when there was a knock at the front door.

And so it came to be that Auntie Lesley and Uncle Pete were babysitting Adam.

They had arrived with beaming smiles and bulging shopping bags containing several bottles of wine. It was one of only a handful of times they had visited the house, but on a day like today the expanse of vivid green lawn was a much better option than their grey paved back yard. George had seen to it that they were both comfortable in the back garden and had everything that they needed to relax. Then, mumbling something about some charcoal briquettes, he had upped and left, leaving his brother-in-law and wife in charge. Lesley and Pete were not averse to babysitting. Childless themselves and not even about to become interested in such things at this stage of their lives, they had waved George off with comments suggesting steadfast control.

Sheila's absence hadn't gone unnoticed, but the couple had assumed that she was out shopping. This was highly likely.

George had lingered on the drive for a moment, ruminating over whether or not to leave. Unfortunately, he had lingered slightly too long and his thought process was eventually interrupted when he realised the spray from the tiny hole in the side of the garden hose had created a large dark patch on the seat of his chinos.

Deciding that the drive to collect the briquettes was only a twenty-minute turnaround, he had eventually climbed into his car and started the engine.

In the back garden the babysitters were doing a fine job. Lesley had poured herself another glass of white wine and retracted her garden chair as far as it would go. Meanwhile, Pete had lit another Benson and Hedges and was puffing away whilst working hungrily through the horse racing pages. From time to time he would lower the paper and squeeze his new wife's bottom as she sunbathed in her bikini alongside him.

"Nice arse," he said, chuckling.

"Cheeky," she replied, smiling, pushing a particularly bubbly permed lock from out of her eyes.

There hadn't been a sound from Adam, which meant, of course, that the childminding was going exceptionally well.

It wasn't until they heard a scream, followed by laughter, followed by a thud, followed by silence that they realised something might be amiss. Pete turned to Lesley and slowly raised his sunglasses from his eyes, as if to bring clarity to the situation. Lesley furrowed her brow and thrust her head upward as if adjusting her own ear volume.

They both heard exactly the same nothing.

Fears for Adam's safety swiftly subsided when they reached the front garden to find him sitting cross-legged and grinning proudly on the single car drive. On the pavement a few feet ahead of him was the motionless body of an old lady. Her right foot was still wedged in a mop bucket, the dirty water having sloshed up her tights to her right knee. A tartan shopping trolley, still zipped, lay on its side to her right. Humanely, Adam had placed a wet chamois leather over her face to preserve her dignity.

George rounded the corner and slowly approached the scene before him. Something odd was happening outside his house. He applied the brake and parked the car on the pavement. The access to his drive was blocked. He couldn't be sure but it appeared that there was a body lying on the path directly in front of his house. This won't do, he thought.

George climbed from the car and approached the scene. Pete, Lesley and George looked at each other and then at Adam. Lying on her back on the gravel, her face covered by the chamois, the old lady didn't appear to be looking at anyone. Someone had to speak, and George decided perhaps it should be him.

"So... er... what's... er... happened here?" he enquired.

"Well," said Pete, lighting another Benson, "the old lady seems to have got her foot stuck in this 'ere, bucket."

Lesley nodded in agreement woozily (wine and sun, probably).

"Right..." said George, slowly and methodically attempting to take in every word of Pete's statement, "... and... er... is she all right?"

"I dunno, should we check?"

"Mmm, that might be an idea," George concluded.

Lesley volunteered to lift the chamois and crouched down to knee level. Gently peeling back the cloth she saw two beady black eyes glaring back at her. The old lady appeared to be in some kind of shock, and had a lump the size of an egg on her forehead.

"Are you all right?" asked Lesley, the alcohol slightly slurring her speech.

"Help me up," demanded the old lady, "and keep that little bugger away from me." She gesticulated towards Adam.

She doesn't seem very happy, thought George as he and Lesley lifted the woman into a sitting position.

"What happened here?" he asked.

The old woman cleared her throat for dramatic effect, and related the tale of how she came to be lying on the floor.

"I'm walking along minding me own business, aren't I, when that 'boy' jumped out from behind the bush and squirted me with the bloody hosepipe," she said groggily. "Well, I lost me footing, didn't I? I'm seventy-two, you know, and I stepped backwards into this bloody bucket which some idiot had left on the pavement. Me foot got stuck inside and before I knows it I'm on me back."

"I'm very sorry," said George, concluding that he should have put away his car washing equipment prior to collecting the briquettes and noting never to make that mistake again. "Would you like some water?"

"I'm up to me bloody knees in it!" the old lady screeched. "Just pass me me trolley."

Lesley picked up the trolley and dusted it down for no particular reason before passing it back. Now back on her own feet under her own steam, the old lady set off slowly away from the scene, muttering something about locks and throwing away keys.

"Adam, I am not in the least bit impressed with you," said George, turning towards the grinning boy.

Adam rose from his seated position and skipped, smiling, down the drive and in through the front door.

After spending the remainder of the afternoon in the safety of the back garden, things had calmed down somewhat and George, Pete and Lesley had cheered themselves with a round of "no harm dones" and "could have been worses". As it was now nearing seven o'clock, Adam had been dispatched to bed still wearing his "I'm exceptionally pleased with myself" grin. Following this, George, Pete and Lesley had settled down in the kitchen.

"You've got to admit it was funny," said Lesley, returning once again to the earlier drama. She now appeared to have now reached the summit of Blossom Hill.

"Well," George mused, "I suppose in hindsight now…"

"Come on, George," said Pete, "it was funny. The old girl on the floor and your Adam, pleased as punch he was, pleased as punch. I tell you what, you'll need to watch that lad."

"You will," agreed Lesley. "Three years old and up to those tricks!" She shook her head and giggled whilst reliving the scene.

George had not really had the opportunity to fully consider whether it had been funny. As luck would have it, the decision needn't be made now anyway because just then the click of the latch meant that his thinking had just been done for him.

A crescendo of "Sheilas" filled the kitchen on her arrival. George, still sipping his green tea, had risen less than a few inches from his chair to greet his wife before her facial expression lowered him swiftly back down.

"Oh, sit down, George!" spat Sheila.

George cheered himself briefly with his own interpretation: that having looked after Adam all day, she felt he was probably exhausted. The rest of the room sensed that Sheila's tone suggested otherwise.

George, ambivalent yet comfortable with his interpretation, continued, "You'll never guess what Adam –"

"You okay, Sheila?" interrupted a slurry Lesley. It appeared she had now begun her descent from the summit and had stopped off at a small town called Rioja for further respite.

"No, Lesley, I am not."

Pete, who was sitting on the worktop, lit another Benson and made himself comfortable for the obvious entertainment that was about to ensue. Perhaps she had forgotten the credit cards. Now, that would explain the deficiency of shopping bags.

"Do you want a drink?" continued Lesley.

"I think I'd better," said Sheila.

Pete pushed himself up off the worktop and reached into the kitchen unit where the spirits were kept. He had remembered its location from Lesley's last visit. He poured a brandy (at times of stress, that's what they did on TV) and handed it to Sheila. Sheila gratefully accepted and gulped it back in one. Anticipating this, Pete switched the bottle back from forty-five degrees to just over ninety and re-poured.

It was only then that George noticed something different about Sheila. Her eyes looked puffy and she was slightly flushed. Unsure exactly what to do at this stage, he led with, "How has your day been, darling?"

Pete glanced at Lesley in the hope he could connect with her telepathically and share the same "my-sister-is-about-to-explode" thought. Lesley seemed to smile at the kettle.

Sheila turned her head slowly towards George, who was still sitting erect and attentive in the chair. "My day? My day?" she snarled, obviously at the quiet end of a soon-to-become-extremely-loud response. "HOW HAS MY DAY BEEN?"

"Yes," responded George, evidently understanding Sheila's question.

"My day, George, has been shit. Utter, utter shit."

"Oh," managed George. Now he too wondered whether the

credit card had been forgotten. He was sure it had enough credit on it, absolutely sure.

"Another brandy?" offered Pete, slightly uncomfortable with his sister's behaviour but more so with his wife's fixation on the kettle.

"Yes, I will. God knows I need one."

George knew the routine now. After many years Pete had also become accustomed to how events would now unfold. Lesley, a recent newcomer to the family, was far less prepared. Sheila wouldn't offer the information immediately. It would be delivered when the scene was fully set. The sighing and gesticulating, the running of her hands through her hair and the staring up to the heavens were simply the theatre lights dimming. There was some work ahead before the curtain call.

"What's the matter, love?" asked George.

"Come 'ere, sis," said Pete, opening his arms slightly.

Sheila feigned a dramatic "I couldn't possibly" before moving across the kitchen to her brother. The next ten minutes were a rally of Sheila being asked whether she was alright and her responding each time that she didn't want to talk about it. Finally, Lesley broke the impasse by slipping stealthily from her chair and onto the kitchen floor in true invertebrate style.

"You must tell us," said George, now feeling quite tired and aware of his bladder's warnings that it wanted to evacuate the green tea. He couldn't hold on much longer, he simply couldn't.

Lesley's physical change of position prompted a conversational fillip, at which point Sheila dramatically blurted out, "I'm pregnant, for God's sake, Pete. I'm pregnant."

George felt instant relief. So it wasn't the credit card, he thought. I knew it!

"Well, aren't you going to say anything?" Sheila continued, now fixing her eyes firmly on George. "Aren't *you* going to say anything at all?"

"Well," said George, "that's wonderful," unsure whether he was referring to his own credit limit intuition or the unborn child.

"No, George, it's not bloody wonderful. It's not wonderful at all."

"Well…"

"Just go to bed, George," said Sheila firmly.

"Well…"

"Go to bed. I want to speak to Pete alone. Just go."

"All right," he offered, and rotated gradually before shrugging his shoulders and aiming one last caring smile towards his wife. The look he received in return made him close the kitchen door without delay.

He slowly climbed the stairs feeling that he had been as useful that day as the charcoal briquettes, which still sat inanimately in the boot of his Chevette.

three

"Aah, another perfect Sunday lunch," George announced whilst gently dabbing the corner of his mouth with a napkin.

Sheila and Sam had already left the table and were continuing their conversation in the lounge. Even though it had been George who prepared the meal, he was well aware that the responsibility for clearing the table and washing up also fell firmly at his door. Delving into the excellent memory he possessed he distinctly remembered Sheila's comment from many years earlier: "Go on, George, you do the dishes so me and Sam can catch up, you know, mother and daughter stuff." At that moment it had become one of Sheila's (many more than) ten commandments and had set the precedent that existed to this day.

After neatly stacking the used crockery to the right of the sink in order of size (which allowed him to wash items in strict order to maximise the space on the drainer on the left) he wiped down the work surfaces and sat for a second at the kitchen table. Pondering his next move, he decided that perhaps he wouldn't join the ladies in the lounge, perhaps he would spend some time in the conservatory. Yes, that's what he'd do: he would finish the dishes and spend some time in there. He was sure the ladies wouldn't mind – they would probably enjoy a little more female time. George rose again and began lowering the pots into the sink.

A cry of "Tea, George!" broke the beginning of a daydream and he hurriedly dried his hands before complying with the request and making his way into the lounge. "Here you go!" he cheerfully announced, carrying through a tray comprising freshly made tea, a beaker of juice for Mollie and a plate of Cadbury's fingers and Garibaldi's which he had carefully arranged into a smiling face.

Without diverting her eyes from the television, Sheila motioned limply with her right hand for the tray to be placed on the coffee

12

table. George placed it down and hovered for a brief moment as if expecting further instructions. As none appeared to be forthcoming he quietly retreated backwards towards the door. Sam's long blonde hair running down to the bottom of her slim back was all George caught as he retreated. She didn't turn her thoughts away from the television to thank him. Mollie, who was lying on her front on the lounge floor, colouring, looked up at her grandpa just in time to catch his smile and wink to her. She reciprocated the gesture (though her attempt looked more like an amalgamation of toothache and an involuntary eye spasm) before returning to her colouring. George, in turn, returned to his dishes.

Once the kitchen was again a perfectly spotless environment, George placed his hands on his hips and smiled contentedly, admiring his sparkling empire. He felt he had earned an hour's rest and crossed the room to the coat hooks before reaching into his anorak pocket for his radio. It had been there since they had been reunited a few days earlier and he was looking forwards to a little time with his own thoughts. Before allowing himself time to relax, it crossed his mind that the girls may need more sustenance and refreshments, so he lingered behind the lounge door as the TV presenter announced that the QVC Diamonique special was about to begin. Thinking better of interrupting Sheila's favourite show, he returned to the kitchen and headed into the conservatory.

After releasing a very satisfied sigh, George settled in his chair and removed his slippers. He outstretched both his legs and wiggled his toes as if to relax his body fully. Clutching the radio, he carefully untangled the wire and slipped on the orange headphones. He was about to switch on the radio when he realised that the rug was not exactly perpendicular with the patio doors. This simply wouldn't do. He removed the headphones and sank to the floor. With his cheek almost touching the rug he eyed carefully down the length of it and similarly down the length of the door frame until he was happy that all was well. Back in his chair, with the rug problem swiftly dispatched, he could now properly unwind.

He replaced the headphones on his head and turned the dial on the side of the radio, waiting for the initial click and the red light on the front to announce that relaxation time was beginning. It was just then that he noticed the vertical blind predicament. "Oh, bother," he softly muttered, removing the headphones once again. Some of the PVC louvre slats had become twisted and weren't hanging quite correctly. George wondered for a moment how this could have happened. Perhaps the wind? Or maybe Sheila had brushed against them when exiting into the garden? Hmm... He couldn't be sure but soon realised that he was wasting time by pondering and found himself straightening the slats one by one until he was satisfied that each was exactly equidistant to the next.

Before returning to his chair (for what he hoped would be the last time that day) he studied the conservatory meticulously to ensure nothing else was awry.

Ten minutes later he let out a second sigh. He was now fully content with his surroundings. The red light illuminated and there followed a few moments of static, crackles and various snippets of music as George turned the dial with his thumb. He was extremely pleased to find a station playing Massenet's *Méditation* and gently closed his eyes, his thin lips pressed together but smiling slightly.

Some time must have passed because the light outside was fading and George remembered hearing a number of overtures and piano sonatas. Feeling extremely relaxed, he switched off the radio and reached down to his side for his book. He was eager to catch up on the latest happenings in *The History of Cogs*; however he had, he felt, had perhaps a little too much relaxation time to himself. He put the book back down and wearily pulled on his slippers. The chapter about helical gears would have to wait.

He made his way back into the lounge where he was surprised to see Mollie alone, still colouring on the floor.

"Where's your mummy and grandma, Mollie?"

Mollie silently motioned to a handwritten note on the coffee table next to the plate of biscuit crumbs. Sheila's handwriting informed George that she and his daughter had "popped out" for a few drinks and would return later that night. It also informed him that Mollie would need her hair washing ready for school the next morning.

"Oh," exclaimed George thoughtfully and lay down next to Mollie to help her finish the picture of a technicoloured unicorn. He would run the bath as soon as they had finished.

four

"Just get out of this fucking room now!"

Sheila meant it; George knew that from the almost satanic look in her eyes. He felt quite embarrassed to be asked to leave. After all, he had mopped her brow and stroked her gradually wetter hair for the best part of eight hours. Indeed, he had even joined in with the same depth and pace of her breathing *and* allowed her to draw blood from the back of his right hand.

"I think your husband should stay," said the nurse.

"Get. Him. Out. Of. Here," Sheila repeated firmly, her eyes narrowing.

George looked at his wife again, trying to gauge whether a final request to stay was worthwhile. To him, despite all the sweat that dripped from her bedraggled hair, she was beautiful. She always had been. He knew, however, that the look on her face meant that he had to leave. Even her brown curly hair seemed to spit venom towards him, not unlike the snakes on Medusa's head.

As he quickly retreated George glanced at the nurse, who gave him a quick, compassionate shrug. Her eyes suggested that his leaving may be for the best.

The double doors swung shut behind him and he sank, his back following the wall down until he reached the floor. The screams continued from within the room, but at a markedly lower volume, probably because there were fewer people for Sheila to perform to. With his head in his hands, he ruminated about his dismissal from the room.

Sheila had clearly said to him that he should guard her handbag closely: she didn't want anything to go missing. As she was hurriedly pushed down the corridor through three, maybe four, swing doors, George had rushed behind clutching the handbag tightly, held up against his chest to ensure that Sheila's instructions were followed to the letter.

When they had arrived at their destination, George had made himself comfortable on a low faux-leather armchair to the left of the bed. Due to the size of the chair, his head was about level with the mattress. Wide-eyed, he peered up at his wife, tightly gripping the handbag. It was George's first experience of this type of situation (he had missed Adam's birth, but that was an altogether different story) and he sat rigidly in the chair, almost catatonic, as he tried to weigh up the drama unfolding around him.

The beginning part was fairly comfortable, he felt. It was all slow breathing exercises and the occasional draw on a tube, which made Sheila light-headed, blurry-eyed and somehow a little friendlier looking. Indeed, she had smiled at him once or twice after imbibing the mysterious elixir.

But then it had got wholly more intense. George, still gripping the handbag, was suddenly aware that the atmosphere inside the room was changing. Sheila's breathing patterns had become much deeper, and the nurses (not dissimilar to a football crowd, he thought) began chanting encouragement. This completely took George by surprise and moments later he found himself chanting along with the nurses. Sheila's draws on the tube became far more regular, yet the smiles she had conveyed earlier were now missing, replaced simply by two angry-looking brows.

"Give me your hand, George," Sheila had demanded.

"Sorry, my love?"

"Your hand, George, give me your hand."

George realised instantly that he didn't actually have a free hand to offer. Both his hands were currently in use, closely guarding the handbag. Momentarily, he thought about asking whether it was more important to safeguard the handbag or hold Sheila's hand, but under these circumstances he knew that this decision must be made alone. George spotted a handle just below eye level on the underside of the bed which would make a good makeshift hook. Fumbling with the bag, he reached out the leather handles and placed them over the lever, which he then used to push himself upward to the edge of the bed where he could give Sheila his hand.

Unfortunately, he had used a little too much force. He was astonished when the lever gave way under his weight, catapulting Sheila and the head of the bed up into an eighty-degree position. Sheila had screamed, the nurses had screamed and George had followed suit. Then George had been told firmly in unison by three nurses to stand back whilst they hurried round and returned Sheila back to the horizontal.

For half an hour or so George had sat timidly in the chair in silence. The screaming and pushing had continued but, not daring to move, he had simply stared at his feet.

And then, suddenly, Sheila had commanded the use of his hand again and George had risen gingerly to be alongside his wife. He had gently wiped her brow and interjected when he felt appropriate with encouraging statements urging her to push and reassurances that it wouldn't be long until her suffering was over. He had, of course, maintained his focus on the stewardship of the handbag and decided (so as to allay any further calamity) to put his foot through the arms of the bag, which was now stowed safely on the floor. This way, should anyone try to make a move for any of the possessions in the middle of this drama, he would feel the movement and avert any potential threat. He eyed the nurses warily whilst he continued his husbandly support. Nurses don't get paid a great deal, he thought. He narrowed his eyes and focused on one nurse in particular who, he suspected, could potentially make a grab for the prize.

It was just then that Sheila had let out what can only be described as a banshee-like scream. The noise reminded George of the period dramas he had seen on television where injured soldiers have limbs amputated on the battlefield without anaesthetic. George, taken aback by the stentorian volume, straightened up and stepped one pace backwards to avoid the noise. His feet, now noosed ever tighter in the leather straps, came to a complete stop, which propelled him further backwards. Trying desperately to stay upright, he grabbed at a metal drip stand, which offered little resistance and quickly followed him on his descent to the hard linoleum surface. The entire contents of the handbag followed seconds later, scattering lipsticks, mascaras and coins across the floor.

It was at this stage that Sheila had ordered him from the room.

Now sitting on the floor outside the room, George realised to his horror that his dismissal had been so sudden that he had forgotten the handbag. A sudden nausea overtook him. Good God, it was still in there! Before having a chance to ponder what to do next, more screams came from inside the room. But these were different screams, tiny screams, from someone who was taking their first gasp of air and their first look at the world they had entered. George scrambled to his feet as the nurse pushed open the door.

Samantha Jayne Poppleton had entered the world.

George walked over and gently stroked his daughter's blonde wispy hair for the first time. He smiled at Sheila and she appeared to smile back.

Three days later Sheila and Samantha returned home from the hospital. George had carefully prepared a chocolate cake on which he had neatly piped "Mum and Sam" in vanilla icing. Both sets of beaming grandparents along with Lesley and Pete were there to greet them. Little Samantha lay small and fragile in her Moses basket in the kitchen whilst the excitable family stroked and cooed and kissed her.

Meanwhile, in the lounge, four-year-old Adam put a claw hammer through the fish tank.

five

Adam finally made his way to his favourite part of the muck stack and sat down on the grass. The muck stack, as it was colloquially known, was not actually as bad as the name suggested. It was a huge pile of earth that had been excavated many decades ago when mining had first started in the area. Originally, it would have been just that – a stack of muck – but now, many years later, grass had grown, trees had self-seeded and the area had become a relatively pleasant hideaway.

Adam loved it up here; from the top he could see the countless houses and streets below, and in the distance it was possible to make out the town hall and the hospital, which stood proudly on the horizon. It didn't matter to him that he should be at school today. To Adam nothing really mattered anyway. He lay back, letting the sun hit his face, and stared up at the clouds. This was where he could really be himself, just him, away from the grip of the rest of the world.

Although locals used the area for walking their dogs, no one would bother him up here, no one would enter his world. The world he hated. He hated the people that he shared *his* world with. He hated their faces, their attitudes, their overpowering dubious version of love and, worst of all, the pressure and guilt that they laid upon him. The world to Adam created a grim feeling of foreboding.

He wasn't sure whether everyone felt like this, and falsely displayed a different façade to the world, or only he felt this way. If it was the former, then why was it that he wasn't equipped to pretend, to outwardly give the impression that life was great? He knew from first-hand experience that his dad could do it. Why was it that he couldn't conceal what he truly felt? Why was he such an open book? But what actually worried him more was that in reality the latter applied and *he* was the isolated one, *he* was the only one who felt this way. If this was the case then there seemed to be no hope. The world had always seemed grey to him, but as the months and years went by the grey was getting ever darker, ever approaching an all-encompassing blanket of black.

He was sure that he loved his parents, but the way they chose to live was the polar opposite of his *raison d'être*. His dad was just so, well… Dad. His mother, quite evidently the matriarch of the family, if not the world, made every decision for everyone, every time. He could not understand how his dad could live like this. He knew that his dad was a good person, but it didn't add up that someone would be happy to live that way; never in control of themselves, their actions or their own destiny. Why would anyone live their life as simply a puppet controlled by invisible strings?

He had tried to speak to his father many times about his worries and fears. However, each time he was met with the same answer: that the feelings he was experiencing were simply part of growing up. Adam couldn't abide this dismissive attitude. He knew that his father's reply was designed simply to be a comfort to him, a reassurance that all would become clearer in time. Surely, though, his dad didn't mean these words literally? Surely his dad wasn't so out of touch that he truly believed Adam's feelings were so inconsequential as to be simply a part of growing up? As time passed this had become a huge conundrum to Adam. This was *the* problem. He understood that a father would wish to shield his son from the world, but at the expense of truth? This was something that Adam just couldn't figure out, and this was the reason that he found sleep difficult and human communication so much worse.

Conversation with his father had now been stripped to the bare essential greetings.

His mother was a different animal altogether. He had heard her, in her usual brash and overpowering way, discussing his "way" (*his* way?) with her friends. Her shameless comments about his demeanour, about how she suspected that there was something not quite right with him. Nothing with his mother had ever changed; it had always been this way. And on the occasions where any well-adjusted person would sheepishly look down, on *those* occasions where she had realised he had heard her, she would simply restate the point directly to him as if to make it absolutely clear that she had no regrets and full confidence in what she was saying. Yes, conversation with Mum was even more sparse than with Dad, and, if at all possible, completely avoided.

Adam sat up, loosened his school tie and reached down into his rucksack, fumbling near the bottom for his tin. Having located it, he pulled open the lid and rested it on the grass, making sure it was level. He carefully laid out the papers and burnt the resin, before adding tobacco and skilfully rolling the paper into a perfect cylinder. He lay back into the long grass, pushing his dark, unwashed hair from his eyes. Lighting the joint, he stared at the clouds that floated effortlessly above before pulling the smoke deep into his lungs.

As the smoke began to take effect, he began to get the feeling that made it worthwhile. The feeling of weightlessness, where the tension in his chest began to subside and the black moths that fluttered constantly in his abdomen began to desist. The feeling that the muscles in his shoulders and neck and arms had become less taut and heavy, less effort to move.

He closed his eyes, the blood in his eyelids spectacularly lit in a bright crimson by the sun, and smiled. This was a feeling he could cope with. The sinister fingers of doom had not disappeared but had, at least for now, loosened their grip.

six

Sheila sat upright on the sofa. Her body rigid, she craned forwards to ensure that the words she had just heard were, in fact, correct. Her right hand crept slowly, spider-like towards the phone on the cushion next to her. This cannot be true, no way, she thought, this cannot be true. She listened intently for what she believed and hoped and dreamed she had originally heard. The television once again repeated its statement. It was true, oh God, it was true! Today, and today only, her "friends" at QVC were offering a year's supply of an American imported anti-wrinkle cream used by the stars of Hollywood (the stars, no less) for a quarter of the price. This was simply too much. Her hand moved blindly, sweeping from side to side to locate the phone, her eyes unable to leave the screen. I need some, she thought.

To Sheila, it had never been about whether she would like something or required something: it had always been about need. Something inside just overtook her entire body and her goal in life was to fulfil and feed *that* need (to the exclusion of everything around her) at *that* exact moment. George had considered on occasion whether perhaps Sheila's need, when satisfied, had lived up to expectations, but that was many, many years ago and now to him, frankly, it was easier just to agree. Sheila, on the other hand, simply didn't have the time to consider whether the need was at all worthwhile, because by the time her need was satisfied another one had appeared and that too required feeding. Twenty years earlier George had likened Sheila to a greedy dog which kept arriving to its master, panting and begging for more. Sheila's reaction at that time ensured that this particular analogy never resurfaced.

Her hand finally located and grasped the phone. Within moments the purchase was made (Sheila, after all, prided herself not only on her ability to recite at speed her own unique customer code but also her amazing capacity to remember product codes).

Her body became limp again whilst her mind cursed the fact that next-day delivery was twenty-four hours too long. She considered phoning Lesley to divulge the details of the covenant she had just made (God knows did Lesley need the cream…) but thought better in the knowledge that she could reveal all when the product arrived and the offer was no longer available.

Satisfied that her need had now been met, she went into the kitchen to arrange some lunch. Her timing, as always, had been perfect and she could now prepare some sandwiches for herself and George while the tedious news was broadcast. They could eat as *Cash in the Attic* began.

"George, lunch is ready."

It was unusual for George not to appear immediately, as if waiting off-stage for his prompt. It would not have been surprising for him to emerge from behind the jackets hung on the coat rack in the corner, as if he had been waiting for his cue all morning. Today, however, was different – he did not appear, and Sheila had to repeat her statement.

It was only on the third cry that George appeared in the kitchen. Still wearing his orange sponge headphones, he made his way to the table and sat down. Noticing the sandwiches on the plate laid out in front of him on the table, he momentarily grinned, before happily selecting a triangle of bread and biting into it.

"*Cash in the Attic* next," Sheila informed him.

George bit again, offering no response.

"It's *Cash in the Attic* next, I said," she repeated, reaffirming to herself that she had not become mute.

George continued to nibble whilst staring contentedly at his ever-decreasing pile of sandwiches.

"GEORGE! GEORGE!"

The volume of Sheila's last dispatch shocked George. His first thought was that there must be a fire. Knowing now that he must have his full wits about him to save his home, he quickly whipped off his headphones and gave his full attention to his wife.

"What is it?" he spluttered, spitting a small piece of cucumber onto Sheila's hand. "Where? Where is it?" he added, alarmed.

"I was just saying that *Cash in the Attic* is on next."

"Oh," said George, now beginning to wonder what the fuss was about yet still plagued by the worrying thought that there was a fire.

"Why are you listening to that radio during mealtimes, George? Do you know how rude that is?"

"Oh, sorry, dear," George said. "I was just enjoying it. I suppose I have had it on rather a lot today."

"Yes, you have," Sheila rebuked, although in honesty she could only testify that he had worn it for the ten minutes that they had been in each other's company that entire morning.

George turned the power off, watching until the little red light faded out, and put the radio and headphones carefully back into the inside pocket of his tweed blazer.

"I'm sorry, dear, that was very rude of me," he offered humbly. "These sandwiches are delicious."

seven

George had been looking forwards to this night all year. There had been times during the last few months when his excitement had got the better of him and he had needed to sit down quietly by himself to gather his thoughts. In fact, on occasion, his mother had firmly suggested that he should do so.

There had also been many nights where he had awoken thinking about it. Many nights of restlessness and anticipation as the day approached. Indeed, latterly, the problem had aggrandised so much that he would find himself getting out of bed two or perhaps three times a night for a nervous wee.

But now the day had finally arrived and his excitement had peaked. In just two hours he would be at the Trainee Mechanical Engineers' Ball. He brushed down his dinner jacket and trousers for the hundredth time and hung his clothes back in his wardrobe before running the bath.

Earlier that day, the talk in the office was the death of Brian Epstein. His colleagues had discussed it *ad nauseam* all day and George was mildly irritated that the demise of The Beatles' manager would somehow usurp the exhilaration he felt about the forthcoming ball. Once or twice George had interjected with a comment regarding the evening's entertainment but it had fallen completely on deaf ears.

It was only in the last five minutes of the working day that he had been able to break into the conversation and finally get everyone's attention.

"So... er... has everyone got their clothes ready for tonight?" he said with perfect timing (although probably more so luck) at the exact point where the previous conversation had faded to silence. It was a particularly insipid interruption even by George's standards.

His three colleagues turned from their dialogue to face him and nodded slowly and somewhat blankly at him.

"Right then! I'll see you all there," George cheerfully proclaimed, putting his jacket on whilst juxtaposing his pencils evenly on his desk.

His colleagues turned slowly back to face each other, still without expression. They weren't sure, but it seemed George was slightly skipping when he left the room.

Outside in the corridor, George saw Norman who smiled as they passed. "See you at the ball tonight, Norman!" said George, his skip developing into a canter as he went through the door and across the car park.

Following his bath, his mother helped him brush his hair before pulling his bowtie straight and taking a step back to get a full view of her son. "George, you look exquisite," she said, then called Walter into the room to have a look.

"Look at your son, Walter, doesn't he look nice?"

George beamed at his father.

"He looks just fine," said Walter, proudly patting his son on the back, "just fine."

The ball was an exciting event beyond George's wildest dreams. Along the right-hand wall was a buffet laden with all food imaginable: ham and egg finger sandwiches, cheese balls, sausages wrapped in pastry and two huge vessels of bubbling cheese fondue. At the end of the table were numerous bottles of different shapes and sizes all containing different coloured liquids. Straight ahead, the wall was lined with gold metal chairs with tasteful maroon-velour padded seats. A large banner was draped across the matching maroon curtains welcoming each guest to the "Trainee Mechanical Engineers' Ball 1967". Smartly dressed attendees stood in small groups chattering to one another. Off to the left was a large empty area with a wooden floor. Bright beams of light shot pinks, greens and yellows across the parquet floor. That must be the dance floor, thought George, his eyes wide. He was completely unaware that his mouth was hanging open.

His sense of awe broke when he heard Norman call his name. Turning away from the dance floor, he made his way over to his colleagues, feeling like a guest at the table of the captain of the *Titanic*. "No icebergs tonight," he chuckled to himself, spotting the lettuce on the buffet.

His colleagues seemed to spend most of the evening adjacent to the drinks table imbibing peculiar sounding drinks such as screwballs, martinis and bucks fizz. They had tried to get George to participate, but following an early brush with a bucks fizz (presented to him on his arrival) he was already feeling frivolous and giddy. As the night wore on his colleagues became more and more difficult to understand, but that didn't deter George at all: he was encapsulated by the people and the lights and the music. And anyway, he himself seemed to be going down a storm. His colleagues seemed to be laughing every time he spoke and so he concluded that he was obviously doing something right. I could get used to this, he thought, glugging back another lemonade.

The night was in full swing and his friends from the office were laughing boisterously, having now attracted a couple of very pretty secretarial types over to their circle to chat. George wasn't quite close enough to hear the conversation but it must have been amusing as the girls were laughing and glancing over in his direction. This made George feel slightly uncomfortable (after all, he had never been in a situation like this before), but the girls appeared to be smiling and George thought it gentlemanly to return the smiles.

Soon after, the brunette girl approached him, flashing a wide mischievous grin, and asked his name. He had no time to answer as at that moment he was grabbed from behind by two of his colleagues and his shoes were removed. Before George could react, the girl (having winked at his colleagues) was passed the shoes, which she proceeded to fill with trifle before sliding them at pace under the buffet table and against the wall.

George, now completely bemused, turned to his colleagues with an expression which begged for clarification. Unfortunately, he was simply greeted with further laughter. He then turned to the protagonist, whose laughter ceased when she saw the look on George's face. She was sure he was about to cry. Internally, George was doing all he could to stop himself.

"I'm sorry," she said, suddenly regretting her actions. "It was just a dare."

George stared blankly. To him it just seemed, well, unkind.

"Come on," she said. "I'll help you get them back."

And that was how, seconds later, George found himself with the girl on his hands and knees eight feet away from his colleagues shielded from the Ball under the darkness of the buffet table. Having retreated from the party and feeling brave enough to speak without fear of tears, George spoke.

"Why did you do that?" he asked innocently.

"I'm sorry," she repeated, "I really am. It was just a bit of fun and your friends (friends? She had wildly misread this, George thought) said you wouldn't mind."

"Oh," said George, slightly puzzled.

"I didn't realise that you'd be so upset about it," she continued. "You looked like, well, you were going to cry."

"No," said George, unsure as to whether or not he was about to now.

"I'm sorry," she said genuinely.

"It's okay," said George. "I suppose I'm well, er, not used to this type of thing."

She smiled fondly at George in a way that reminded him of his mother. "Have you got a girlfriend?"

"No," said George, "no, not yet."

"Come on," said the girl. "Let's get these shoes cleaned up."

George nodded and crawled out from under the table behind her.

He decided that perhaps it would be best if he took some time away from the party and made himself comfortable in a cubicle in the toilets for a little peace and quiet. He sat forwards, arched his back and sighed. He hadn't been expecting this was the type of thing that happened at such auspicious events. His eyes lowered and he stared at his clean shoes, which were now empty of dessert but still a little on the squelchy side.

Towards the end of the night his colleagues insisted that they all get up to dance. George didn't care too much for the rock and roll music that was now playing, but after a little coaxing from Norman (who assured him it would be alright) the five of them made their way to the dance floor.

George liked Norman. He wasn't like the rest of his colleagues, who were a little too raucous and sometimes quite coarse. Granted, Norman was a little older, but he had a steady way about him which George respected and largely aspired to. It was for this reason that George (with no prior experience to draw on in the amphitheatre of dance) decided to follow Norman's lead on the dance floor.

Within moments, however, the five had separated as his colleagues quickly honed in on girls dancing nearby. George continued to dance alone whilst trying to emulate Norman's distant moves. All this movement felt very unusual to George, who fervently observed the etiquette of the dance floor for the first time. His colleagues repeatedly leaned over to the girls, who giggled following each whispered remark. Although they were still slightly damp, George curled his toes into the end of his shoes to ensure they would stay in place should there be another heist.

All of a sudden a loud cheer went up which made George jump slightly, his eyes darting from side to side as he tried to figure out what the fuss was all about. His confused appearance must have been evident, because at that moment the trifle girl (who had been watching him since the earlier incident) came over and explained, "Penny Lane." She nodded towards the speakers.

"George Poppleton," replied George, nodding towards the speakers as if to complete the ritual.

The girl laughed, again flashing an attractive smile at him.

He couldn't possibly have had any inkling at the time, of course, but this was the night that George became forever known as "Sheila and George".

eight

Adam had not left his bedroom for nearly three days – not for food, for the bathroom, for television, for anything. He had lain on his bed with the curtains fully closed and tried desperately to ignore the thick fog which now seemed like it was grimly hanging just above his head. There had been concerned knocks on the outside of his door asking whether he was alright, which he had deflected with grunts of "fine" or "not feeling well". He had listened to his mother's muffled voice becoming more exasperated and telling him his behaviour wasn't normal for a sixteen-year-old. He knew this already.

He didn't feel like he had chosen to be in the bedroom: it was as if something unknown had placed an anvil on him which rendered him catatonic. Every part of him felt heavy and lifeless. Even his blood seemed different. It felt like lead apathetically pumping around his body as though even *it* didn't have the energy to move. This lethargy was in contrast to the insects which lived inside him. The black moths now lived with him daily, in his chest, in his abdomen, each hour ever stronger. They had boundless energy and seemed to feed hungrily on the energy which the rest of Adam's body was not using. He felt that their larval stage had taken place at the moment of his birth and the inactive pupal stage had only perhaps lasted until he was four or five. From then the metamorphosis had taken place and they had wholly inhabited him. He had lost track of the amount of times that he had wanted to reach for a knife and plunge it into his chest as a way of releasing them. Perhaps this action would finally make them happy so they would leave him alone.

Time no longer mattered. In his bedroom he didn't know whether it was day or night. He had slept for long periods at a time only to be awoken when the rest of the house was asleep, sweat dripping like candle wax down his body, the sheets sodden, fear pushing him further into his mattress.

He had tried to read, but the words played tricks on him, moving in and out of focus, getting smaller and smaller before all of a sudden getting larger and larger and larger until the page seemed to turn completely black. He would then throw the book to the floor and bury his head deep into his pillow again.

Time.

Meant.

Nothing.

For years Adam had clung desperately to an image that one day he would wake to find the world bright again. That his life would be illuminated and all the dark colours would suddenly burst into glorious colour. The sky would turn from grey to a brilliant blue and the sounds around him would become less muffled and reveal their true clarity. But Adam was now beginning to believe that this wouldn't happen. He was giving up. It was almost as if a vulture had swooped down and grabbed his hope between its giant claws before arching its wings and flying high into the black sky above.

Then, there was a different knock at the door.

nine

George sat in the conservatory completely at ease with life. He had been overjoyed to tune into the final movement of Fauré's *Requiem* and now was busy conducting the beginning of Boccerini's *Minuet*. Life couldn't be better, he beamed to himself, accentuating each wrist movement in a dramatic fashion. He could almost hear the audience rise to their feet clapping euphorically as the strings subsided and he turned to take his bow. Life, simply, could not be better.

Life in the kitchen, however, was altogether different. Sam, sobbing and histrionic, had just arrived with Mollie in tow. Sheila had heard the front door bang (a little more loudly than usual) and come through from the utility room to investigate. There at the table sat Sam, her face bruised with a freshly stitched wound running an inch down from the top of her nose.

"My God, Sam, what happened to you?" Sheila asked.

"Carl," she spluttered. "Carl."

"What has he done to you?" she asked (although the answer to her question seemed fairly obvious).

"Last night." Sam managed before theatrically throwing her head backwards then forwards and burying her head in her hands.

Sheila, now slightly unsure what to do, noticed George through the kitchen window. At that moment he appeared to be bowing to the bird table.

"George!" she shouted. "George!"

There was no response from George, who was concentrating on ensuring that the bassoons and violins were beginning in time. Sheila stormed into the garden and dragged the headphones from George's head from behind. George spun, confused, and Sheila instructed him that he was needed "NOW!" in the kitchen. George followed through the conservatory and into the kitchen, his headphones trailing behind him.

"Look at your daughter, George, look!"

Sam refused to remove her hands from her face. George plonked Mollie in front of the television in the lounge and then sat down beside his daughter to try to get to the bottom of the problem. Resting his arm around her shoulders and pulling her closer towards him, he spoke calmly and gently.

"What's happened, love?"

At this point, it could have been any number of things, George thought, quickly racking his brain. Did she need money? Had she lost her job? Had she actually got a job? (He wasn't sure on this one, but didn't think so.) Had her favourite dress shrunk in the wash? He was used to these displays of life-engulfing emotion – they had always been a regular occurrence around the kitchen table – and decided to bide his time in gently coaxing the problem from Sam whilst simultaneously rubbing a circular pattern around the top of her back. Rather like polishing the car, he thought. Sam, who had suddenly transformed from a woman to a little girl again, sobbed and wailed inarticulate sounds.

Sheila's patience with the situation was beginning to wane and she spoke in an attempt to accelerate the current situation directly to the main event.

"It's that bloody Carl, George, isn't it, Sam? Tell your dad… tell him what's happened."

George ignored the statement and continued softly rubbing Sam's back whilst offering encouragement to his daughter in a low, considered voice. Sam remained with her face in her hands, still refusing to unveil her injured face to her father.

Mollie wandered in, nonplussed, and helped herself to some milk from the fridge. George looked up and winked, and Mollie responded with a smile and a shrug before returning to the lounge.

Sam's sobs were now beginning to settle and George adjusted his position so his face was opposite hers. "What's happened, Samantha?" he asked again, using her full name to add extra gravitas. Sam slowly removed her hands from her face and stared at her father. Expertly covering his shock, George studied his daughter's face for the first time that day. Her eyes, although not helped by the puffiness caused by tears, were both black. She had a small cut on her top lip and her nose had been bent slightly over to the left. The cut, which was currently being pulled together by black thread, was deep and would surely leave a permanent scar.

"Oh, Sam," George offered sympathetically.

"It was Carl, Dad. I didn't do anything. He just hit me. I didn't do anything."

"I'll tell you what I think – he wants bloody locking up, that's what I think," said Sheila, not considering for a second that nobody had asked her what she thought. "I've always said he's no good for you that bloody Carl. I don't know why you even got involved with him. He's no good, that lad, no bloody good."

George wanted to respond to Sheila's outburst, but was conscious that this wouldn't help the situation and certainly wouldn't make Sam feel any better. He was acutely aware that up until now Sheila had never offered anything but glowing praise for Carl when from time to time George had expressed his doubts. He was also aware that the chances of Sam "not doing anything" to provoke this type of reaction were extremely remote. Granted, nobody deserved this type of treatment at the hands of another, but there was no possible chance that Sam had simply *done nothing*. Regardless, his main concern was for his daughter. But he knew that he would have to tread carefully with his words to contain the potential lynch mob which Sheila and Sam would soon become.

"What would you like me to do?" asked George, focusing his question wholly on Sam.

"What would you like me to do?" mimicked Sheila. "Go round and rip his head off, that's what she wants you to do, George."

George again ignored Sheila and looked deep into Sam's bruised eyes, as if trying to find the answer himself deep within her mind.

Sam spoke. "No, I don't, Mum."

"Well, what do you want?" asked Sheila, frustrated with what was fast becoming a very disappointing finale to a performance with such early promise.

"I just want him out," Sam said, resigned. "I just want him out."

"You heard her, George, she wants him bloody out."

"Okay," said George, patting the back of Sam's hand as he stood. "I'll go over there now."

In the car, George was extremely pleased with the way Sam had sought a peaceful and non-dramatic resolution to the situation. He was also extremely nervous about approaching his daughter's boyfriend and asking him to collect his belongings and move out of the rented flat they shared. Carl was far bigger than he was and he certainly didn't want a scene in front of the neighbours. However, this man had inflicted serious harm on his daughter and it was this thought that spurred him and kept him driving towards the flat. He had considered telephoning Norman to join him (for back-up, no less), but Norman was eight years his senior, and the appearance of two men with a combined age of over one hundred and thirty may appear a little too heavy-handed in this situation. Norman had also had a few heart murmurs in the past and George had thought better than to endanger his friend's life by calling him up for active service. No, George concluded, this is something I will deal with myself. He selected *Ride of the Valkyries* on the stereo and accelerated his speed up to thirty-four.

Minutes later he was outside the flat and he felt his hands tremble as he fumbled with the key and finally clicked it into the lock. He paused briefly, glancing around, in the hope he would catch the attention of one of the neighbours as he entered. There would at least then be a witness to what could well be his final moments. Unfortunately, there wasn't a soul around. He took a deep breath before pushing the door open.

Inside the flat things were different somehow. It wasn't as if he went over there often; in fact it seemed to him that most of the time Sam and Mollie themselves spent little time there, preferring to while away their time at his home. But it felt different here. Something was missing. His heartbeat quickened as he sheepishly opened one door after another, bobbing his head into each room to look for life. As he made it through the flat and into the open-plan kitchen-diner at the back he realised that the place was definitely empty.

This presented a problem to George. How could he return

home to report that he had thrown Carl out, when Carl wasn't actually there to throw out? He now realised that this mission would have to be aborted and he would have to return to base camp to report his failure. This just won't do, he thought. But then, as if sent from above, he spotted a handwritten note torn from a foolscap pad on the side of the worktop. The note was being weighed down by an apple. He unfolded his reading glasses and perched them on the end of his nose, swiftly bringing his eyes into focus. It read:

ive left Carl

This didn't quite make sense to George. He read and reread it but it didn't become any clearer. His attempts to understand it by holding the paper at different angles and different distances from his face didn't seem to help either. "Hmm… some punctuation would help," he thought out loud. Now what could this message mean?

There were two possible solutions to the riddle. The first was that Sam had written the note, perhaps as a statement of intent whilst she got her thoughts together. The statement was a way of empowering herself and writing it down in black and white perhaps made it more real and final to her. If this was the case, George concluded, no punctuation was in fact necessary and the note made perfect sense. However, the second option was that the wordsmith was actually Carl and the note lacked a full stop between words two and three.

Now this was a muddle, thought George, sitting at the breakfast bar to gather his thoughts. He felt a little light-headed. He was hugely relieved that he hadn't needed to confront Carl over the issue, but his task was far from over as he couldn't work out *who* had left *whom*. This added further pressure on what to tell his daughter on his return home. George folded the note and put it inside his jacket pocket.

Meanwhile, back at home, Sheila was offering her own style of assistance to her distressed daughter.

"I've always said he's not right for you, love. Always. But would you bloody listen? No. You wouldn't listen to your mum, would you?" It was amazing how any situation could be strategically rotated back to Sheila. "I said to you time and time again that he was bad news. It was those eyebrows, or eyebrow I should say. There was just something wrong about him. Never treated you right, I'll say that to you, love. Never. And now where are we? You've got a smashed up face, our Mollie hasn't got a clue what's going on, and how does this look for me, eh? My only daughter in another failed relationship, battered and bruised. How does it look for me? I told you, Samantha, but you wouldn't listen. You wouldn't listen, would you?"

As it happened, Sam wasn't listening now either. She stared out of the window, wondering where her dad might be.

Twenty minutes later and after some extremely deep thinking, George decided on a course of action. The note didn't make any sense but he had no choice but to somehow solve the riddle. He thought about the book he had just finished, yes, that was full of mysteries and clues. He fully focused his attention, resting his elbows on the breakfast bar and holding his hands to the side of his head, pushing his index fingers into his temples. He closed his eyes and tried to think in the same way Dr Robert Langdon would.

After a further twenty minutes of meditation-like thinking, George came up with the solution. He rose with purpose and went into the bedroom. Pulling across the ceiling-high mirrors of the built-in wardrobe, he made his discovery. There in front of him was a full row of empty hangers. He closed the door and repeated the procedure on the next door. In front of him was row upon row of hanging clothes. "Girls' clothes," he exclaimed and realised for the first time the true meaning of the note. He carefully unfolded it and, taking his biro from the inside pocket of his jacket, added a full stop after the word "left". "It's all about simple punctuation," he said, extremely pleased with himself.

He briefly checked the drawers in the bedroom, which reinforced his interpretation of the note. Happy that the coast was clear and the enemy averted, he made his way into the hall, clicked the latch down and closed the front door behind him.

Climbing back into his car, he started the engine and checked his mirrors before easing the car forwards. *Elvira Madigan* would accompany him home.

ten

It had now been six months since the different knock at the door and in this time plenty had changed.

The knock, as Adam now knew, belonged to Kelly. She had popped her head around his door at the moment he felt that the ceiling and floor were about to meet one another with him between them, smiled and asked him what he was up to. He had turned slowly to lift his face from the pillow and adjusted his eyes to see who the voice belonged to. He recognised Kelly from school immediately, her messy fringe covering her eyes and her sweet smile lighting up her fairly pudgy face.

"Not much," he had replied sullenly, "just hanging out."

"Do you wanna hang out somewhere…," she paused, "…not so dark?"

Adam had pushed himself up and sat on the edge of his bed, rubbing his eyes to waken himself. He had forgotten how it felt to be upright again. He scratched around in his bedroom looking for something to change into, picking up and discarding the various balled up items from the floor, until Kelly interrupted and informed him he looked fine and suggested "let's go somewhere… like, now."

Adam's demeanour since that time had changed dramatically. It was a slow transformation at first, but within a week or two it appeared to George that his son had made it to the other side of puberty. This puzzled George immensely. It wasn't as if he hadn't offered his help over the many months of darkness. However, George was wise enough to know that children of that age weren't exactly open to listening to the helpful guidance of their parents.

Further, George was aware that Sheila, for all her faults, had tried to connect with their son as well. It was, however, a fact that her connections usually began with a quiet knock on the door and a gentle glide across the room to sit adjacent to Adam's stomach. She would then fix her understanding face (complete with cocked head and raised eyebrows) and focus her gaze on the duvet, stroking it methodically as though trying to flatten out all the creases, before whispering bedside assistance to her son. Her comforting words, though not dissimilar to everyone else's, were invariably met with a wall of silence. Within minutes Adam's inaction would lead to Sheila slamming the door behind her and a raised cry of "Well, if you won't talk to me, what am I supposed to do?" or "You're just bloody lazy, Adam, bloody lazy" or even "Do you know how hard this is for me?". George had tried once or twice to explain to Sheila that her lack of patience "wasn't, er, well how shall I, er, put it – very helpful". On each occasion, this was met with a flattened raised hand, which seemed to push George's words away, followed by a "Don't" through gritted teeth. From then on George "didn't".

Even Adam's friends had tried to coax him from his room, but they had given up when girls became a more favourable diversion than trying to talk in half-light to someone who still looked like their friend but seemed different. Some had blamed it on his regular cannabis use, whilst others perhaps less vocal on the subject due to their own 'hobbies' had retorted that he had simply changed. The truth of the matter was that Adam hadn't actually been using cannabis for quite some time and the reason for this was fear. After all, he was too scared to leave his room and, mainly due to the unmistakable aroma, smoking in his room was not an option.

These feelings of isolation and despair, however, were now a thing of the past.

Kelly had appeared and, in Adam's mind, had rescued him. Adam had known Kelly for some years through school and various mutual friends and she had called that day because (as she later admitted) she had heard he had some weed. This had turned out to be the case and after some persuasion the two of them had gone up to the muck stack to smoke and talk. It hadn't taken long for the two of them to be giggling almost manically and for Adam to notice a slight return of colour in the world which was wrapped all around him.

Since that time the two had become inseparable, spending day after day after day with one another. Adam now had a reason to dispel the inertia which enveloped his life. He had a reason to leave his room: he had Kelly now and they were a team. Kelly's

41

exuberance and glowing nature completed Adam and, little by little, seemed to stir his inner characteristics of humour, sensitivity and consideration; characteristics that he had long forgotten he possessed. Adam's relationship with Kelly sparked feelings inside him that made him suddenly think about *and believe in* the future. He secretly planned their future together and when they kissed he felt love pour from his chest through his mouth and into hers with overwhelming intensity. It seemed that the vulture had returned, dropping its carrion at his feet.

It worried George that Adam rarely seemed to be at home any more, arriving back only very late at night after he and Sheila were in bed and then leaving again at sometime around lunchtime the next day. The only indication that he had been there was the shout of "I'm off out" as the front door thumped closed behind him. But when their paths did cross, George felt that Adam was positively cheery, albeit he and Kelly talked extremely quickly most of the time, usually allowing no space between the end of one word and the beginning of the next. On one occasion George had been downstairs in the kitchen getting some warm milk to help himself sleep when the two of them bounded in. He had to ask them to "slow down, please" so he could understand their youthful banter and excitement, and after their whirlwind chat he'd had to have a little sit down due to feeling slightly dizzy. He was bemused as to where they got the energy at such a late hour. They were just so full of life, he had eventually ratiocinated, before returning with his milk to bed.

So it was a surprise to encounter a less-than-excitable Adam and Kelly in the kitchen one afternoon. They both looked extremely tired with eyelids which seemed to hang almost right to the bottom of their eyes, their view on the world nothing more than a squint. You could almost see the whites of their eyes (through the red) on the small proportion of the eyeball you could see. But nevertheless, George concluded, they both seemed happy.

"Hi, Dad."

"Oh, hullo, Adam. Hullo, Kelly."

Kelly tittered. George wasn't sure why.

"You both look extremely tired today, been out having some fun?"

Adam tittered, which caused Kelly to again.

"Yes, Mr Poppleton, we've been out with friends," she said sweetly.

"You kids must have been having fun to look so tired. Your eyes look like you could do with forty winks, if you ask me."

Kelly tittered again and then stifled her laugh, which unfortunately led to Adam letting out one of his own as a replacement.

"Your eyes look huge, Dad," tittered Adam, "like giant space saucers or plates or space plates!"

Kelly now let out a loud noise similar to a raspberry as an impressive opening to a laugh she simply couldn't stifle any more.

"Space plates," she repeated, "space plates!"

"You wouldn't be able to eat your dinner off space plates," Adam giggled, "the food would just keep floating up off the plate. You'd need anti-gravity gravy!"

George looked utterly confused.

"Space plates!" laughed Kelly. "Gravy!" She was now laughing so much that she hadn't realised that she was leaning into George as a way to keep upright.

Adam noticed this, which in turn set him off into further hysterics as he watched his girlfriend steady herself on his dad.

Kelly laughed.

George smiled awkwardly with absolutely no idea why.

Then, suddenly, Adam became very serious.

"But, Dad, can you imagine it, man? Like all the debris floating above us all in space. Just floating, like endlessly?" His eyes focused on a small area of the kitchen ceiling as he imagined the night sky above it. "It's kinda too hard to imagine, Dad, all the debris which kinda just hangs in the sky above us, floating from planet to planet with no control over its own direction…"

Kelly and George were silent as they listened. Kelly was fascinated. George was bewildered: he'd had no idea his son was so interested in the solar system.

Adam continued to stare through the ceiling to the night sky. "Just crashing endlessly, man. It's unreal. Debris floating to eternity. Just floating. Too much to take in man…" His sentence drifted off as his eyes lowered. He noticed Kelly leaning into a wide-eyed George and burst into giggles again. "Fucking space plates," he said.

"Space plates!" laughed Kelly as her concentration on Adam's space fantasy was broken. Her shoulders instantly moved up and down rapidly with laughter again.

George watched as his son and son's girlfriend's faces became an ever deepening scarlet as tears streamed from their eyes. Each bout of laughter set off some kind of chain reaction in the other, which seemed to up the stakes in an unusual laugh-off competition. It was a happy scene, thought George, and he almost giggled himself, but didn't. He hadn't understood a word of it.

George excused himself and set off out to his shed, wondering where today's children got their wild and wacky ideas from. He smiled and as he slid the patio door shut he could still hear the young couple back in the kitchen laughing.

"Space plates!" snorted Kelly as she embraced Adam tightly.

eleven

The journey home had been much more satisfactory than the outbound journey. George felt far more relaxed knowing that his fatherly duties had been performed and he could return somewhat of a hero back to his wife and daughter to proudly inform them that the evil Tsar Carl had been overthrown. However, this in itself presented George with a problem. His difficulty now was how he would present the facts of his mission to the family. On the one hand, Carl was gone and in truth he hadn't *actually* had to do anything. This was not strictly true, George corrected himself; he had after all been forced into deciphering a particularly complex cipher. On the other hand, did Sam actually want Carl out? He did seem to remember that these were his instructions when he had left earlier that afternoon, but he was also aware that women sometimes say one thing when they actually mean the exact opposite.

He could recall a number of instances when Sheila had spoken to him and he had followed her instruction to the letter only to have been screamed at shortly afterwards and then be met with long, drawn-out sighs and tuts for the rest of the afternoon. "Don't bother getting up and helping me," she had once said, wobbling on a stool whilst trying to reach a box of Family Circle on top of the kitchen cupboards. In George's mind this was a straightforward simple and clear statement. But after toppling from the stool and falling heavily onto the lino floor, swiftly followed by a monsoon of Garibaldi's, Bourbons and Jammy Dodgers, she had directed a storm of abuse at George before salvaging the biscuits and banishing him from the lounge for the rest of the day.

The sound of a car horn behind him brought his wandering mind back to the present time and George lifted his hand to the rear-view mirror to apologise before putting the car into first gear and pulling away from the traffic lights. The car passed with its occupants gesturing and informing George that potentially he was too old to be on the road. It was unlikely that the passengers heard George reply "I'm only sixty-three" as the car was nearly out of sight by the time he wound his window down. The incident had shaken him slightly and, deciding that perhaps he needed a little thinking time, he pulled off the main road and into the car park of a local country park to settle himself. He wished that he had brought his radio to soothe him, but unfortunately it had been left behind in his coat pocket when the earlier drama unfolded.

George began to weigh up the situation. He turned the wheel on the side of his chair and reclined backwards slightly, closing his eyes and whispering his father's rhyme, which would help him bring clarity to the situation: "A problem can be solved, with no haste it'll be resolved, tune your brain so you'll think logically, and deal with it methodically."

George began to put the predicament into a neat and tidy order in his mind. Carl had left, and Sam had wanted Carl to leave. This was good. Sam had instructed him to get Carl out of the house and he had managed to do this without any incident. Carl had indeed answered the call of both George and Sam and had left before anyone had to get him out. This was very good. Did Sam actually want Carl out of the flat? George was not so sure about this. Carl had, after all, attacked his daughter, and who would wish to spend another moment in the company of a person who would do that? But George had seen the television shows that Sheila watched where all manner of less fortunate people stuck with their partners who were, let's say, less than kind to them. They stayed because they loved them, they said. But this situation was different. In all the time that Carl and Sam had been together there had appeared, at least to George, no inkling whatsoever of love. Sam had never been even remotely kind to Carl in George's company. He also knew that Mollie wasn't very fond of Carl: any mention of him to his granddaughter was usually met with silence and a look of blank indifference. There could be no question in this circumstance that love would keep them together because it appeared that there simply wasn't any.

George thought back to the first time he had met Carl. He had gone to Sam's flat to collect her and take her into town for a night out. He had sat outside with the engine running whilst Sam put the finishing touches to her face. He had been trying to guess the age of a nearby tree when he had been startled by the back doors of the car being opened.

"Hullo, Samantha, hullo, David," he had said without turning when the passengers were safely inside.

"It's Carl," came the brusque response from just behind George's right ear.

"Oh," said George, visibly freezing before managing a stuttering, "Hullo, Carl." He was confused as to why David would suddenly take on a different name. Fortunately for George, his confusion would be expelled with the next sentence.

"This is Carl, Dad," said Sam. "Me and David have split up. I'm with Carl now – we're together."

"Oh," said George.

"Yeah, she dumped him, pal."

"We kinda grew apart, Dad," said Sam. "Things haven't been going that well for a while and then, well, I met Carl and told David that we were finished."

Kind of grew apart? thought George. They didn't seem too apart when they returned from Greece last week. In fact, they seemed very together. Sam had been in his kitchen parading the new jewellery David had bought her and David had watched her adoringly. This was all very sudden, he thought, at the same feeling his face visibly reddening. This simply wouldn't do. But George knew better than to speak his mind in front of Sam. He knew that he could be trounced in seconds by a vicious diatribe from his daughter, learned directly from the School of Sheila.

"Oh," said George again, suspecting that his thinking time had brought about a suspiciously lengthy pause in the conversation.

"Carl's a bricklayer," said Sam for reasons that even she didn't understand.

Say *something* George implored himself and not "Oh"; *something, think*, George, *THINK!*

"I wonder how old that tree is over there," said George, nodding in its direction, relief flooding through his body as he slowly pulled the car onto the road.

On the trip into town George had remained mute as Sam and Carl chatted in the back. He had managed a few glimpses in the rear-view mirror to try to get a better look at Carl. Although the light outside was fading he could make out that Carl's head looked somewhat like a breezeblock with straw-yellow spiked hair stuck on the top. He wore what looked like a gold bicycle chain around his neck and had a nose that looked like it had been ironed. He was nothing like David, George surmised.

"Stop here, pal," Carl had barked and the two of them had left the car in seconds without another word.

It wasn't exactly the best of first impressions, but fortunately for George's future mental stability that day was to become typical of every exchange he had with Carl in the future. And now, four years on, the only thing he knew was that his daughter's ex-boyfriend was called Carl and he was a bricklayer.

The relationship throughout this time had been through many ups and downs with the emphasis firmly on downs. Sam mostly didn't appear to like him. Mollie just didn't like him. George himself didn't like him. Sheila flipped between like and dislike simultaneously with her daughter's mood. No, George concluded, there was no possibility that on his arrival home he would be met with anything other than a family relieved to be rid of this character.

"Thinking time over," George announced to himself with a contented grin on his face. He wound his seat back into the upright position and checked his mirrors before signalling and manoeuvring back onto the main road towards home.

The house was a hive of activity on his return. He let himself in and was greeted by a huge smile from Mollie, who was lying on the sofa watching television.

"Hullo, Mollie."

"Hi, Grandpa," said Mollie. "Has he gone?"

"Yes, sweetheart, he has."

Mollie beamed, letting out a quiet celebratory "Yay", before turning back towards the screen.

There was a buzz of excitement coming from the kitchen, accompanied by various tones of cackling laughter.

"Hi, Dad!" exclaimed Sam as George entered the room, feeling every part the war veteran returning from the frontline after many years away.

"George, you're back," said Sheila, stating the startlingly obvious once again.

Four empty bottles of wine made a fine centrepiece in the middle of the kitchen table, with numerous bottles of beer scattered around them like toddlers standing alongside their mothers. Lesley made up the last of the coven, sitting half slumped at the far end of the table. Sheila must have telephoned her with the news and she had immediately travelled over to offer support (though it was more likely that she had smelled the bouquet of the wine and simply followed her nose).

"Hi, George!" she slurred, neatly managing to put together a sentence by fusing together words from the two preceding greetings.

The three women turned and continued their conversation as George stood slightly uncomfortably off to the side. He certainly hadn't expected this. Perhaps they had forgotten he was there? He was, after all, out of visibility to them and thus it was likely that they may have thought he had left the room to dress his war wounds. The women continued their chat, apparently oblivious to George's presence. He stood for a minute longer before mustering his maximum confidence and then pulled out a chair and sat at the table.

"So," he said, "I see you've had a few glasses of wine, ladies."

"Just one or two, Dad," laughed Sam. She looked remarkably happy despite her own war wounds (though admittedly these were numbed from imbibing a natural anaesthetic).

George expected that someone would ask him about his trip to the flat so he could give them in depth details of his mission, from the initial drive to its wonderful conclusion.

No one did.

Even though George was fully visible to each of the women he was perplexed as to why he wasn't the main attraction in terms of conversational participation. He summoned all of his courage to speak again. This had been a most difficult mission for him and he simply must share the details.

"Well, I've been over to the flat," George interrupted.

"We know, George," said Sheila dismissively.

"There was a note," said George, wondering whether he would have to tell his entire tale in staccato bursts of sentence. In truth, he would much rather tell the story from beginning to end than in this way – it would make it much easier to follow, you see. George knew from experience that if he didn't follow a story from beginning to end in chronological order, it became far too confusing. Some of the films nowadays started at the end (*the end!?!*) and he quickly found that he was lost and in a terrible muddle trying to work out what was happening. This was why he no longer watched films.

"We know, George," said Sheila wearily.

"The note was from Carl," said George proudly, as if revealing an unexpected ace at the end of a card game.

"We know," said Sam and Sheila in unison.

"… know," slurred Lesley, just off cue.

"Dad, Carl phoned just after you left. He said he had taken all his stuff from the flat and left me a note. He said that he wasn't coming back and it was over…"

"So she told him," interrupted Sheila, realising that as usual it was her turn to usurp the zenith of the story, "she told him she wouldn't have him back after what he did to her, didn't you, love? She said she's glad he's moved out and he couldn't finish her and tell her it was over 'cause she'd already finished him, didn't you, love? And you're not bothered about him at all, are you, love?"

"Do I look bloody bothered?" shrieked Sam and all three women burst into further crow-like laughter.

"Not bothered," slurred Lesley.

"Anyway, Dad, we were waiting for you to get back 'cause we're going out to celebrate, aren't we, Mum? Auntie Lesley?"

Both nodded in eager agreement and the three were up from the table in seconds.

"You'll have Mollie tonight, won't you, Dad?" said Sam as they left the room. The cackling continued until the front door closed.

George was left alone once more. "Glass of milk, Mollie?" he offered as he popped his head around the lounge door. Mollie nodded, smiling. George turned and plodded back to the kitchen and began clearing the bottles into the recycle bin.

twelve

"It's getting bloody ridiculous," said Sheila. "Absolutely bloody ridiculous."

Sheila stood alongside Pete, who had called in to see his sister for the first time in months. He observed the scene in the conservatory quietly and Sheila filled him in on the details.

Sheila had thought at first that the radio was to be a short-lived hobby. In fact, she had been quite pleased when he had first found it because it gave him a little hobby ("He doesn't have much in his life, you know"). But now the situation was getting increasingly annoying and marginally worrying to her. The problem was that George had taken to listening to the radio most of the time.

"He's constantly wearing the bloody thing," she told Pete.

Pete was well aware of Sheila's predilection for drama and he divided most things of the statements she made to him by an exaggeration factor of three. However, in this circumstance Sheila was as close to factually correct as she would ever be. It was true, George *had* begun to listen to the radio far more often. In the early days, he would settle down for an hour a day to relax and clear his mind with some gentle classical music. Now it was a different story. He had begun to wear it during every meal time and now, even in bed. If Sheila was unsure where to find him it would always be in the conservatory with his eyes shut and the orange headphones concealing his ears. If that wasn't enough, only that morning she had popped into the bathroom to find George perched on the toilet, eyes closed and humming quietly to the music playing into his ears.

She was beginning to feel that his anodyne existence had reached a new record low.

"Well, if he's happy...," said Pete, "... I can't see the problem," still observing clandestinely through the window.

"The problem... Pete ...is that, well, he doesn't listen to me any more. He doesn't, well, do things for me any more."

"Hmm," said Pete, half-listening. He was now preoccupied with a sudden change in events in the conservatory.

George had risen to his feet, eyes still tightly shut, and lifted both his right and left arms to the corresponding side of his head. He was standing completely still as if portraying a giant fork.

"Oh, God," sighed Sheila, resigned, "he's going to bloody conduct."

Seconds later, George was jerking around from side to side, his hands pointing to nothing in particular, and moving his head in appreciation of the efforts of the orchestra. Every so often his left hand, which remained raised, would become motionless whilst his right bobbed up and down to the rhythm of whatever instrument he was directing.

The two of them watched in silence for three or four minutes before Sheila interrupted with, "What do you think, Pete?"

Pete was puzzled. He didn't really know what to think. It was unlike George to have any kind of hobby which impinged on Sheila's needs. However, this whole situation was probably incredibly healthy for George, who, it appeared, was simply learning to relax. For all their differences, Pete liked George and knew that it could not have been easy for him to live with his sister for all these years. The discovery of the radio had probably come just in time to save George's sanity.

"I think he's fine. Nothing wrong with letting off some steam, is there? I must say I prefer darts, though," said Pete, winking. "Anyway, I'd better get off. Tell him I called, won't you?"

Sheila sighed, watching through the lounge window as Pete wandered down the path and out of the gate. She wasn't exactly worried about George – it was just, well, he was changing, and not for the better.

She paused for a second, deep in thought. Whilst staring into space she noticed that the sideboard was beginning to gather perhaps too much dust, so she removed all the family photographs and laid them to one side. In the kitchen she glanced through into the conservatory to see George still in full flow and decided for the first time in years that she would do the dusting.

On returning to the lounge, she sprayed a large haze of

furniture polish onto the coffee table and began circular motions with her yellow duster.

"Do you think your dad is acting oddly, Adam?" she said to her son, who was lying on the sofa.

No answer.

"Adam. Do you think your dad is okay? He always seems to have that radio on nowadays."

No answer.

In all honesty she didn't really expect an answer, but perhaps she hoped that she and her son could put behind them their unwritten pact of non-communication and that today he may offer some guidance. She moved over to the sideboard, firing another burst of spray.

"He seems to always have it on," she continued. "He never really listens to me any more and he just seems so... well, distracted."

Again there was no answer, and for the first time she could remember she felt she had lost a little control. She looked down at the sofa and smiled at her son, who smiled back. The dusting now complete, she retrieved the photographs and carefully polished each frame individually before neatly rearranging them back on the sideboard.

thirteen

Kelly was gone and Adam knew she wasn't coming back. A six-month sabbatical from darkness had abruptly and quite definitively come to an end. Adam was now back to where he had started.

He had enjoyed a hiatus in his life where colour and noises and sounds and conceivably even joy existed. This was now finished. The dark black blanket which had provided no comfort was now laid grimly over his life and all thoughts of colour had again disappeared.

Kelly had been the bright hope of the family to help their son to believe in the world and believe in life. George and Sheila had, within their own limitations, done their best to help Adam move forwards, but both would admit without question that maybe the task was for someone else. Someone not so close. Someone better equipped. Someone from Adam's peer group.

During the previous three or four months Sheila had been heard to say that Kelly was just what Adam needed, and George had agreed. George had expressed his feelings on more than one instance, stating "Kelly is just the type of girl to give Adam some hope and belief" and Sheila had nodded.

And so was the problem. Kelly had been pedestalised and had become some kind of deity in the minds of the Poppletons, yet the truth was that they knew little or nothing about her. Kelly had felt this idealisation, and as time went by she too had begun to believe that Adam's entire existence relied upon her.

This was a difficult situation for anyone, but for a sixteen-year-old girl who had only intended on scoring some soft drugs that little time ago, well, it had been a lifetime. And so, over the last month, the regular teenage girlfriend/boyfriend conversations had begun to arise between the two: "You don't have to see me every night, Adam, it's okay," she would reassure him; or, "Go out, have a good time with your friends, see what they're up to," she would encourage him; or, "I'm going to see my friends tonight, I'll see you tomorrow instead," she would inform him; and then, "We're not glued together, you know. We're two separate people with our own lives," she would warn him.

Adam didn't see it that way, though. For every moment that Kelly appeared not to want to be with him was another hammer blow that suggested who he was wasn't enough. Every time she encouraged him to be away from her was another accolade achieved in reduced self-worth. And in the latter months, Adam began to slowly feel the monotone greyness re-enter his life. It started slowly, then quickly it seemed that the remaining colour was being sucked, as if by some colossal vacuum cleaner, permanently from his life.

Then, one night, it all went black.

Adam had arrived at Kelly's house. He just wanted to see her smile, which always pierced the fog of gloom that hung over him. But Kelly hadn't invited Adam over that evening, and indeed had made it quite clear that she wasn't seeing him that night – she was spending time with her friends. So when she heard Adam's knock from her lounge, her temper rose and she threw open the door with a look of bitter resentment on her face. Adam had quickly realised that the intended visual purpose of his visit was unlikely to be achieved.

"What do you want?" she had snarled.

"I just came to…"

"To what, Adam, to what?" she interrupted. "To check up on me, to see what I'm doing, to WHAT?"

"To see…"

"Go, Adam," she instructed.

Adam nearly spoke but the words wouldn't come.

"Just go," she said resignedly, closing the door.

Head down, Adam traipsed back up the front path. He wandered the streets for hours, trying to work out what the exchange of just over thirty words had meant. But he couldn't. He couldn't work it out and his skull felt like it was beginning to grip his brain from the inside. He had simply wanted to see her smile. This wasn't too much to ask, surely? He hadn't intended on staying for longer than the moment it took to see her mouth curl up and her dimples become evident and the look in her deep brown eyes that reassured him everything was alright. That's all he had gone there for. Why couldn't she understand this? Why couldn't she have just smiled at him?

But then it struck him. She had not smiled because she didn't feel like smiling. Because of him. Her eyes could not show everything was alright because it wasn't. Because of him.

He suddenly had the sinking feeling that the "just go" was a final instruction, her last request.

Adam returned home. He had thought better of going home in the state he was in; after all, he was open to all manner of nonsensical encounters with his parents and he simply didn't want that. He didn't want to get engaged in any type of "How's Kelly?" or "Have you had fun?" conversations. But the cold crisp winter night finally took its toll and he realised home was really his only option. It wasn't actually home he wanted, he simply wanted his room.

Climbing into his bed, his brain endlessly swayed and rolled and rotated those two words, "just go", trying desperately to unravel his future.

Sheila opened the front door early the following morning to collect the milk. The used Tesco bag containing the few possessions that Adam had left at Kelly's house would solve her son's puzzle.

fourteen

"Oh, Jesus." Sheila exhaled wearily as she looked through the lounge curtain. The doorbell had forced her to avert her attention from the final moments of a 'miracle' facial-hair removal cream infomercial and the view on the other side of the window was not what she hoped for. She dragged herself up from the sofa and opened the front door.

"Oh, hullo, Sheila, my dear, how are…"

"Walter," she curtly interrupted.

"Would you help me?" he requested, motioning to the doorstep.

For God's sake, Sheila thought, why can't you make it up the step, it's ONE step, not bloody K9 (or whatever that mountain was called).

"It's my legs, you know, they're not so good now. Not so good."

Sheila wasn't listening; she could hear the presenter about to announce the product number of the cream.

"Come on," she said abruptly, stepping out of the house and down one step in her slippers. She yanked his stick away and threw it into the house, feeling it would be quicker to simply march him in.

"There are limited stocks available…" the television continued.

Sheila quickly linked her arm with Walter's and began pulling him forwards into the house.

"It's my legs, you know," Walter continued, "they're not so good now. It's a nice day, though, isn't it, dear?"

Surely you can lift your foot six inches, thought Sheila, her forthcoming purchase beginning to evaporate. Walter felt like a deadweight. She tried to move him but his feet would only move the slightest of fractions. Walter saw this as an achievement and stopped to give another useful insight into the state of his legs, the weather and the fact that he was nearly ninety.

"…your last chance to hear the product code," the television mocked.

"Come on, Walter," Sheila hurried. She was beginning to feel frantic about her cream purchase disappearing in front of her eyes. For Christ's sake, she thought, if she didn't get it *she* would look nearly ninety.

Walter continued to shuffle millimetres at a time. Sheila by this time had certainly had enough and was attempting to manually lift Walter's right knee high enough to at least get it onto the step. Walter – at least, it appeared to a now extremely agitated Sheila – was concentrating his entire body weight into any part of him that Sheila tried to move.

"Did you see that lovely old pocket watch on *The Antiques Roadshow* yesterday?" continued Walter, oblivious to Sheila's now frenzied state of mind.

"…we have had a deluge of orders from you all… thank you… only fifty now remain so be quick."

Walter's right foot was now on the step but Sheila knew all too well that she was now supporting his full weight from behind. She had one hand on his hip and if she stepped back he would simply fall over to his right into the garden. The cream was disappearing – it was time to call for back-up. Cries for George were interspersed with useful titbits from Walter such as "Oh yes, good idea" and "He'll come and help out, won't he, my dear?"

The exclamations and shrieks must have gone on for at least five minutes before Sheila realised George wasn't coming. It must have been five minutes because somewhere between shouts Sheila had heard the programme return from a commercial break and the television announce glibly that they were down to their final stock.

Had George known, he would have been more than happy to come to assist his wife and ensure that his father got into the house safely. But George hadn't heard any of this commotion. He was in the garden enjoying Haydn's *Seventeenth Opus*.

Sheila now knew that to get the cream she had to act quickly. No one was going to come to her aid and rescue the situation as had happened so many times before. It was all down to her, a feeling that was entirely alien to her. In an instant she decided that the only possible hope was to take a step back and literally push her father-in-law forwards. At worst he would fall sideways onto the grass where she could leave him for a few moments (enjoying the weather) whilst she made her way into the lounge. At best he would settle at least in part in the house and she could get George to finish the retrieval. She could, after all, blame it on "a fall".

With one almighty push and without prior warning, Sheila shoved Walter forwards towards the open door. The momentum was a little too much and she tumbled with him, ending up straddled over his back in a kind of horse-riding style pose. Miraculously, they both managed to make it into the lounge (aside from Walter's calves, which stuck horizontally out of the front door). Now, thought Sheila, make the call – I NEED THIS CREAM.

George was shocked as he entered the lounge to see his wife apparently pushing his father's head into the deep pile. Sheila needed to get to the phone and using her father-in-law's head as leverage seemed more than reasonable in the circumstances. It was only by chance that George had even seen this spectacle. Quite coincidentally, he had been passing to go upstairs to use the bathroom. He hadn't been aware that his father had even arrived.

"Oh, goodness," exclaimed George, quickly removing the orange headphones and rotating the dial to the click that switched off the radio. "Whatever's happened here?"

Sheila grabbed George's jumper and pulled herself up desperately, standing on Walter's back in the process.

"Where's the phone, George? Where's the bloody phone?" she screeched.

George hadn't time to even look when Sheila spotted her mobile on the coffee table and leapt headlong over the corner of the settee to retrieve it.

"Dad? Are you okay?"

Walter spoke but George couldn't make out his response, which was muffled by the carpet. All he could hear was Sheila breathlessly recounting the product code to the call centre operator at the other end of the phone.

George knelt down to carpet level and spoke again to his father. "Dad?"

"No, no, no, twenty-nine, ninety-six, fifty-one, THIR-*TY* not THIRT-*EEN*!" Sheila continued. "It's the cream I want, THIR-

TY, as in the number after twenty-nine!" she gasped, trying to catch her breath.

"Are you okay down there?" George was beginning to worry that his father was still face down in the carpet.

"Thank goodness, you finally understand," she panted. "Is there any stock left?" There was a tension-laden pause, then, "There are!" said Sheila exalted, her face suddenly transformed from resembling a screwed-up piece of paper to that of a child let loose in a chocolate factory. "That's wonderful – yes, I'll take both of them. Thank you."

Walter finally looked up and tried to focus on his son above him.

"Dad? Are you okay? What happened here?"

"It's my legs," replied Walter, "they're not so good, you know." In all honesty, it was unlikely that Walter had any idea why he was where he was.

"Come on," said George gently, helping his father from the floor, "let's get you a nice cup of tea."

"Good idea," said Sheila, now slumped back in the armchair. "Get me a vanilla slice to go with it as well."

It took two cups of tea and the careful removal of numerous biscuit crumbs and pink carpet fluff from Walter's cheek before Walter was back in the same condition as when he had arrived. Father and son decided to spend some time together in the shed at the bottom of the garden away from the hustle and bustle, as George put it, of the house.

It took over twenty minutes to walk the thirty foot path to the shed, and along the way George encouraged his father, agreeing that it was a nice day and that he was doing extremely well for nearly ninety. Once in the shed George settled Walter comfortably in an old armchair to the side of the workbench.

"Well, it's nice to see you, Dad," said George, poking around in a jam jar packed full with nuts and bolts and other bits and pieces that men accumulate over a lifetime of tinkering.

"That's my boy," said Walter, proudly. "Always a little job to do, always on the go."

"I've been meaning to mend this old thing for a long time,"

George said, motioning towards the pocket watch on the bench in front of him.

"What is it?" said Walter, craning his neck to see his son's project. George held the watch up towards his father.

"Ooh, a beauty," said Walter cheerily. "There was one like that on television the other day."

George had picked up the pocket watch over a year earlier at a local antique fair and had tried to fix it on a several occasions.

"The problem is, Dad, that I can't seem to get this little spring to stay in place. It keeps, well, popping out."

"Oh dear," sighed Walter, removing his glasses case from the inside pocket of his blazer.

"You see, I put this little screw in here and that should hold the spring to this cog, but it doesn't seem to do the trick."

Walter motioned for the watch and George passed it over to him. In his day, Walter would have been able to solve this conundrum in a second, but nowadays his hands were a little shaky and his vision was beginning to fail him. He was very proud of the fact that his hearing was crystal clear, but his ears weren't much help in repairing a watch.

George continued to delve in the jam jar trying to feel around for perhaps a more suitable screw.

"The smallest screws – and that's what you need here – will be at the bottom," said Walter helpfully, still eyeing the timepiece in his hand.

George carefully tipped the contents of the jar onto the workbench and studied the metallic jewels in front of him. Each potential screw was held aloft towards Walter, who shook his head one by one, coupled with helpful responses of "too long" or "too wide" or "not for this job".

"Just the ticket!" Walter beamed as George held aloft the winning screw like a miniature World Cup. George smiled back at his father.

Walter handed back the watch as George painstakingly removed the cog and the ill-fitting screw and laid them to one side. He then fitted the tiny spring in place, reattached the cog and meticulously screwed the victorious screw back in place.

"There!" he said proudly as he laid the watch on the work surface, followed swiftly by "Oh bother!" as the screw catapulted out and the spring sprung after it. "This simply won't do!" said George angrily. "I just can't seem to get this thing to work." He banged the watch down on to the workbench, defeated. He was beginning to wonder why he was actually doing this.

"Now then, George," said Walter quietly but nevertheless sternly, "your mother will be looking down and she won't want to see you behaving that way."

"I know," said George guiltily. It had been many years since she had died and George knew how proud she had been of him.

Walter smiled at his son, "George…"

George glanced back to his father and returned the smile.

"… a problem can be solved, with no haste it'll be resolved, tune your brain so you'll think logically, and deal with it methodically."

George knew his father was right and retrieved the rogue parts from where they had scattered. On the advice of his father he removed two further cogs (which up until this point hadn't occurred to him) and quickly set about replacing the parts in a different order before proudly displaying the now restored watch.

"As good as new, Dad." George grinned.

"Your mother would be proud, son," said Walter gently.

George glowed with pride.

"Incidentally, how long have you been repairing this old thing?" asked Walter innocently.

"Oh, some time now, Dad, nearly a year, I'd say," said George.

"Well, I can't understand it, you'd usually have had this fixed in an hour."

George was aware of this but knew that he hadn't spent much time doing anything just recently. He usually loved his time in the shed repairing bric-a-brac (or junk as Sheila called it) but recently, well, he just didn't seem to have the time.

"I've been spending a little more time listening to an old transistor, Dad, and a little less time, well… in here."

"Oh," said Walter, raising his eyebrows ever so slightly.

fifteen

It seemed as though black smoke was billowing into the room, coming from every possible angle. It came in from the landing and under the door, blocking all light from the world outside. It came from inside the wardrobe as a surging mass which overcame the room quickly. It poured from the minute cracks in the walls and flooded across the room, seemingly attracted to the bed. The room quickly became darker and darker as the swell of the smoke covered everything with a dark residue, removing the colour instantly from the furniture which lay inside. The room was already entirely black, but it seemed like the smoke was depositing its debris thicker, ever thicker.

The figure in the bed was slowly suffocating and although nothing was physically stopping him from moving, he also knew there was nothing he could do. He lay, catatonically, as time passed without his knowledge or participation.

The figure in the bed now knew that he couldn't stop this.

sixteen

It seemed an excellent idea to George to make contact with David in his daughter's time of need. Sam had been single for more than a month, and although she had coped very well in this time, George felt she may need a little boost. David had immediately sprung to mind.

Following Carl's departure, George had covertly noted that his daughter seemed to be longing for something. It had been a difficult time for her and she had kept herself busy, admirably pursuing many evening activities. George had certainly noted a swift rise in the number of evenings he had spent at home alone with Mollie. But each day, Sam (and Sheila for that matter) had seemed a little distant and George felt perhaps a little fatherly focus would put her back on track.

The idea had come to him one afternoon whilst sitting in the conservatory. Having listened to the radio solidly for five hours he had removed his headphones and sat back in his chair. He heard his daughter and wife chatting together in the kitchen.

"I know it's hard, love, but you will meet someone one day. You deserve that."

"I know I will, Mum. It's just, well, men are just interested in themselves. They don't care about what a woman needs."

"You're right, love. All they care about is themselves, they just don't know what a woman needs."

"Take Carl, for example. He was more bothered about his mates than me…"

David wasn't, thought George.

"… and he used to keep all his money to himself…"

David didn't, thought George.

"… I mean, how long were we together? And we never put all our money together even though he earned more than me…"

David did, thought George.

"… and he never bought me anything, like a surprise or gifts or anything."

Bingo! David did.

And so George's plan was hatched. He had listened intently for a good fifteen minutes and now believed he knew the solution to his daughter's problems. She wanted a man who would share with her. She wanted a man who would treat her as an equal. She wanted a man who would surprise her with gifts. She wanted a man who was thoughtful and kind and caring.

And of course, David could provide all of these things and more. George was suddenly filled with excitement – he could solve everything for Sam and he could do it right away. "George's Marvellous Medicine," he had delightedly said to himself as he cantered through the kitchen and upstairs to the quiet of the bedroom where he could make the call.

It took some time for George to get through. There was a lot of bother with dialling codes and not using zeroes (when they were evidently part of the number) and adding a plus sign at the start of the number (of all things!). He also had to endure at least three recorded American voices that had instructed him to "please replace the handset and redial using the correct caller information". So when the long, drawn-out ring of the overseas phone network finally sounded George almost fell off the bed with excitement. The ring of the phone seemed to take a lifetime to George, who was by this time near wetting himself with anticipation. Finally, though, he heard a click and he knew that he was connected.

"Hello?" said a voice heavy with sleep at the other end of the phone.

"David?" enquired George.

"Who is this?" asked David, shocked by the intrusion so late into the night.

"David, it's George, George Poppleton, Samantha's father," George gushed. "You know, Mollie's grandpa, Sheila's husband, Adam's dad." (He was beginning to run out of family relationships to articulate.) "It's George Poppleton!" he triumphantly concluded.

"Hello, George," David replied sleepily.

"How are you?" asked George enthusiastically.

"I'm, er, okay, thanks," replied David. "It's, er, well, sort of the middle of the night here in Tokyo. Is everything okay?"

Apparently not noticing David's time difference hint, George continued, "Everything's fine, just fine, thank you. Er, we've all been, er, talking about you a lot."

"Oh?" said David suspiciously.

It had been many years since he had been dispatched from Sam's life without a moment's warning and headed overseas to lick his wounds. Indeed, it had been a long time since he had heard anything from the Poppletons. He did, as always, send Mollie birthday and Christmas cards and a little present each year but he had never heard anything in return from either her or Sam. He had always carefully written his telephone number on the bottom of the card just in case she or Mollie chose to respond. He had done the same with Mr and Mrs Poppleton, and at the other end of the phone George held such a card in his hand.

It wasn't as if Mollie was even his daughter – she was already born when David had arrived on the scene – but he had taken to her in an instant and since that day had protected her like his own precious gemstone. As far as he knew, not even Sam knew whose daughter she was, but in his short duration as father figure, she may as well have been his.

And then one day, right out of the blue, he had been dispatched with strict instructions not to get in contact and to forget about Sam and Mollie. But something inside him had not allowed him to follow these instructions. He couldn't just cut in two the bond he had formed with Mollie. And so, from the safety of six thousand miles, he had for the first time disobeyed Sam and continued his contact in the hope that one day things would change.

This was that day.

"Yes," continued George, "we've all been, er, talking a lot about you."

"Right," confirmed David sleepily but now significantly interested. "Mr Poppleton?"

"George, please."

"Er, George, would it be okay if…"

At that moment the telephone line began to crackle and a

whirring sound began which seemed to rise and fall, copying yet distorting the sound of both George and David's voices.

"…if…" David continued.

"Pardon?" asked George.

"…if I called…"

"I can't understand you," said George, straining to follow David but instead hearing a strangely robotic version of his own voice reflected back down the line into his ear.

"…reasonable time…"

"Sorry?"

"…and say, er, we could…"

"No, David, I can't quite make out your words."

"…day time…"

And then George was greeted with the familiar elongated monotonous tone which indicated that David was no longer there.

"This simply won't do," lamented George to himself.

Unbeknown to him, in Tokyo, another voice said exactly the same thing.

Two days had now passed since the phone call and the bright lights of Tokyo were now beginning to dim for David. He wondered why George hadn't called back the next day to continue the dialogue. George's call had come deep into the darkness of a Saturday morning and David had cancelled all his plans for the weekend so he could ensure that he was next to the telephone when it rang. Then perhaps he could get an idea about the little mystery which had been unfolding at the Poppletons' home back in England. He had hurriedly ended sporadic phone calls from friends over that weekend, desperately trying to keep the airwaves clear for the call he was expecting. There had been times where he had found himself standing over the phone desperately willing it to ring until his glasses slipped to the end of his nose and he needed to push them back into place with a speedy index finger. But it hadn't rung and the hours had continued to pass.

David's time alone with the mute telephone had started to play tricks with his mind. George's telephone call had been vague to say the least. "We have been all been talking about you a lot." This wasn't particularly helpful at all. David was satisfied that there was no immediate hysteria taking place. He prided himself on his logical mind and knew from the telephone conversation that no harm would have come to Sam or Mollie. This was obvious from George's tone and the words he had used. If Sam had been in grave danger or unwell it was quite evident that from six thousand miles away David could not do anything immediate to make things better (even if he was willing to do anything in his power to assist). Furthermore, if a serious drama was unfolding he couldn't think for the life of him why the entire family would switch their focus from the individual in need to David of all people. He had, after all, been consigned to the other side of the world with strict instructions not to return. At low moments he cheered himself by likening his plight to that of Papillon. Perhaps his story would end the same way. No, it was quite clear that there was something happening (but not something too big) which somehow may require his assistance.

David was fully aware that dramas in the Poppleton house, at least from the female gender, were immense occasions which blew up into a storm of the utmost importance. Seemingly innocuous situations were debated in great detail (and always with incredible volume); mother and daughter recharging one another's spirit to enable them to stand shoulder to shoulder against any perceived enemy. Tactless opinions were openly shared between the two with little thought for anyone else in the room who may wish to interject a little logic. Those wishing to proffer a little reasoned judgement would become the object of scorn and would be guaranteed an instant rebuke for siding with the enemy. It was truly very difficult to say the right thing without just agreeing. The storms that at one stage threatened to destroy everything in their paths would then gently peter out into nothing. Sheila and Sam – being right as usual – would suddenly become distracted by something else and the likes of David, and more so George, would have to forget the scornful words invariably thrown in their direction and continue on as usual. Sheila and Sam, of course, would have already forgotten the words they had used and had no patience for the injured party ruminating over such conversations at a later date. The men had learned that, apparently, the accidental raising of an eyebrow or a mistimed cough could indicate an allegiance to the enemy. And so George, and latterly David, would find it much easier to take cover during the storms, being careful not to move and certainly not to profess any opinion at all.

A sleepless Saturday night had followed the call, during which David estimated he had slept for no more than an hour. He was still slightly grouchy from the previous night's interruption when he was woken from a particularly pleasant dream (he was the slightly reluctant hero and centre of attention at the opening of a new dam he had designed). Then, conversely, he had longed the phone to make itself known again in the darkness – terrified that falling into a deep sleep could result in him missing the call and spending another frustrating day trying to solve the riddle.

On the Sunday morning he had returned to the lounge of his apartment unshowered (he couldn't risk the sound of the water drowning out the telephone) and set about designing a spreadsheet to solve his problem. Down the left he had listed the names of all the individuals who may have a part to play: George, Sheila, Sam, Mollie, Walter. Then across the top of each column he had listed potential issues which may have prompted George's call. He then neatly ranked each with a score of one (least likely) to five (most likely) numerically across from each individual. Then, using a system of intricate formulae and logarithms (which David himself wasn't sure he understood entirely) he had statistically calculated in percentage terms the likely reason why George had telephoned. This process had taken the majority of the day and David had felt extremely pleased with himself when the spreadsheet was finished. The activity had taken David's mind off the phone, which was still subdued to say the least and continued to deny him his answer. Admittedly, though, he had found himself on more than one occasion on his hands and knees under the table ensuring that the wall hadn't somehow spat out the telephone wire whilst he wasn't looking.

Now, in the early hours of Monday morning, David removed his glasses and rubbed his blurry eyes before stretching back in his chair and staring at the screen again. "Statistics don't lie," he said resolutely to himself. As if to reaffirm David's thoughts the laptop screen stared back, its display clearly presenting the unshakeable fact:

REKINDLE RELATIONSHIP WITH SAM   71.24%

And with that David saved and closed his masterpiece before opening the Nippon website to research flight times back to England. He would sleep well tonight, regardless of whether George telephoned back – the spreadsheet had, after all, proven that his return was now imperative.

On the other side of the world, George had spent the weekend listening intently to his radio. There was no reason at all that he had left David stranded in Tokyo longing to hear the sound of George's voice. There was no reason aside from the fact he had simply forgotten. George had sat through two breakfasts, two lunches and one evening meal, glued to the radio throughout. He had smiled vacantly at Sheila as she had served up the food, his foot tapping along to the sound of the orchestra whilst Sheila sat opposite. Sheila had attempted one or two conversations and when no response was forthcoming she had loudly scraped her chair back from the kitchen table and made a show of carrying her plate through into the lounge to dine alone. This had gone largely unnoticed by George, who had continued smiling throughout whilst enjoying Brahms or Chopin or whoever else came next.

Over that entire weekend the only time that Sheila and George had any meaningful conversation was when Sheila stumbled upon George hunched over the sink. She could see from behind that, for the first time since he had woken that morning, he was not wearing the headphones.

"George!" she said, more loudly than necessary with the full intention of making him jump.

George jumped.

"Oh, hullo, dear," he said, turning his head.

"What are you doing, George?"

"I'm, er, well, you see, the whatdoyoumacallits, were, er, getting a bit, er…"

"George," Sheila interrupted.

Sheila moved to one side, hoping to catch a glance into the sink, but George turned and skilfully adjusted his body so as to block her view.

"George," Sheila continued, "would you like to perhaps come to the garden centre with me?" She used a tone tinged with a slight hint of pleading that George would have realised he hadn't heard for many years if, indeed, he had been paying attention.

"Sorry, dear?" George said, his mind firmly fixed on whether leaving the orange headphone sponges in the sink too long with the Fairy Liquid may cause them damage.

"The garden centre, George, would you like to come with me?"

"Er, no, thank you, love, I'm, er, a little busy, you see."

The truth was that George had calculated that the radio would be out of action for around an hour whilst the necessary maintenance took place. He was hoping to use this time in the shed glossing an old piece of dowling which he had shortened and sanded down earlier in the week. He had even saved a cork from one of Sheila's bottles of wine to attach to one end.

"Oh, okay," said Sheila, turning to leave the room, feeling rather rejected, "I'll go by myself. See you soon."

George turned swiftly back to the sink and retrieved the sponges, wringing them out and carefully checking them for signs of damage. They seemed to have come through their submergence completely unscathed and George lovingly laid them on top of the radiator to assist them in expanding back to their original state.

Outside in the car, Sheila was worried. She couldn't remember the last time George had turned down the offer of a trip to the garden centre. Usually, the slightest mention of the garden centre would have been met in the same way that a child would react to the offer of a trip to Disneyland. Indeed, his usual fervent enthusiasm had generally been greeted with a great degree of annoyance by Sheila, who often had to snap at him to calm down as he skipped across the kitchen to put on his coat.

No, Sheila thought, something was certainly not right.

seventeen

Sam was sitting in the pub with her friend Angela. The darkness of the sky outside suggested it was some time after nine o'clock, but due to the amount of alcohol consumed neither could be entirely sure. What they did know was that they had been sitting in the same position since they had left Mollie with George at around teatime.

The two had sunken upwards of five pints of lager, each accompanied by a shooter, and they were deep in a conversation which centred around the hateful nature of men, how men don't understand women and bemoaning the fact that now, thirty years after their introduction to the world, they were as single as the day they arrived.

Angela and Sam had been friends since school and they shared everything together. Although Sam thought extremely highly of Angela (this was proven by the empty sounding "I love yous" each time they parted) she found it difficult to talk about any life issues because, in her opinion, Angela hadn't really started her own life as yet. Angela had been single throughout school and college and ever since. This made it difficult for her to offer any advice to Sam, who had basically been part of one couple or another since she was fourteen. The perceived naivety of Angela worked in Sam's favour very nicely because any advice received which didn't quite fit Sam's preconceived vision could be easily disregarded with a patronising, "Ange, you wouldn't really know, would you? Because you've not been in my situation."

Sam, on the other hand, ever the reluctant listener, didn't have much advice to give to Angela because it was rare that Angela required any. Sure, from time to time Angela would become glassy-eyed and stare wistfully into space, wishing that she had a relationship with someone else, other than her cat. Generally, though, she had become comfortable in the fact that she was alone, and as each year passed she felt that her perfect man would have to become that bit more perfect if he was to infiltrate her insulated cocoon.

And so on this evening, as the drinks began to flow and the tongues became a little looser, the two girls chatted – as was the norm – about Sam.

"You've just been unlucky, Sam, that's all..."

"I know," interrupted Sam, "it *is* just bad luck. I mean I put everything into my relationships, you know, make sure that my man has everything he wants and well, they just end up being bastards."

"There must be someone out there for you..." Angela replied selflessly.

"There will be Ange, there will be. There'll be loads of men who'd kill to be with me, but you know, I'm pretty picky about who I see. I don't just want to end up with any old tosser."

It was a shame there wasn't a third party available to point out that latterly this was precisely what Sam had excelled in.

"And," she continued whilst Angela was drawing breath, "I deserve more don't I? My mum agrees, she says, 'Sam, you deserve much, much, much better', and I know I do, but it never seems to work out, and I know it's not me, all the men I meet just, well, change."

Angela listened.

"Take Carl, for example. When we first met he couldn't buy me enough. Always paying for my drinks or pizza at the end of the night, but towards the end he was like, well, out with his mates all the time and, well, you know, not bothered about me. Then what did he do?"

He hit you, thought Angela.

"He bloody well cracked me, didn't he. For like, nothing. They're just all bastards, all of them."

As David settled himself in the hard plastic chair of the departure lounge he realised with a stab of horror that he had forgotten his in-flight earphones, which meant he was faced with the choice of either wasting three pounds on another set or finding a new pastime to fit into the programme of activities he had mapped out for the eleven-hour flight ahead. Some more Sudoku puzzles, perhaps, or a mental recital of Shakespearean soliloquies?

On any other day, he would have felt extremely displeased with himself for not being organised and meticulous in his pre-flight planning. Indeed, he couldn't remember one single occasion when he had forgotten anything. But today was different; it had all happened in such a rush. One minute he was thinking about Sam and Mollie maybe just twice or three times a day; the next, following an unexpected phone call and some pretty tricky calculations, he was about to embark on a new chapter in his life and finally be allowed to unleash his undying affection back towards Sam. I always knew this day would come, he thought as he gazed at the passengers milling about around him. Though, he reminded himself, "hoped" would perhaps be more honest than "knew".

It had been a long day already. David had arrived at the airport four hours before check-in to make sure that he was well prepared should there be a sudden gate change or announcement that he needed to hear. On arrival, he had realised that his flight hadn't yet made it onto the departure board. Taking this in his stride, he had settled down directly in front of the board and stared at it until finally his flight arrived on the bottom. After enquiring about the check-in desk number he had proudly marched down the airport and positioned himself opposite the desk until it opened. Proud to be the first in the queue, he had carried out the formalities, confirming his details and that no one had tampered with his case. They couldn't possibly have, he thought, reminding himself that the night before he had slept with the case next to his bed. He had awoken nervously in the night, worried that a case-tampering intruder may break into his apartment to fill his case with I-don't-know-what and bid a stealthy retreat without his knowledge. At that point he had got out of bed and unlocked both padlocks before thoroughly checking nothing untoward had been surreptitiously inserted between his clothing. Satisfied that all was intact, he had climbed back under the duvet and, ever vigilant, decided that he would bring the case in alongside him. To be completely sure he had tucked his arm under the elastic luggage strap, which recurrently displayed his name, happy that he would feel a tug should anyone try to interfere. It wasn't comfortable but it was effective.

His journey through security (for which he had left a possible two hours) had been a non-event and he had found himself in the departure lounge with just over three hours to spare.

He smiled to himself contentedly. Everything was going like clockwork.

"I'll have another, if you're buying, Ange!" Sam slurred.

Having bought four more drinks at the bar, Angela was curtailed on her return by the smiling face of her friend's Auntie Lesley.

"Ange, how are you, love? Is one of those for me?" she laughed, nodding at the drinks which Ange was struggling to hold in front of her.

"Well, they were for me and Sam…" she replied, nodding over in Sam's direction.

"Pass 'em here, Ange…" Lesley continued, taking the drinks without waiting for a response, "I'll take 'em over for you, love…"

"It's okay…"

"Oh, and be a good girl and get your Auntie Lesley a large glass of wine as well," said Lesley, disappearing off over to the table.

On Angela's return a few moments later, she noticed that her shot of tequila had already been consumed. She returned to her seat beside her friend.

"So, what are you two girls talking about then?" Lesley continued, seemingly unable to stop one word from flowing into the next. "Lads, I bet." (Not waiting for an answer.) "Lads, eh? Well, you'll never get one sat on your arse in the corner, will you? You need to put yourselves out there, get up and mix with 'em."

Angela glanced at Sam, hoping to catch her eye. It was her intention to somehow transmit her thoughts that they should drink up and move on. To her dismay, however, Sam appeared to have taken the bait and was laughing along with Lesley.

"Is that how you did it, Auntie Lesley? Put it about a bit to snare Uncle Pete, did you?" she joked.

"That I did," she proudly repeated, "that I did. First night with Pete, first night! But, I tell you what…" She suddenly looked serious. "I've never bloody looked back!" And with this her face cracked and she threw her head back laughing.

"But, I always pick the wrong ones…" Sam continued, as if her evening's conversation was on a tape loop which had returned to the beginning.

"Well," interrupted Lesley, "you need to be a bit more careful, doesn't she, Ange?"

Angela was unsure how to respond to this. An agreement could be met with a barbed comment from Sam about her lack of experience, and a contradiction could end up with well, God knows what, from the Jekyll and Hyde-like Lesley. As it happened, Angela didn't get the chance to respond as Lesley's question appeared to be rhetorical and her conversation rapidly moved on.

"You need a good fella, Sam, to look after you. Someone who can put up with you going out, will look after your Mollie, someone with loads of cash who'll treat you like a princess."

Sam smiled at Lesley, nodding after each trait as though Lesley had described her dream man exactly.

Lesley continued, "Someone who won't argue with you over shitty little things, someone who'll put you before them, someone to take you on holidays and give you everything you deserve, love."

"You're right, Auntie Lesley, you're right!" Sam agreed excitedly. "She's right, isn't she, Ange?!"

Angela nodded in agreement. Someone like David, she thought.

On board the plane, David neatly stored his hand luggage in the overhead locker before sitting down in his seat, a broad smile plastered across his face. He pulled the buckle across his waist, feeling like the butterflies in his chest were going to fly out of his mouth at any time. A lady in her fifties sat down next to him and he greeted her with an even wider smile and a polite "Hello". The lady returned his greeting and immediately began flicking through the in-flight magazine, making it clear that she wasn't in the mood for a chat at that moment. Slightly disheartened that he wasn't able to tell her of his wondrous romantic adventure immediately, David put her demeanour down to nerves and vowed to fill her in with all the details once they were airborne.

Moments later, the plane was taxiing out of the airport and the pilot demanded everyone's attention as the safety demonstration took place. As he always did, David reached for the laminated card in the pocket in front of him and studied it, pointing to each picture as the hostess talked them through its meaning. The woman alongside him continued to read her magazine and, glancing quickly around the cabin, David noticed that very few of those in his line of sight were following the pilot's orders. He was horrified to see the couple in front of him were actually snuggled up together, asleep. This simply won't do, he thought to himself. Why, when the cabin crew were openly offering clear, straightforward advice to their passengers on how to save their *own lives*, were people treating this so flippantly? The cabin crew didn't have to tell everyone this information. The crew were obviously extremely experienced in all aspects of aviation, and should the plane drop from the sky they could simply exit it without any thought for the people on board. But no, they had chosen to share their years of training with the rest of the plane, and the vast majority of passengers were simply ignoring it! Why, the cabin crew's selfless advice could actually mean that in the event of an accident *they themselves* may perish trying to save the general public! How extremely noble, he thought.

With that in mind he felt it his duty to intervene and tapped the lady alongside him on the shoulder. She glanced at him and he gestured at the laminated card he was holding. She looked at the card then rolled her eyes before focusing back on her magazine. He tapped her again, waggling the card up and down. She looked at him and glared.

"They're demonstrating the safety procedure," he whispered.

"I know," the woman snapped.

"Don't you think you should listen?" David asked considerately.

"No," said the woman.

"It could save your..."

"Listen," snarled the woman (with a look on her face that made her feelings more than clear). "Leave. Me. Alone."

"But..." (David had obviously missed the look.)

"Do. Not. Talk. To. Me. Again."

David got the message and sank back into his chair, disappointed that his good Samaritan role had failed. He studied the card one last time before returning it to the pocket in front of him. It seemed he wasn't going to get the opportunity to tell his starry-eyed love story after all. Just then he noticed that the woman next to him was wearing black stiletto shoes and he was suddenly gripped with panic as he wondered whether she would know to remove them for the inflatable yellow slide should the plane crash-land into the sea.

"So this is where you got to!" said Uncle Pete, approaching the table.

"I'm just giving our Sam some relationship advice," slurred Lesley.

"I bet you bloody are! Don't listen to a word, Sam love," Pete advised, winking.

"Hey! Cheeky," responded Lesley, grabbing her husband's bottom as he helped her to her feet.

"Come on," said Pete. "Let's get you home."

The two said their goodbyes and disappeared through the crowded pub towards the door. It seemed that Lesley had put her entire body into italic mode, leaned at a forty-five degree angle from the floor to meet at Pete's shoulder. Using all his strength Pete tried to pull her waist to his to keep her upright.

The two girls got yet another four drinks (two lagers, two tequilas) and returned to their seats.

"You know what your Auntie Lesley was saying about your perfect man?" Angela asked.

"Yeah?" said Sam, interested.

"Well, I was thinking, if the man she described was your perfect man, like your really perfect man, like all the things that your auntie talked about, well, I thought maybe…" (She knew she was rambling, but we can put this down to alcohol.)

Sam leaned forwards impatiently.

"… well, and you agreed with her that it was your perfect man…"

"Spit it out, for God's sake, Ange."

"Well…" She was going to have to say it. "Well, wasn't David all those things?"

"David who?"

"You know, your David. David Cross, David."

Sam seemed to visibly deflate, immediately realising that, as usual, Angela wasn't going to provide her with any kind of useful advice.

"David?" replied Sam.

"Yeah," slurred Angela. "He was all the things she mentioned. He wasn't tight with cash, and he took you away and he looked after Mollie *and* he treated you like a princess."

"David?" repeated Sam, still not believing that Ange had brought him up. "David-who-I-used-to-live-with David?"

"Yeah, that David."

Recognising the subject matter, Sam immediately held her hand to her forehead with her thumb and forefinger held out at right angles.

"What a loser! David Cross? He was like my dad. In fact, he was Dad Version Two. I used to think they'd be better off together than me and him."

"But he was all the things your auntie listed."

"He might have been but he was just nothing like me. We had nothing in common whatsoever; in fact, I don't know why we ended up together in the first place. God, he was so fucking boring. So fucking boring... He liked cogs and collected drill bits for fuck's sake!"

"But..."

"Listen, I'd rather be dead than back together with someone like David Cross." Sam laughed. "I'd rather be single forever. Back with him? Not a fucking chance."

The excitement David felt about his return to England straight into the arms of the girl he had never stopped loving made the flight pass extremely quickly. Throwing caution to the wind, he abandoned his careful timetable of distractions for the flight and whiled away the hours re-enacting their relationship from the time they first met to all the happy times that they had shared together. He remembered birthdays and holidays and Christmases. He remembered the smile she always used to greet him with when he returned from work and the cuddles they used to share on quiet nights in. It was simply idyllic and he couldn't wait for it to all begin again. Sure, he thought, there would be questions to be asked when the right time came and there would be trust to be built, but he knew that he was strong and they, as a couple, could overcome anything. He would be back where he belonged, with Sam and Mollie.

As David stared out of the window he recognised the bright lights of London glimmering below him. Soon he would be back, and he couldn't help but imagine Sam's wide grin and the dazzling shine in her beautiful brown eyes as she opened her door to see him standing there.

This was going to be some adventure, he thought to himself.

eighteen

Entirely gripped by his own circumstance, the figure rolled over to his right and left the bed for the last time.

Everything was now black.

nineteen

"Where's Dad?"

Sam breezed into the kitchen with a smile on her face that was, at the very least, manic. Smiles all round – it was evident that something had happened.

Sam's appearances at her parents were usually moments of sunken shoulders, lazy walks and deep heavy sighs which were designed to beg questions from an observer as to what could possibly be the matter. The first sigh was usually enough for a concerned voice to ask Sam whether she was okay. If, God forbid, the observer were wrapped up in their own thoughts and didn't enquire after Sam's welfare after sigh number three, Sam would lead into the conversation with a confrontational, "Don't ask what's the matter then, will you?" This was almost always enough to demand immediate and full attention on Sam's mood and disallowed any further thoughts that the observer may privately have been having. It was rare that this methodology failed as Sheila could be relied upon (usually prior even to the first sigh) to leap and desperately devour every detail. This was entirely self-serving as it did, after all, give her more material to pass on to those willing to listen. On retelling a story, Sheila also had a deft knack of somehow positioning herself in the story as if she had been a first person witness in the events which Sam had related to her. On the rare occasion (and always in front of George) that Sam's slouch, triple sigh and rhetoric self-absorbed question routine did not work, Sam simply turned and left the house, slamming the door behind her. (There was no way that she would have lowered herself to beg for the attention, after all.)

Today, however, Sam had breezed into the house with Mollie in tow and radiated an extreme level of joy and happiness that was somewhat off-putting. Mollie herself looked extremely pleased, and her demeanour mirrored exactly that of her mother. (It was possible that this was because her arms were full of sweets, chocolate and comics.) Sheila couldn't remember Sam looking this happy for some time and she wasted no time in enquiring into her daughter's blissful rapture.

"You look happy, Miss Poppleton! What's got into you?" she asked playfully, yet desperately intrigued.

Sam continued to grin with delight. "Where's Dad?" she repeated.

"What do you want your father for?" Sheila teased, now smiling herself; her daughter's attitude was contagious.

"Can I have these now?" Mollie interjected, rustling the sweets in her arms.

"Of course you can, darling. Do you want the telly on?"

Mollie nodded and Sam skipped back in from the lounge after settling Mollie in front of the television with a year's supply of sugary snacks.

"So where is Dad? Is he in the shed?"

"Why do you want your father?" said Sheila. "Can't I help?"

"No, it's Dad I need. I need to see if he'll have our Mollie for the night."

"Oh, yes?" asked Sheila knowingly, sensing that Sam may have a romantic liaison of one kind or another planned. "He can't tonight, love, I'm sorry."

Sam's face dropped immediately. "What?" she clarified.

"He can't tonight…"

"Well, why not?" The sunshine of Sam's mood had now been interrupted by unexpected dark clouds and heavy showers. "Why can't he babysit?" she demanded. "He always looks after our Mollie for me. What am I supposed to do now?"

Sheila thought back to the events of earlier that afternoon. She had been watching a particularly interesting show demonstrating the qualities of a new fabric used for tights which was guaranteed ladder proof. The presenter had put the tights through their paces, using sandpaper, inserting paperclips through the fabric and even stretching them across the top of a wheelie bin. The tights, however, had been impenetrable and had shown no signs of the reckless abuse they had endured for over half an hour. It was something to do with the infusion of lycra into the denier, Sheila remembered.

Usually, such a show would have Sheila glued to the screen for at least one packet of ginger creams and perhaps two or three cups of tea lovingly made and delivered by George. But this afternoon, she simply couldn't concentrate on the programme in the way she might usually. True, she hadn't had any cups of tea delivered to her, and also true, she had eaten all the ginger creams the previous day, but something had just felt wrong. It had been many weeks since George had checked on her every quarter of an hour to see whether she needed something, and her afternoons of whiling away endless hours shopping via television had somehow become a little lonely. For many years in the daytime she would watch these shows alone with her feet up in the lounge. But she had never really felt alone because she knew that George was somewhere around, pottering about and making his presence felt. This no longer happened and Sheila now felt both lonely and a little disconcerted. Nowadays, an hour or two could easily pass without Sheila speaking to anyone at all. She didn't like this one bit.

That afternoon, after feeling that her concentration had finally given up on the tights (but after ordering the black, brown and natural colours), she had decided to find out what George was doing. In her heart of hearts she knew what he was doing and she resisted shouting his name as she knew that he rarely responded now. There was no sign of him as she walked through the kitchen and conservatory. Following her intuition, she slid open the patio door and headed for the shed.

On arrival, she was momentarily unsure why she had made the journey. She knew that if George had seen her he would, as always, enquire whether she was alright and ask whether he could get her anything. She could think of no reason for her to engage with him, though. She didn't need anything; she just felt like, well, seeing him. Just for a moment perhaps.

Peering through the window, Sheila had been surprised to see George dressed so smartly. He was wearing the same black tuxedo that he had worn on the first night that they had met. A winged collar with a black bowtie finished his outfit and in his right hand he held what appeared to be a homemade baton. He swung this wildly from side to side whilst using his left hand to orchestrate the symphony in which he was deeply engrossed. Sheila stood for five or six minutes watching as George confidently took the piece to its crescendo before finishing with a bow, the sweat pouring from his temples. At that point she decided that she wouldn't interrupt him and went back into the house to telephone Norman. Yes, she confirmed, George would be playing bridge tonight, and yes, it had been a few months, but he was feeling more like himself again.

When George returned to the house half an hour later, Sheila had explained that Norman had telephoned and was very excited to hear that George would be back on the old team later. Once he had removed the radio George had tried to remonstrate that he was happy with his new hobby and didn't, well, you know, mind not playing bridge, but Sheila was resolute and insisted that he go. George, ever the conciliator, had agreed and thanked Sheila before popping his headphones back on.

"So, I'm afraid he's gone over to Norman's to play bridge," Sheila informed Sam.

"But what about me?" Sam was enraged. "I thought he'd given up that shit. What am I supposed to do tonight? What time will he be back?"

It was quite staggering how quickly the initial sunshine had become an all out storm.

"Listen," said Sheila sternly, "it's only six now. Your dad won't be back until at least eleven tonight – he can't babysit for you. You'll have to make other plans." (Sheila knew, of course, that her bingo night was not about to become a sacrificial lamb for Sam's cause.)

"Oh, that's fine then! I bet you're off to bingo as well. You and Dad do what you want to tonight then, don't worry about me."

Sheila heard a trenchant "Come on, Mollie" from the lounge before finding herself in the house alone.

Sheila sighed. She was sure she had done the right thing tonight – George needed the company of his friends.

Not long later, Sam arrived at Angela's house with Mollie and an overnight bag. "You don't mind, Ange, do you?" she enquired. "I've got a date tonight with Luke, you know, Luke Davis from school. I bumped into him at the petrol station and he asked me out. It's really, really important to me. You know how down I've been." Angela had little choice as Mollie had already been thrust into her hall and Sam was leaving down the path. She managed to a blow a kiss across the passenger seat and through the open car window in the general direction of her Mollie (who had already made for the television) before pulling away with an overly dramatic look of hurt on her face. Without speaking, Angela closed the door and joined Mollie in the lounge.

The phone rang and rang. Norman hung up, apologising to his friends, and suggested a game of knockout whist instead. It was already seven o'clock and it wasn't possible to play bridge with just the three of them.

Two hours later George finished his latest overture and suddenly realised how dark it was outside. Condensation covered all the windows and the full moon outside was just a blur through the windscreen. "This simply won't do," he muttered, reaching for a chamois from the glove compartment.

twenty

It was still dark when Sam was woken by her father stroking from the top of her forehead down to her eyebrow. The stroking was gentle and repetitive, over and over again, coaxing her patiently from her sleep. Rubbing her eyes into focus, she blinked, and when her eyes adjusted she could see her mum sitting next to her dad on the bed. It looked as if she had been crying. Sam awoke from her dreams and sat up.

George and Sheila had discussed this moment for a number of hours and even at this point had not agreed on a resolute plan to break the news to their twelve-year-old daughter. When the hours of discussions in the early hours of the morning had come to an end they had walked back up the stairs to Samantha's room to softly wake her.

That evening, both parents had headed to bed a little earlier than usual at around nine o'clock. It was early January and the late afternoon darkness and cold winter chill in the air had persuaded them that the day was over and sleep would be the best option, closing one day to open the next. After reading for an hour they had switched off the lights and fallen asleep, George's light snoring for once going unnoticed in the dark hours. They had not heard the sound of their son rising and dressing quietly in his room. They had not heard the sound of Adam pulling on his trainers in the lounge and quietly clicking the front door closed behind him.

Adam had waited patiently as the house had finally wound down to silence. Hours earlier in the evening he had felt the darkness and the suffocating fog which had surrounded him so much recently, unexpectedly and very rapidly lift. He had suddenly felt totally in control, knowing that no longer would the blackness be a part of him. Lying in his room, he had listened to every movement in the house, waiting until one by one they had all ceased. The muffled buzz of the television in the room below him finally ended and the key in the front door was turned. The first click of the light switch signalled the lounge light being extinguished before the second click allowed the landing light to burst into life. He heard the pull of the bathroom light and the sound of water as his parents brushed their teeth and prepared themselves for sleep. He continued to listen as the toilet flushed, and finally, after they had checked on Samantha, he heard the latch on their bedroom door sink into its cavity. Eager to leave, Adam knew that he couldn't until he was satisfied that his parents were unequivocally somnolent. Other than the odd grunt, he hadn't spoken to his parents for many days now, and at this point, now he had realised that the worst was behind him, he did not want to risk a chance encounter on the landing. They were more than aware that Adam had not left his room or dressed or seen his friends for goodness knows how long, and to see him awake and dressed outside his bedroom door was guaranteed to raise suspicions and, worse still, questions that Adam simply did not want to answer.

Confident that silence now ruled over the house, he had carefully studied the gap underneath his parents' door. Satisfied that there was no glow, he had walked gingerly down the stairs before leaving the house.

"There's been an accident," said George, still stroking his daughter's hair.

Sam's eyebrows furrowed and her nose scrunched up. George noticed his daughter's confused expression and repeated himself.

"There's been an accident, Samantha."

Samantha began to cry. At this stage she didn't know exactly *why* she was crying, but the grave sound of her father's voice and the soft sniffling from her mother had prompted this involuntary emotion. With one hand on the back of her head and the other on her lower back George held her tightly to him, constantly stroking her hair. Sam continued to cry, each stroke from George and each excruciating second of silence a signal for her tears to increase. She still didn't know what her parents meant by an accident, but she couldn't yet force the words out to question their statement. As

88

every lingering second passed and her mother's sobbing became more audible, she begged and urged that one of her parents would form words and expand on the little they had told her. George held her tightly, pulling her ever deeper into his chest, and the three of them cried as the early morning half light became evident.

Finally, George loosened his grip on his daughter, wiped his eyes on his pyjama sleeve and then cupped his hands on each side of her wet cheeks. Gently rubbing away stray tears with his thumbs, he looked deeply into her eyes, searching for inspiration.

"There's been an accident," said George.

Sheila wiped under her nose and gripped Sam's leg through the covers.

"It's Adam."

Adam hadn't realised that the January evening was to going to be quite so cold; he had left the house in just his jeans and a jumper. As he made his way through the darkness of the night the streets were all but deserted, but despite the gloom of the evening and the bitter cold, for once Adam's world finally felt illuminated. His emancipation that evening had come unexpectedly: something had finally broken through to him, showing him the way to go, the path he must take.

His breath hung in the air as he continued swiftly down street after street, alley after alley. As he got closer to his destination an occasional taxi passed by before disappearing quickly behind him. The lights ahead became brighter as he cut through the small park, kicking empty cans of lager that had been left there by previous visitors. Soon he had made his way across the precinct, continually staring at the block paving beneath his feet to avoid catching the eye of the late night drinkers who were making their way home.

He made his way through the empty markets until he reached his destination. Looking up at the building, he was struck by how brightly it was lit. This wasn't what he had expected. He had imagined that a place like this would be shrouded in darkness when all the shoppers had gone home. But each storey shined brightly into the night. There seemed no logical reason for this as the barrier was down, showing that no cars would be allowed in until the following day.

The lights in the building hummed as Adam made his way under the barrier and across to the first ramp. Up the ramp and then back on himself and up another. His breathing became heavier as he continued his journey ever higher. On each floor the buzz from the lights grew louder and louder inside his head as rogue fluorescent tubing flickered and went out before reigniting again. Ever higher he went as the floor numbers increased from three to five to seven to nine.

He felt increasingly uncomfortable that his act was to become a spectacle, illuminated for all to see. He had lived his entire life in darkness and it did not seem appropriate that he should be showered in light for his epilogue. He had hoped to arrive here and then simply disappear into the blackness, become one with it. Jesus, he thought, I can't even get this right.

Then, suddenly, the light disappeared and night stars were above him. He had reached the top.

twenty-one

It was an annual tradition. George and Sheila, along with Sam and Mollie, enjoyed a cooked lunch together before spending a few hours looking through old photo albums of times gone past. Mollie, who understood the tradition a little more each year, wondered at photographs of a young Sam buried up to her head in sand and laughed at pictures of her mum at the same age as Mollie pulling a sulky face, adamant that she shouldn't be captured on film. The family looked happily at old photographs of George from when he and the rest of the male British population had felt it acceptable to sport moustaches. The favourite shot depicted George totally oblivious to the fact that Adam, perched on his shoulders, was poised to thrust his ice cream complete with nuts and juice directly into his father's face. The following shot (which was over the page as if for comedic effect) showed George part-man-part-unicorn with the glistening cone sticking up towards the sky from his forehead. Adam, high above him, had his head back with his mouth wide open, cackling with laughter. There was a glint in his eye even then.

Following a few glasses of wine (tea for George), George helped put the cases into the back of the car and drove the three girls to the station for their annual trip. In years past George had gone with them for their overnight stay, but this had all stopped when Mollie was born. At that stage, George had offered to stay back and look after Mollie and this had been accepted by Sheila and Sam without protest. He was sure that the girls would enjoy their time better at the hotel without him around. This was the first time Mollie had been away on the trip and Sam had made sure that she had packed a bag with activities for her to ensure that she wouldn't be short of things to do while she and her mother whiled away an afternoon and evening in the hotel bar.

At the station George waved them goodbye. Only Mollie

returned the gesture; Sheila and Sam were already in deep conversation. He drove back towards the house, looking forward to his own company. All this reminiscing had made him feel that an afternoon in the conservatory with some nice classical music would be just the thing. He was sure from an advert that he had heard earlier in the week that the afternoon would be dedicated to the works of Franz Schreker, which would mean an afternoon at the opera for George. Schreker would be most appropriate.

After making himself comfortable in the conservatory, George realised within seconds of tuning in that something was wrong, something just didn't feel quite right. Looking down, he noticed he had forgotten to change when he arrived back home: for the trip to the station George had been forced, under heavy pressure from his wife and daughter, to swap his tuxedo for a shirt and some slacks. He placed the radio on the wicker coffee table before heading upstairs to change back into his tuxedo. Moments later he returned to the conservatory, replaced his headphones and settled down to relax.

The first *liberetto* concluded and George rose to his feet to ensure that the orchestra was prepared for the crashing music which followed it. Standing with his head bowed and baton in his right hand, he drew breath in advance of leading the orchestra through a lengthy and complex piece. Looking down at his shoes, he noticed that he couldn't see himself in the black gloss shine as he usually could. In fact, his shoes were positively matt. George felt immediately angry. Good God, he thought, no composer would take to the stage for this type of performance and forget to polish his shoes. What does this say to the rest of the orchestra? What must they think? The conductor is supposed to lead the rest of the orchestra and the members of the ensemble admire and respect the conductor. That is why, after all, he is high up on a pedestal above them all. "No, this won't do," he angrily said out loud. He wouldn't have been surprised if on noticing his shoes the orchestra refused to play. He could almost visualise the bassoon player nudging the flutist and nodding towards his shoes. The word would quickly go round and each musician would slowly lower their instrument and look blankly up at George. He imagined a solemn-looking cellist slowly shaking his head at him. He put his baton down, removed the headphones again and went into the kitchen to find the tin of black Kiwi polish.

After spending about an hour scrubbing and rubbing and polishing George was satisfied that his shoes were of performance standard and he returned to the conservatory to continue, hoping that the orchestra had forgiven him. Again he replaced the headphones and, standing proudly, he retrieved his baton and nodded solemnly toward his musicians to convey his most sincere apologies.

The afternoon seemed to pass quickly and the relentless rain which bounced from the conservatory roof slowly persuaded George that he needed a wee. He had held it in for some time, refusing to let the ever growing urgency in his bladder stand in the way of what had been, latterly at least, a world class performance. When George felt that perhaps he could wait no longer, the radio presenter interrupted the close of the opera, thanking the listeners for tuning in, and George bowed before removing the headphones. He rushed upstairs to relieve himself, eager to get back after the news bulletin for Wagner's *Faust Overture*.

On his way back downstairs he heard the desperate sound of banging on the front door and, sighing to himself, reluctantly went to open it. It was difficult to make out the man in the torrential rain, and to make matters worse George wasn't wearing his glasses. The man standing in front of him was absolutely drenched. The clothing he wore was completely sodden and his hair looked like an upturned crown, with four or five triangular points each collecting rain which dripped down his face. George pondered for five or six seconds before slowly drawing the conclusion that he was unsure who this person was. He decided to lead with an especially probing, "Yes?"

"Hello, Mr Poppleton," the man said.

"Hullo," said George, now a little wary that the man knew his name but still entirely in the dark as to who he was.

"Mr Poppleton, it's David, David Cross."

"Oh," replied George. It had seemed like the correct answer to use so as not to give away the continuing lack of recognition. The rain bounced on the doorstep outside, spraying George's freshly polished shoes.

David quickly realised that George hadn't any idea who he was and continued, "Mr Poppleton, it's David Cross, Sam's old boyfriend. I'm back from Japan. You telephoned me?"

All of a sudden somewhere in George's mind the penny dropped and he realised who the wet stranger was. He offered his hand out to David to greet him. "Hullo, David," he said, retracting his hand after realising that the arm of his jacket was getting wet. "How are you?"

"Could I possibly come in?"

"Yes, of course, where are my manners? Do come in."

David stepped into the lounge. "It looks like you're just on your way out, Mr Poppleton," he said, noticing George's attire. "I'm not interrupting anything, am I?"

"No, I'm in all night, David," George replied. "I'm not about to go out in all that rain."

"It's just, well, you look like you're dressed for a dinner or something. Are you sure you don't want me to come back tomorrow?"

"No," said George, smiling, "it was just a quiet night in for me."

Not expecting the sudden downpour, David had left the luggage containing his clothes at the hotel so George kindly offered him a bath. Whilst David bathed, George prepared him a towel and change of clothes outside the bathroom door before going downstairs to make some warm cocoa for the drenched traveller. It was whilst George was carefully spooning the cocoa into the mugs that he remembered for the first time that he had spoken to David so recently.

Half an hour later David appeared in the kitchen. Unfortunately, he was a good six feet tall to George's five feet and six inches and the clothing George had left for him was not entirely suitable. The beige chinos finished at least an inch from the top of the grey and red diamond-patterned socks. The cuffs of the olive turtle-neck slowly strangulated David's forearms. At least now he had been able to get his hair dry and clean off the steam and rain from his circular metal-rimmed glasses.

"You look more comfortable," offered George.

David lied in agreement.

"Come and sit down for your cocoa."

"It's been a long time since I sat at this table."

"I'll say, a good few years, I think."

"Mmm, I didn't ever imagine I would be here again," David probed.

"No, neither did I. When did you arrive back?"

"Only this afternoon. I left London at two to fly up here and then got a train across and got into my hotel about two hours ago."

"Oh really, so soon?"

If this was the case then Samantha's high spirits a few days earlier were probably not due to David's arrival, thought George. Perhaps she had somehow been notified that he was on his way back and her excitement was down to his impending visit. George made a mental note to mull this over further before commenting.

"Yes, then after dropping my things off I came straight over here."

It was only half an hour from the station to the Poppletons'. It appeared to George that there may be some confusion with the times. He would certainly investigate this fact further. Perhaps David had seen Sam before he arrived at the house.

"Oh, where are you staying?"

"Over at the Mallory Inn on Talbot Road."

"Very nice. That's not so far from here. Did you walk over?"

Nice and subtle, thought George, pleased with his tactic. He knew it was only a ten minute walk from the hotel.

"I did, yes," said David, smiling. "That's when the heavens opened, though. It's a shame you weren't in earlier, Mr Poppleton. I've been walking around the area and knocking sporadically for a good few hours."

"Oh," said George, suddenly extremely confused about various times which had been thrown at him. He concluded that there were too many variables to consider and he quickly shelved his plans to interrogate further.

Instead, the two spent hours chatting like old friends. George validated his initial confusion at the front door by explaining that he recognised David's name but expected that after such a long time David may "look a little more Japanese". They spoke about David's job and how the lifestyle over there must be so much different from that in England and David confirmed that it was. David rhapsodised about his visits to Karayoshi Park Square and the Yokohama Landmark and George drank in David's descriptions of the minutiae of the tonnes of steel needed and the hundreds of blueprints prepared down to the numbers of screws used to build such engineering masterpieces. David tried to steer the conversation towards Sam and Mollie countless times but not once did George take the bait. George seemed a lot more interested in Japanese excellence in the electronics industry and the country's relationship with China. David was far too polite, however, to ignore George's questions and direct the conversation to the real reason that he was there. It was a little frustrating, but David was patient enough to travel his host's circuitous route. After all, he had waited this long.

David refused George's offer of a fifth cocoa and asked whether there may be any red wine available.

"Oh, the hard stuff, eh?" George commented winking before reaching for a bottle of Shiraz from the wine rack and placing it on the table in front of David. It was now past nine.

"Let's retire to the lounge," said George, momentarily picturing himself as the lead man in an old black and white movie. "I think I might have a glass with you."

George put the fire on and dragged a coffee table over so that it was adjacent to Sheila's chair and the sofa. David was holding a picture of Sam and Mollie he had picked up from the sideboard.

"Is this recent?" David asked, captivated by the size of Mollie and how her beautiful brown eyes stared out at him from the picture. Sam sat alongside with her arm around her daughter. She wore a long green summer dress and the sun glimmered off her natural blonde hair.

"Yes, that was last summer, in the garden. Doesn't the Rhododendron look lovely?"

"It does, Mr Poppleton, it does. Tell me, where *are* Sam and Mollie?"

"Oh, they're away at the moment. You know, the annual trip to the hotel, once a year. I used to go myself…" George's voice trailed off thoughtfully.

"When are they back? I'd like to see them."

"Tomorrow afternoon. I'll be picking them up from the station at one twenty."

"Right," responded David in a long and drawn out way. He was now aware that he wasn't going to see them that evening. This was probably a good thing, he thought to himself, noticing the clothes he had found himself wearing. He suddenly felt very relaxed and replaced the photo before sitting down on the sofa.

"How about a game of chess?" George (ever the cordial host) offered.

"That would be great," said David, holding up and gently rocking his empty wine glass from side to side. "And another glass?"

"Ah, yes, another glass for us both!" agreed George, feeling slightly reckless. He hadn't had this much fun in a long time.

It took at least an hour to set up the game of chess. George managed to find the set on top of a wardrobe in Mollie's bedroom but on opening it he soon realised that there were more than a few pieces missing. David shouted up from the bottom of the stairs to see whether George was alright as he had been away for quite some time. George, meanwhile, was lying on the carpet partway under Mollie's bed desperately searching for the missing pieces. He had already moved the wardrobe out and was disappointed to see that the rogue pawns hadn't made a quick escape from the box down the back. Whilst walking the wardrobe back against the wall he was unable to stop a tin of felt tip pens sliding off and emptying themselves in a rainbow of colour over his head. These were quickly followed by a wave of little green houses and red hotels from the Monopoly set which moments earlier had also been balanced on top. George cleaned up the debris and eventually gave up on the missing chess pieces, concluding that they could literally be anywhere. He apologised to David for keeping him waiting and explained about the missing pieces. David set up the board, noting that although a full set of white pieces were available, there were two pawns, a rook and the king missing from the black side. George wasn't about to give up and generously let David play as white whilst he went to find replacements.

Once the game was underway David poured the last of the Shiraz into his glass. The opening moves were slow and cautious with each opponent carefully weighing up each move. Both sets of eyes focused on the chequered board on the coffee table between them.

"Shall we have some more wine?" David asked whilst taking the pink plastic thimble which doubled up as George's pawn.

"Why not?" said George, feeling extremely relaxed.

George returned from the kitchen and poured two more glasses.

"Do you like classical music, David?"

"I do, yes, Mr Poppleton…"

"Call me George, please."

"… Sorry, Mr, er, George, yes I do. I listen to it all the time. There's nothing quite like it. So very relaxing." David was pleased that after this length of time they were finally on first name terms.

"Relaxing. Yes, that's right. I find it extremely relaxing. In fact, it's probably the only time I do relax."

"You used to relax in the shed at the back, Mr, er, George. Tinkering I think I would call it."

"I don't tinker very much any more."

"Oh, shame," said David.

"Not any more," replied George sedately.

The game continued along with the wine consumption. George couldn't remember the last time he had consumed more than a glass and that was usually to be polite at a wedding or a christening or a wake. George had always somehow found himself driving at such events, which would usually conclude with Sheila's slurred summary of the day in the car on the way back. George wasn't averse to alcohol, he just never seemed to get the chance. But tonight he was certainly enjoying himself. He was in good company, was under no pressure and was enjoying the conversation with someone with whom he felt a connection. He wondered whether the wine had assisted this process, but concluded not – he simply liked David's company.

His momentary bout of day dreaming had unfortunately taken his concentration away from the game and he was disappointed to see his salt pot taken by David's knight.

"Tut, tut, tut," said David, jokingly shaking his head.

"Bother, I should have seen that coming."

"That you should, er, George, that you should," said David knowingly. "So tell me a little more about what's been going on while I've been away."

"Well…" said George, staring at the board.

There was a long pause whilst David waited for George to continue his sentence. He believed that the "well" had signified an opening to a potted history of the last six years. David waited patiently for George to continue, but looking across the board he began to think that George was concentrating on the game instead of the conversation. He was desperate to encourage George to continue his dialogue but felt that perhaps he should let George take his next move first. The silence continued for some time whilst a quick exchange of pieces took place. It was finally broken by George.

"I've been thinking, you should get in touch with Sam and Mollie whilst you're back, David. I'm sure they'd like to see you."

David hesitated. This *was* the reason that he was back. Up until this point he had been feeling slightly merry and eager for further clarification of the exact purpose of his summoning back to England. George's comment had instantly sobered him.

"Do you think so, George? I mean do you *really* think so?"

"Yes. I think they would very much like to see you, David."

George looked down at the swiftly emptying board and then back up at David. He was sure that they would want to see him. After all, he was enjoying David's company and who wouldn't? David was polite and interesting and friendly and kindly and everything that, in George's opinion, a gentleman should be – why of course they would be pleased to see him. George imagined that perhaps his own son may have turned out this way. It was something that was impossible for him to know, but for Adam to return at *this moment* and spend an evening *like this* with his father would mean everything to him. He would be proud for his Adam to have turned out like David. Extremely proud.

"Good, because I would very much like to see them. I've missed them, you all," David corrected, "very much while I've been away. If I'm honest, I'd like things to go back to the way they were."

David poured out the rest of the wine and moved his rook forwards into an aggressive attacking position. George noticed and loosened his bow tie before moving his bishop into a final desperate attack.

"I think you have the measure of me, young man."

"I think so too," said David confidently, smiling at the man he hoped would soon become his father-in-law. He allowed himself the brief indulgence of imagining their future weekly chess matches before moving his rook again.

"But I'm not finished yet," chuckled George, as if ready to unveil a master strategy to bring David's white monarchy down. He moved forwards his pine cone to counter.

"We'll see," said David knowingly and in a swift and wholly unexpected move, David put George's maroon nail polish in check.

George sighed. "This simply won't do." He smiled at David, in awe of his opponent's strategic thought process.

Defeat was now obvious and the two went through the motions of David cleaning up all of George's pieces before finally putting the nail polish in check mate.

"Well done," said George proudly.

"A good game, thank you."

"No, thank *you*."

David's clothes weren't yet dry and he arranged to collect them the following day before George picked up the girls from the station. The two shook hands and David left for the hotel to get some sleep.

He would need it.

Tomorrow would be a big day.

twenty-two

At the top Adam knew that it was time. Although it was cold he now didn't feel it. He kicked an empty bottle of Becks across the floor, smashing it as it hit the low perimeter wall which surrounded the top level of the car park. The wind flicked through a discarded magazine before neatly closing it again as he made his way past empty crisp packets to the edge. He inhaled a long, deep breath and pulled himself up onto the top of the three foot high wall. It was about a foot wide and made from concrete which was showing the early signs of decay. From here, across the landscape, he was able to see the town he had grown up in, but instead he chose to focus on his feet. There were perhaps three or four inches between the end of his toes and the edge of the wall. Little by little he gently shuffled his feet forwards, ever closer to the edge. His mind pushed him to keep moving, to edge closer, to get nearer. His feet, however, were not obeying his brain's orders. Although they managed to move slightly, they were no closer to completing the task. He lifted his right foot purposefully to move it the required distance, but when he replaced it back onto the surface of the wall it had simply reverted to where it had previously been. He craved an almighty gust of wind to crash into his back, forcing his body forwards regardless of the cooperation of his feet.

When he had been on the wall for nearly ten minutes he could feel the anger rise inside him over his inability to finalise his task. He felt his chest tighten and his arms and legs become rigid. His upper and lower teeth bit hard against one another and the muscle in his jaw began to ache with the force. His neck became taut and his shoulders ached as every muscle in his body became tighter and tighter. His head pounded around his temples, spreading to his forehead as each long second passed. Tears ran steadily from his eyes as his frustration increased. His entire body shook from tension. He again tried to edge forwards. One last step. One last step. His body swayed forwards until he felt that from his ankles up he was literally hovering above the roofs of the market stalls so far below. Again his feet refused to move. "One step, Adam," he quietly sobbed to himself pleadingly, "just one fucking step."

His muscles were relieved of tension immediately as he turned and climbed down from the wall. He walked slowly across the tarmac, the toes of his trainers dragging with each step. When he reached the middle he turned, drew a final breath and ran back across the car park before throwing himself head first over the wall and into the night sky.

"Is he alright? Where is he?"

It was the first time since being awoken more than an hour before that Sam had been able to speak. Her throat stung and her eyes were sore. George still held her tightly as she sat up in bed. It had taken everything that she had to get the words out. Her voice had cracked as she forced them, the words seemingly not wanting to leave the back of her throat. In the end her questions had come out as no more than a barely audible croak.

"He was found," George forced out through his tears.

"Found?" questioned Sam. "Found where?"

"In town."

Her tears had now stopped as her brain focused on collecting information from her parents. Her father sat with her head in his hands, staring at her and crying and shaking his head, unable to provide more than small pieces of information, each short sentence he offered inadvertently tormenting Sam. She looked at her mother whose head remained bowed, her tears streaming down her cheeks and onto her nightie. Her mother was usually so strong, so forceful, and now the vision that Sam had in front of her was of a different person.

"Mum?" she pleaded. "Mum, what happened to Adam?"

Sheila looked up at her daughter and silently shook her head. Her whole body trembled. She tried to force a comforting smile but was unable to do so with any conviction and silently bowed her head again.

"Dad? Please."

George breathed in deeply. He knew that he owed his daughter an explanation as to why the three of them were sitting in her room, shattered and broken, at that exact moment. But he didn't want to believe the words he knew he must say. His young daughter's pleading eyes drilled into his own and he knew that he had to put aside his own pain and summon all his strength to retell the events that had unfolded after he and Sheila had fallen asleep that night, the events that had been related to him via a phone call pulling him from sleep, by a stranger's officious voice. Taking a deep breath, he explained in slow, considered words the dreadful situation that the family now found themselves in.

"There was an, er, accident," he began. He knew that the use of the word "accident" wasn't strictly correct; however, using the actual word was too horrifying for him to think about. The accident misnomer would have to do. "There was an accident. In town." George drew a deep breath. "A couple found Adam lying next to the multi-storey car park…"

As he spoke, each word a huge effort, Sheila gripped deeper through the duvet into her daughter's thigh, unable to make a sound, her red eyes saying everything.

"What happened to him?" whispered Sam.

George pulled Sam's head away from his chest and held her face in his hands so he could see her. He looked directly into her eyes as tears poured from his.

"What happened to my brother?" she wailed.

At that moment, for the second time that evening, the telephone rang across the landing, its shrill tones abruptly halting the conversation.

George rose from the bed and touched his wife's shoulder lovingly. "That'll be the hospital."

Adam had frantically tried to turn in the air to ensure that his fall continued the way it had started. His body spun through the sky and he desperately adjusted the position of his body to land face first onto the ground below. His body twisted and spun through the blackness over and over again. The increasing acceleration didn't allow him to make his own choice as to how he fell and he rotated again and again. The lights of the car park blurred and became dark again as the earth became ever nearer. At the last moment he made one final effort to push his head forwards to take the full impact, but gravity denied his last wish. His feet smashed into the ground, immediately forcing his left femur upwards, shattering his pelvis. His right fibula disintegrated, forcing his knee directly into his face, instantaneously breaking his nose and jaw. A rib broke off and forced itself inwards, puncturing his lung.

And then it was quiet.

Adam lay crumpled on the floor. He scraped the fingers of his right hand along the floor, feeling the slight indentations in the concrete, and then slowly lifted his hand in front of his face. The dull light from the bottom floor of the car park lit the area where he lay. He stared at his hand, moving his fingers backwards and forwards slowly and precisely. He was just able to make out the silhouette of his hand moving in the near darkness through the blood which dripped into his eyes. This confirmed to him something that he had never once contemplated could occur. He was still alive. This grim realisation quickly removed the numbness he had felt and agonising pain surged through his body. Tears welled, diluting the blood in his eyes as he rested his head to one side.

He lay on his back, unable to move, and stared for what seemed like a lifetime before two figures rounded the corner and approached him. As they knelt over him he wanted to scream to them to keep walking, to leave him there until his blood finally stopped flowing, but his shattered jaw made it impossible for him to speak. He was trapped. Then, how much later he could not say, a mask was placed over his mouth and he was transferred into an ambulance. The bright lights on the ceiling above him seemed to burn into his eyes as the paramedic inserted a drip into his arm and began cleaning the blood from his face. He flapped his hands in an attempt to communicate with the paramedic to stop what he was doing and to leave him back where he had found him.

"You need to be calm," the paramedic told him. "I'm doing everything I can for you. You've had a nasty accident, son, but you're in good hands, you're going to be okay."

The final five words hit Adam like a hammer blow.

"That was the hospital," said George standing in the door frame, "he's out of surgery. I think we better go over there now."

Neither Sam nor Sheila moved. George walked into the room and gently peeled Sheila's fingers away from their grip on the duvet. "Come on, dear."

Sheila was helped slowly from the room to get dressed for the trip that none of them wanted to make. Sam got up from her bed and made her way across the landing to the bathroom to get washed. After cleaning her teeth and quickly pulling her hair into a tight ponytail she went back to her room to get dressed. George knocked whilst pushing her door open slightly and smiled weakly. "I'll be in the kitchen. Do you want tea?"

Sam nodded, pulling on her jeans. She smiled weakly back at her father. Her eyes filled again.

As Sam left her bedroom to go downstairs she heard her mother's voice for the first time that morning. Sheila was speaking in a low quiet tone on the telephone in her own bedroom across the landing. Sam paused on the top step and craned her neck to hear but it was difficult to make out the words through her mother's sobbing. She turned and walked back up the stairs and stood directly outside her mother's door, which was slightly ajar. She could see her mother standing with her back to her, facing out of the window.

"It happened early this morning, Pete."

Sheila wept as she recounted the story.

"I'm not sure whether he'll be okay, Pete... Broken bones in his face and his legs, punctured his lung, broken his pelvis... He was found by a couple on a night out... We're going up there now, he's just come out of surgery... I never thought he was so unhappy that he'd jump off the multi-storey..."

Sam froze. Had she heard this correctly? *Jump off* the multi-storey? This was something that she had not even considered. She had spent the last half an hour desperately wracking her brain to fathom how her only brother had managed to be so badly injured in town. She had concluded that it must have been some kind of fight he had been involved in: maybe a group of men had attacked him or perhaps he had been fighting with someone at the top of the car park and he had fallen. It was true that Adam had had his fair share of scrapes and fights at school in the past and therefore this scenario would not be entirely out of character. However, she had not been able to understand why he had been in town that night in the first place. He had hardly left his room for the last month and so it seemed odd to her that he would even be in town. Her mother's words had now cleared up the entire mystery. Adam had been in town with one specific purpose and that was to end his own life. Sam began to weep and went downstairs, straight into her father's arms.

The journey to the hospital was quiet and Sam decided not to mention the phone call she had overheard. George purchased a ticket from the machine in the car park and the three of them made their way through the main doors and up one floor in the lift to the Intensive Care Unit. At the reception desk the nurse called the doctor who had operated on Adam through the night. He arrived moments later and took George and Sheila to one side to update them on their son. Sam sat a few yards away on an orange plastic chair and waited.

"He's in a very bad way, I'm afraid," the doctor explained. "He's lost a lot of blood and he's extremely lucky to be alive. The next forty-eight hours are critical."

The doctor explained the injuries Adam had sustained and agreed that George and Sheila could go in and see him. As he left he smiled at them sympathetically and reassured them their son was in the best place that he could be.

"We can see Adam now," George almost whispered to Sam.

Sheila pushed open the double swing doors and George grabbed the handle to stop her. He turned to Sam. "Your brother isn't going to look very nice, Samantha. Do you want to wait here instead?"

Sam shook her head. She needed to see her brother. George gripped her hand tightly as they entered the room. The ward had six beds of which only two were in use. On the left a grey-haired man lay upright with his eyes closed. A labyrinth of tubes and wires came from his body ending in nearby machines. In the far right-hand bed was Adam.

Sam approached the bed and stared at the figure which was purportedly her brother. Adam's face was twice its normal size and completely flat. It was impossible to make out any identifying features which corresponded to her brother. Both of his eyes were closed and his eyelids were entirely black. Strange wire protruded from within his mouth, holding his jaw together. A long transparent tube ran from a hole in his neck to a machine to his right which emptied and then refilled with air. Dried blood flaked and crumbled from below his ear. From his shoulders down he was covered by sheets and blankets which rose from his waist before draping over a large square frame.

George pulled up a chair and sat to his son's right, stroking his hair, still matted with blood. Sheila stood frozen at the end of the bed sobbing, unable to go any closer, unable to accept what had become of her only son. Sam stood opposite her father staring at her brother, trying to understand what he must have been thinking the previous night. She held his hand and was surprised that it was cold. She rubbed it between hers to warm him up.

The nurse explained that Adam was heavily sedated for his pain and was unlikely to be able to hear anything they said. "But," she encouraged, "we don't know for sure – he may just hear you."

Twenty minutes later she returned to say that the family would have to leave for a couple of hours as more tests were to be carried out on Adam.

The three walked slowly away from the bed.

No one had spoken.

No one could begin to find the words to say.

twenty-three

Despite the previous night's excesses and the mental effort required to overpower George in the chess department, David rose extremely early the following morning. He peered from the window of his hotel room, eyeing the world outside from behind the net curtain which offered a small amount of privacy to residents. It was still very dark and a crisp frost had gathered on the windscreens of the cars in the hotel car park below. It was the time of year when it could be one a.m. or seven a.m. such was the blackness outside. There was no sign of sunrise and David observed the world outside for some time to try to find clues to give him a suggestion of the time.

Over many years he had meticulously calculated that specific defining noises allowed accurate prediction of the time after midnight in winter without the use of a watch (he did of course have a watch, but enjoyed the challenge much more). If it was dark and there was louder than usual talking outside or voices from several people which involved *either* laughing or shouting it was likely to be between eleven p.m. and one a.m. (two a.m. at weekends) and would almost definitely be people making their way home from a night in a pub or restaurant. One a.m. (adjusted for weekends) and four a.m. would be the quietest time of the night. Usually, at this time the hum of the traffic would have subsided and taxi and bus drivers would have long made their way home to prepare for the next day. Although the traffic noise would never subside completely, it was noticeably reduced between these hours. Voices in the world outside would also significantly reduce at this time as well, limited to the odd shout or less frequently a drunken interpretation of a popular record. Between four a.m. and five a.m. the world would slowly begin to come alive again. The sound of voices remained unusual at this time – an early riser would usually wish to keep his early morning mood to himself and ponder the day ahead in silence (although admittedly there were few people to converse with at this time). The engine sounds would gradually increase as the morning shift workers populated the streets, quietly cursing from within their cars that their rota had forced them out at this ungodly hour. From five a.m. to six a.m. the world began to stretch its arms to welcome a new day. The quiet, but audible, whoosh of the milkman's float was a familiar sound along with the clinking of bottles. The traffic noise continued to rise steadily. Suddenly, voices could be heard again and at this time brief exchanges of greetings would be heard between dog walkers or those who chose to collect their newspapers rather than accept the local newsagent's offer of delivery. From six a.m. onwards the noise escalated every few minutes, and – almost as if the noise had awoken the sun itself – the sky would gradually become lighter. Soon after, the sun would finally rise to see what all the fuss was about.

David observed for five minutes more before smiling to himself and exclaiming "Five eighteen, David" to the empty room. He left the window and picked up his watch, which was laying face down on the bedside table. Clutching each end of the straps, he slowly spun the watch towards him until he could see the face. The bright green digital figures stared up at him through the darkness, displaying:

5:18 37

"Bingo!" he chuckled, smiling knowingly to himself. This was going to be the perfect day!

After showering and pulling on some everyday clothes (he would change into his best outfit for that afternoon's liaison later on) he made his way to the breakfast room just as the swing doors were opened. Ah, more perfect timing, he thought to himself. Everything was going like clockwork. The waitress seated him near the window and passed him a menu, taking his order for coffee at the same time. She walked away from the table grumpily wondering to herself why someone would choose to have breakfast at six a.m. on a Saturday morning.

David was nervous about the day ahead and coming face to face with Sam and Mollie again after all this time, but he also felt excitement at the prospect. It really was going to turn out alright, he calmed himself; after all, if his early morning time prediction wasn't an omen then he wasn't sure what was.

"Are you ready to order, madam?" a waiter asked, approaching from behind.

David's eyes met those of the waiter on the word "madam". He looked up, slightly narrowing his eyes and furrowing his brow in genuine confusion. The waiter tried to hide his surprise that David's hair from behind certainly didn't match the slight stubble at the front.

"I'm sorry, sir," said the waiter, immediately correcting himself.

"Why did you call me 'madam'?" asked David, puzzled.

"A genuine mistake, sir."

"No…" said David slowly, unable to leave the waiter's statement unchallenged, "…why did you say madam? Did you think, that, er, I was, er, a lady?"

"No, sir, of course not," said the waiter, a beaming smile spreading across his face in a "trust me" type of way.

"You did, didn't you?"

This simply wouldn't do, thought David. It was true that since moving to Japan he had kept his hair more shoulder length than neatly trimmed into the neck as was previously his practice. His new start overseas had required a change and he had settled on this style a good number of years before. Well, in all honesty he hadn't even settled on this style: his mind had been on other things and the hair growth had carried on regardless without David paying much attention to it. The first time he had stepped in a Japanese barber's the only word he had researched was "trim" and the barber had cut it this way. David hadn't had the courage to ask for any more taken off (mainly because he didn't know how to) and had just accepted the cut. From that moment on, he had visited the same barber every couple of months and used his standard phrase, "trim", each time. Even as the years went by and his Japanese improved significantly, this pattern never changed. David was used to his new hair, and the barber wrote his client's name in the appointment book simply as "Trim".

"Well, okay," said the waiter, conceding that his winning smile had failed. "I did think from behind that you were a woman…"

"Oh?"

"… but as soon as I got alongside you it was clear that you weren't, sir."

"Right."

"Anyway, what would you like for breakfast, sir?"

"Do I really look like a woman from behind?"

"Like I said, sir. For a split second, that's all."

"Really?" reiterated David incredulously.

"To be honest, I don't think the shirt helped," offered the waiter, gesturing with his hand towards David's lemon silk shirt.

"Oh?"

David was in a muddle. He had never really taken much interest in his own appearance, preferring to concentrate on matters more important to him. Matters such as the calculation of structural loads, the use of spectrometers and the efficiency of relativistic society (and other such useful things). He had, however, never been confused with a woman in all his thirty-eight years. He found this concept extremely difficult to understand.

"Well, it's a nice shirt, sir. Looks nice quality, but, well, I don't know. It's…"

"You needn't say anything else," said David gently. "Perhaps it is about time for a haircut."

"Okay, sir. Now what would you like for breakfast?"

Prior to the confusion over his gender David had mentally settled on a light breakfast of tomatoes, scrambled eggs and mushrooms. Something light, he had thought to himself; after all, he didn't want to be too full when he met Sam. Too much fatty food could cause him to belch or, God forbid, worse than that. But the short gender confusion had now catapulted him into further confusion, this time in the breakfast department. Perhaps he should have a hearty meal? That's what a true man would have before rescuing his waiting damsel. Sausages and bacon and fried bread and black pudding. By God, the Vikings wouldn't have gone to sea on an egg and a few vegetables. Yes, the full English breakfast would be the way to do it. After all, he would need all the energy he could muster to pick Sam up and spin her around whilst locked in a long embrace. But the possibility of unwanted bodily functions drifted quickly back into his mind.

The waiter did exactly what his job description required of him, and waited.

This is such a jumble, thought David, his eyes darting up and down the menu. Fresh fruit? Selection of cured meats and cheeses? Porridge? Yoghurt? His head was beginning to spin.

"Do kippers smell?" he eventually blurted out.

"Sorry, sir?"

"Do kippers smell?"

"Do you mean under the sea, sir?"

"Er…" David looked at the waiter, puzzled. He could feel himself beginning to get very flustered.

"I'm not sure if any fish can actually smell, sir. I don't think they even have noses."

"No," corrected David, "I mean do they smell on humans?"

It was now the turn of the waiter to look puzzled. This was becoming a very unusual breakfast order. The waiter began to wonder whether the man in front of him was actually sane.

"I mean," David continued, "I know that they smell when they're being cooked, but after, you know, consumption, do they smell on the consumer. Of them?"

"I don't know, sir. I'm sorry. Would you like me to find out?"

"Well, er…"

Before David had the opportunity to consider this, the waiter (perhaps sensing his own opportunity to escape) left the table momentarily and grabbed the head waiter, who at that moment was conveniently passing. It was possible that he could provide an answer to David's conundrum and end this convoluted breakfast order.

"This gentleman is about to order his breakfast," said the waiter in slow, drawn-out words as if to convey that David was perhaps a little unhinged, "and wondered whether it would be evident to someone else later in the day that he had eaten our kippers."

The head waiter's eyes quickly darted at his colleague with an expression of "what?!" before focusing on David.

"Sir, is there a reason that later in the day you may wish to hide the fact that you've enjoyed our kippers?"

David could tell from the tone of the head waiter that he didn't take kindly to the suggestion that he was embarrassed to admit that he had dined at the hotel. He felt his neck turn a deep crimson.

"No, no, I'm not embarrassed to have eaten here," stuttered David.

"Why then, sir, would you wish to hide the very fact you've eaten here?"

The head waiter suspected that David may be a mole for a competitor. David suspected that the head waiter suspected that he was a mole for a competitor.

"I'm not a mole!" blurted David.

The original waiter rolled his eyes. Jesus, what a fucking nutter this guy is, he thought.

"I just want to know whether kippers would smell on me later in the day?" David couldn't remember a time he had ever felt so flustered. He immediately regretted booking into such a lavish establishment and made a mental note to stay three star or less in the future.

The head waiter's face relaxed. "Sir," he asked, continuing the slow tone for David's benefit, "if you're asking whether kippers may carry on your breath today, I would think so."

"Oh," said David, struggling to comprehend why he had panicked and asked the question in the first place. "Thank you."

"I'm happy to help, sir," said the head waiter entirely unconvincingly.

"Now what can I get you for your breakfast, sir?" said the waiter, glancing at his watch and noticing that he had been at the same table for nearly fifteen minutes.

"Er, I think… I'll have… the, er, tomatoes, scrambled eggs and mushrooms please."

"Wonderful choice, sir," commended the head waiter, smiling through gritted teeth. "Do enjoy your breakfast, sir."

Both waiters turned and left. David felt exhausted from all this decision making but was glad that the order was finally placed. He had only scheduled half an hour into his morning itinerary for breakfast and now realised that by the time breakfast had been consumed he would be running nearly an hour late. He pulled out his notepad and reworked the morning – saving five minutes here and there. He would also have to fit in a haircut which he hadn't previously accounted for.

Following breakfast the rest of the morning went surprisingly well and David's confidence began to grow back to the success of his early morning time prediction. He managed to get into a hairdressers' at short notice and pulled out the photograph which he always carried of himself, Sam and Mollie on their first holiday together. He reasoned that Sam had liked him at that stage and therefore presenting himself with the same haircut could only tip the scales further in his favour. After bathing for the second time that morning (this time to include a shave) he pulled on his best clothes and headed from the hotel to Sam's flat.

It was unusually warm for February and David decided he would walk the short distance to the flat. His watch told him that he was right on schedule and, assuming there had been no hold up at the station, Sam would have been home for just under three hours – plenty of time for her to unpack and get settled. As he crossed the park his heart beat ever faster, each step taking him closer to the only place he had ever felt true love. It had been many years since he had been in the flat and he wondered if much had changed. They had always talked about making the kitchen open plan and he felt excited over the prospect that an island had been installed. No doubt the flat would have had a number of colour changes over the years. Decorating was always something that Sam had been keen for him to do. The very fact that she let him get so involved with all the manual work whilst she shopped for soft furnishings was another example of perfect teamwork.

He crossed the road and stared up at the stone built flats. His stomach flipped as he picked out the black railings which stretched across the French windows on the second floor. This was *their* flat. The outside door was ajar and so he let himself into the warm vestibule and took a deep breath as he placed his hand on the banister. His heart began to pound ever quicker as he made his way up the steps to the second floor. The excitement and nervousness overwhelmed his entire body and his hand visibly shook as he reached for the bell. It rang, a long, constant, monotonous, buzzing noise not dissimilar to an angry wasp. It wasn't until David heard an irritated cry of "I'm bloody coming" from inside the flat that he realised he hadn't removed his finger from the button. He quickly retracted it and put on his most casual yet sincere smile as the inhabitant removed the door chain and turned the key from the inside. As the handle lowered, David took a deep breath.

"No need to ring the bloody bell for so..." The door opened.

It was Sam. The anger which had been so evident in the beginning of her sentence faded into an expression utterly devoid of sentiment.

"Hello, Sam," said David, smiling.

twenty-four

The scene in the kitchen reminded George of a coven. Sheila, Lesley, Sam and Angela were sitting at the table drinking coffee. George had heard the voices from upstairs and, much to his dismay, realised that he would have to pass through the kitchen to get to the conservatory. He had grabbed his radio from the shoebox at the bottom of the wardrobe, where it was covertly stowed each night, and slowly walked down the stairs. As he pushed open the kitchen door the laughter and excitement quickly turned to silence.

"Oh, don't mind me," he said to the room.

Sam looked up and smiled sheepishly. George offered hot drinks to the ladies but was informed by Lesley that he was five minutes too late and they had all just got one. So as to let the ladies continue their conversation with the least amount of fuss, George forwent his drink and hurriedly bustled through to the conservatory for some radio time. He closed the door adjoining the kitchen to the conservatory and made himself comfortable. He was sure that the excitement would begin again as soon as he vacated the room and in anticipation he turned his radio up to full volume before tuning into the morning programme. He closed his eyes as the sound of a lonely cello filled his ears.

In the kitchen Lesley and Angela were almost at bursting point as they awaited the reason they had been summoned to the house. To achieve maximum dramatic effect Sam had decided to begin the story at the moment she and her mother and her daughter had arrived at the hotel three days earlier. Sheila nodded at the end of each sentence as if confirming that the statements Sam had made were indeed factual. It was true that the early nods were a confirmation of fact. The later nods, as Sam continued her story, were less and less likely to be factual, as the consumption of wine at the hotel bar had made Sheila's memories increasingly fuzzy.

At the hotel, Sam and Sheila had left their bags in the room and settled down on a brown leather sofa with a beautiful view of the lake outside. Mollie knelt at the far end of the oak coffee table, busily drawing. The waiter had delivered the first bottle of Chardonnay and poured a glass of wine for each of them before replacing the bottle in a fancy looking metal ice bucket. Half an hour passed and the waiter made the same trip and removed the empty bottle, replacing it with a full one. Sam's phone beeped and she removed it from her Radley bag with the intention of switching it off. This was a day for her and her mother and she was not about to have this special time ruined by numerous irrelevant text messages from friends bemoaning that they had hangovers or that their boyfriend hadn't come home the previous night. On any other day these communications would be a welcome interruption in Sam's life, but today was different. This was a mother and daughter day and nothing would interrupt that.

Looking down at the phone, Sam noticed that she had received a text message from an unknown number. She concluded that it wouldn't hurt to read it before switching off the phone and pressed the green button to open the message. The words on the screen were clear.

wud be gr8 to c u

Puzzled, Sam looked at Sheila, who looked back questioningly. Unaware of the beginning of yet another drama, Mollie continued colouring the legs of the farmer she had drawn. His body wasn't visible; it appeared to be mangled under the combine harvester which lay above him.

Without speaking, Sam held the phone out with the screen facing her mother. Sheila cupped her hands around the phone as if to steady it. She then narrowed her eyes to try to see the message, but unfortunately she had taken a little too long and the background display had automatically reduced its brightness.

"I can't see anything, love."

This immediately annoyed Sam, who snatched the phone back and hit the relevant key to brighten the screen. She then thrust it back at her mother, who read the message, nodding. The drama of receiving such a message was lost on Sheila. She had noticed her daughter's quick temper briefly flare and wasn't sure what the relevance of the message was.

"Who is it?" Sheila asked.

"It's an unknown number, Mum, how should I know?" Sam snapped back.

Sam was intrigued. She wanted to turn off the phone but couldn't resist the temptation of finding out who this could be. The knowledge of a deactivated phone lying silently at the bottom of her bag with a mysterious message would eat away at her all afternoon. She wouldn't be able to concentrate on anything. She had to know. She tapped the keys on the phone, explaining to Sheila that she would only be a moment.

who r u?

Seconds later the phone beeped.

me lol

Tap, tap, tap.

who's me?

Beep.

you know who it is x

Tap, tap, tap.

i don't, who r u?

Beep.

you do sam x

Sheila finished her wine and looked at Sam for more information. Sam was visibly annoyed with her lack of progress and slammed the phone onto the coffee table. The noise startled Mollie, causing her to colour the red blood of the farmer onto the blue windscreen of the combine. She sighed, without looking up, before deciding that it looked quite effective and continuing the red scribble onto the door and bonnet. Sam, now extremely frustrated, finished her wine and called the waiter over for a third bottle.

"Everything okay, love?" asked Sheila.

"Does it look okay, Mum?"

"Who was it?"

Sam's eyes narrowed. "If I knew who it was…"

Beep.

Sam?

Sam ignored the phone.

Beep.

It wud be gud to get 2getha sam just for a drink x

Ignored.

txt me bak sam please x

In a matter of minutes the tables had turned. Half an hour earlier Sam had been desperate to know who the mysterious communicator had been. With a little cunning she had now forced the communicator to become desperate for a response. This was a tried and tested method Sam had used on numerous occasions before and to date it had always worked. She smiled slyly to herself, switched off the phone and returned it to her bag.

Thick veins protruded through the wrinkled skin on Lesley's neck. If she craned any further forwards it was likely that her head would simply snap off. Angela, although far more reserved, was equally eager for Sam to continue the story. Sam had everyone just where she wanted them.

"Another coffee, anyone?" Sam asked.

All three women gasped as if they had just reached the end of part one of a two-part television thriller and now had to wait a full twenty-four hours before uncovering the murderer. Sheila wasn't entirely sure why she gasped (as she already knew the end of the story) but it seemed the appropriate thing to do.

Sam sprang over to fill up the kettle, a large grin covering her face. Lesley excused herself for a visit to the bathroom, informing Sam in a serious tone that under no circumstances should she continue the story without her.

Sam brought the drinks over to the table and waited for Lesley's return. For a few moments no one spoke. Angela broke the silence.

"Do you think your dad wants a drink?"

"He'll be alright," said Sam, slightly annoyed that for a second the attention had switched from her.

"Okay."

Lesley returned at speed through the kitchen door, still tucking her t-shirt into her jeans. She would wash her hands later. Sam waited until everyone was back in position and when she felt happy that the focus was back on her she continued her narrative.

"So, I waited for about two hours…"

"And another bottle of wine!" interjected Sheila.

Sam shot her a disapproving look. Sheila mouthed "Sorry".

"… and then I decided…"

Directly behind Sam, the telephone on the kitchen wall rang.

"… to text…"

The phone persevered.

"… back…"

Sam realised that the interruption had caused her to lose the attention of the table.

"For fuck's sake," she sighed as she grabbed the receiver.

"YES?" she snapped.

The voice explained that Mr Poppleton was the person required and Sam left the phone hanging from the wall before marching in to the conservatory. She grabbed the headphones from her father who was standing with his back to her, arms outstretched.

"Dad, phone!" she shrieked angrily.

George made his way into the kitchen, forced from behind to move more quickly. The caller informed him that his delivery had arrived and that he could collect it the next day.

"Tomorrow?" said George excitedly.

The caller responded positively.

"That would be, er, fine, yes. Thank you. I have been waiting some time for it to come, you know," he responded slowly.

Sam glared at George, who smiled sheepishly.

"Thank you so much, yes, er, so tomorrow it is."

"Jesus!" Sam sighed loudly, making her irritation quite clear to everyone in the room. Angela sighed for a different reason.

"Right, well, it'll be, er, tomorrow then."

"Yes, Dad! TOMORROW!" shouted Sam, grabbing the phone from her father and slamming it into its cradle.

George smiled. "I can collect it tomorrow," he muttered to no one in particular as Sam forcibly assisted him back into the conservatory and closed the door.

twenty-five

George stared out through the front window of the car. He was sitting behind the driver's seat with Sam alongside him. Sheila was next to Sam. He held Sam's right hand tightly, her fingers crushed into his palm. He strained his neck to the right, trying to see past the driver to the black car in front. The driver coughed before removing his hat. This allowed George to see the black car more clearly. It was perfectly polished and for a moment the winter sun poured through the grey clouds lighting the matt black box which rested in the back. George noticed that the windows which surrounded the box were also sparkling and spotless and this allowed him the chance to see the three chrome handles down the right-hand side of the box. The sun disappeared back behind the clouds and the surrounding atmosphere returned to dark grey.

George felt a hand from behind him on his left shoulder giving him a squeeze of encouragement. He glanced down and noticed the old wrinkled hand resting there. He recognised his mother's wedding ring and lifted his right hand to return the squeeze. He turned and caught his fathers' eye before smiling uncomfortably. His father returned the smile and noticed the pain in his son's eyes, quickly followed by a look of hopelessness. The car was eerily silent, each passenger lost in their own thoughts of how they had come to be in *that* car on *that* day.

George, Sheila and Sam had stepped into the lift and pressed the button to take them back to the ground floor. There were no words any of them felt were appropriate to say. The lift bell rang and the voice from the small metal grill informed them that they had reached the ground floor. Sam shuffled forwards first, followed by Sheila and then George. All were unaware that they would not be needing the lift the next time they returned to the hospital.

Back at home, George sat in the lounge with his head in his

hands. Sam sat on the sofa alongside him, sobbing quietly. She felt helpless in her inability to do anything to make the situation better. Both could vaguely hear Sheila's voice coming from the kitchen informing various family members of the unthinkable situation. From time to time George lifted his head and rubbed his face repeatedly with both hands in a concerted attempt to rub away the overpowering feelings and pull himself together – to give him the strength to support his daughter. He would look up at Sam and force a distressed smile for a moment before returning his gaze into his cupped hands. After repeating this pattern for more than an hour, George finally mustered all his resolve and stood, shaking his hands down at his sides.

"Right!" he said, as though to convince himself that there was something he could do.

Sam looked up at her father; his eyes were red.

"It's very quiet in here, Samantha," said George.

Sam nodded.

"Would you like the television on or something?"

Sam stared at her father and shook her head slowly. It *was* quiet in the room, but the television wouldn't be able to help her. She wouldn't be able to concentrate in this situation. George noticed the small black radio that he had received from his children the previous Christmas on the coffee table. He picked it up and stretched his arm out, offering it to Sam.

"Maybe some music, darling?" he said softly, hopelessly trying to offer some solace to his daughter. He was her father after all and he knew that she needed him to be strong for her. This situation was too much for him, though. He was already broken.

In the distance, the telephone rang.

Sam shook her head again, blinking more tears away from her eyes. She was unable to speak and longed for her father to tell her that Adam was going to be alright. That Adam would one day come home and they would be a family again. That Adam would regret his actions and tell the family reassuringly that it had been a mistake and that he had not known what he was doing. That he loved them all and that he wanted to put it all behind him. And that she and Adam would become close, like a brother and sister should. And that they would always be there for each other, inseparable. These were the only sounds she wanted to hear. She knew her father was trying to help, but only his words of reassurance would be sufficient.

George placed his hands on the windowsill in the lounge and sighed heavily. Sam stared at her father's back. He again steeled himself and turned slowly to attempt to comfort her. At that moment Sheila returned to the lounge. She didn't have to speak. George knew from her face what had happened. She stood paralysed in the doorway of the lounge, her mouth open wide. George began to shake his head, the rest of his body motionless. Sam noticed that her father's eyes were fixed on something above and to her left and spun round to see her mother standing behind the sofa.

"Mum?"

Sam's eyes darted back towards George's. His chin began to shake. The saliva which joined his upper and lower lips split as his mouth opened and he let out a long, low wail. Sam stood and the three met together in the centre of the lounge. Fingers and arms gripped tightly around one another, George and Sheila pulling Sam deeper into the embrace. At that moment, the closeness of their bodies symbolised how they would never, ever let harm come to their daughter. "He's gone," Sheila repeated in a mantra into George's neck. When there was no strength left in their arms the three crumpled down onto the sofa, crying and wailing. All time ceased until eventually Sheila broke the embrace.

"We have to go to the hospital," she said.

George rose and steadied himself.

"I'll do it," he said regretfully.

Sheila smiled gratefully at him. She would see her son later. For now, she must concentrate on her daughter. She left the sofa to get some tissues and a drink for them both.

Sam pulled her knees up to her chin and remained on the sofa – her tears became heavier until she gasped for each breath.

Outside the church, people had already gathered. Adam's friends stood nervously off to one side, huddled together in a group. They smoked and talked, quietly avoiding eye contact with the other mourners. Friends and neighbours nodded their respects towards the family through the car windows as the black car pulled up in front of the church. Sam caught the eye of Kelly who was standing alone, staring at the car which contained Adam. Kelly smiled uneasily and looked away before she had chance to notice Sam return the smile.

Phone calls had commenced on the day that it had happened, with people offering their condolences and of course *any* help that the family needed. People had offered to take Sam to school or to sit with her should George and Sheila need time. The family were welcome to come and stay when they felt up to it, to "get away from it all". The kind offers were one by one politely declined; George and Sheila were resolute that they would do anything to be alongside Sam, to protect her, to stay near her. Cards and flowers began to arrive at the house the next day. Everyone had been so kind.

In the past week, and just so suddenly, the familiar pattern of everyday life had been rapidly destroyed, replaced instead with daily meetings to make decisions that no parent should ever have to make. Burial or cremation? *We don't know, it's never crossed our minds. What do you think, George? I don't know, darling. I don't like the thought of our son being burned. Neither do I, darling. Shall we say burial? Do you think? Yes, burial, please.* What type of flowers? *Lilies? What do you think, George? Er, yes, that would be okay.* Food for the wake? *Something light? Sandwiches, George? Yes, I think so, Sheila. A buffet would be fine, please.* How many people would that be for? *Well, the cousins from Suffolk will be coming, and I expect that my cousins will be coming down with their families from Scotland as well. So about fifty, George? No, I think there'll be more, there'll be Adam's school friends, of course. I'd say about a hundred altogether, Sheila. Okay, we'll cater for a hundred, please.* The colour of the coffin? *Well, he liked black, didn't he? Yes, black. It should be black.* We have two different shades of black, would you care to see? *The matt one, I think, Sheila? Yes, matt, George, he'd prefer that, he wouldn't want the shiny one.* Chrome or gold handles? *I think chrome, Sheila. I agree, chrome, please.* And the headstone? Granite or stone? *I don't know. You choose George, I really don't know. Er, well, er, something simple, something straightforward. Okay, well, granite sounds fine. Granite, Sheila? Yes, that's fine.* Would you like a picture on it? *Er, do we, Sheila? No, the pictures fade and go out of date. I agree, no, I don't think so, just words.* And the verse for the headstone? We do have a selection of standard verses if this makes it any easier? *No, we'll write our own, I think, yes, I think it would be more appropriate if we wrote our own. Will you write it, George? I don't know if I could. Yes, darling, I'll write it.* We don't need that right away, Mr Poppleton. Over the coming weeks is fine. *Oh that's good, thank you.* And any special piece of music for the service? *I hadn't thought about that. What do you think, Sheila? Any ideas? I don't know, George. He did like heavy metal. The posters on his wall, erm, Metallica or Nirvana? I don't know, Sheila, I don't know much of that thing. Can we decide later on?* Yes, of course. There's no rush, as long as we have it to the church before Friday. *Oh good, that's a relief. We'll have a think about it. Thank you.*

And this had been the overwhelming, all-encompassing emotional haze of the last five days. A flurry of questions that *had* to be answered which neither respondent ever thought they would be asked. Questions asked with answers given which they couldn't be sure were right. In truth, there were no wrong or right answers – just answers – tinged with an underlying unease that they should try to give the answers their son would have given. It was almost impossible to correlate the questions to what Adam would have wished for. Neither George nor Sheila had any inkling that Adam had actually wished to be where he was at that very moment. Unknowingly, his final wish had been to have his parents make these devastating decisions on his behalf.

George helped Sam from the car and once again grasped her hand tightly. He was aware of the people around him but couldn't raise his head to look. Instead he focused on the wet February ground in front of him. He was joined by Sheila and his own parents as they made their way slowly into the church. They were greeted at the door by the vicar, who smiled kindly and briefly explained the order of service to them, as he had the day before at their home. Still staring at the ground, the five walked reluctantly through the back doors of the church and down the centre aisle towards their seats at the front. Sheila linked arms with George as they approached and pulled down sharply to let him know that they had arrived. They were all seated when George finally managed to lift his head for the first time. Looking around him, he was suddenly aware that the large church was packed. At the sides people who had arrived a little late, or had given up their seat to someone they thought more deserving, were standing facing the front. George was careful not to catch the eye of any of the congregation and quickly averted his eyes back to the floor.

The vicar spoke briefly to welcome those in the silenced room before introducing George. George hadn't heard his prompt; he was completely engulfed in a deep grey fog which seemed to surround him. His hearing seemed muffled and he was conscious only of the sound of his own heart which pumped loudly and slowly within. Sheila tugged at him and smiled sadly before motioning him to the front. George stood uneasily and walked slowly to the altar. His son lay in the black casket just feet away. The vicar had assured George that if the situation became too distressing or too difficult then he would step in and continue the eulogy on George's behalf. He mustn't worry, the vicar had said, he would be here for George. George stared down at the people in front of him, grasping the altar to keep upright as he felt his legs wobble slightly beneath him. He opened his mouth to speak, but a croaked exhalation was the only sound. Panicked, he glanced across to the vicar, who motioned towards the glass of water on the altar. George took a small sip and shuffled the papers which contained his speech in front of him. Again, he tried to speak and again the words wouldn't come. Tears welled in his eyes. He smoothed the creases on the page again and glanced across to the vicar. The vicar clasped his hands in front of him, raising his eyebrows questioningly, inviting George to allow him to assist. George looked across to his right at the matt black box in which Adam lay. Whatever this may take, he would do this for his son. He would speak on behalf of his son and tell the people who had come today how he felt, in the hope that his son would hear and finally know in death what he hadn't known in life. He took a final look at the congregation before taking a deep breath and speaking.

"Thank you all for coming today. It's very kind of you. Today is a very sad day for us all. My son, Adam, lies to my right. His final moments are now. Adam, as you will all know, was our only son. Just over a week ago, Adam made a decision that would be the catalyst to bring us all here today. I did not know he was making this decision, and had I spent more time with him I perhaps would have been able to help him not make it. But I suppose I didn't spend enough time finding out how he felt and what he needed from me whilst he lay in his room…" George's voice cracked as the tears came.

He continued, "… I didn't understand his needs then and I don't understand the situation we are all in now. I loved my son, but didn't manage to find the right words to let him know this. And now we are all here in this mess. I know that I have failed him as a father, that I could have done more. Don't let the same thing happen to you. Talk… talk to each other."

He glanced at the coffin again before glancing at Sheila and Sam. He steeled himself one last time, then continued, his voice ringing strong throughout the church, "We all loved Adam. His sister, Samantha, is now without a brother and Sheila and I, without a son. His grandparents won't get to see him grow into a man. None of us will. I am so sorry, Adam, so sorry. Goodbye, son. May you finally be at peace."

The church was silent. George stood staring at the coffin as tears streamed down his face. After a few moments, the vicar approached him and gently helped him back to his seat. He folded the speech that he had written the day before and replaced it back inside his suit pocket. His written words had been unused, instead replaced by those which came more naturally.

twenty-six

There was going to be a party (an engagement party, no less) and it was going to take place in two weeks' time. At first, Auntie Lesley and Angela had been surprised when Sam had explained to them that Carl had been behind the mysterious text messages and that he was sorry for what had happened. Sam hadn't noticed Angela's eyes widen and her mouth fall open because Angela had cleverly covered it with a cough. Auntie Lesley had been about to comment when Sheila had burst into the conversation, exclaiming how she hadn't seen her daughter this happy for a long time. Sam had laughed and thrown her arms around her mother's neck. It was all so exciting.

Angela hadn't been able to sleep that night. And she couldn't eat all the next day. She spent the day on the sofa staring up at the ceiling and pondering her best friend's forthcoming mistake. She was acutely aware of Sam's failings but this decision was probably the worst she had encountered so far. The facts were clear to her. Firstly, her best friend was engaged to someone who had previously broken her nose and blackened both of her eyes. The scar at the top of her nose had only recently healed. Secondly, she presumed, they would be returning to life under one roof back at Sam's flat. Her thoughts turned to Mollie. She knew from her brief conversations with Mollie that the little girl was pleased that Carl was no longer around. It was true to say that Mollie lived much of the time in her own imaginary world, but from the few words she had uttered, the absence of Carl was certainly a positive. Thirdly, and perhaps most shockingly, Sam appeared to have the full support of her family in this decision. Sheila had waxed lyrical about Carl and about her daughter's happiness without, it appeared, any thought of the ramifications of Sam's decision. Nobody had thought to discuss whether either Sam or Mollie could be in danger from the violent individual they were about to cohabit with again.

In fact, nobody had even thought to ask Mollie's opinion about this sudden turnaround. Mollie, as was always the case, would simply be expected to go along with her mother's decisions. Mollie was no more than a bag that Sam was duty bound to carry around with her from place to place.

Angela ignored the flashing light on her phone which indicated she had missed calls. She poured some fruit juice and returned to her sofa.

Actually, she concluded, it wasn't fair to say that all of Sam's family were wholly supportive of the decision. Auntie Lesley at first hadn't spoken when the news had been delivered. Soon after, though, riding the wave of enthusiasm, she had let herself be engulfed by the excitement. It was Auntie Lesley, after all, who had suggested a celebratory drink at the pub. The thought of an early afternoon drink was enough to sway her allegiance regardless of the validity of her niece's decision. When the foursome had arrived at the pub, Lesley had immediately ordered two bottles of champagne and brought them over to the table. This sudden injection of opulence into the usually prosaic bar had awoken a number of regulars from their alcohol-induced slumber, and they had then slowly drifted over to enquire into the fuss. Before long, the size of the group had trebled as people arrived to offer their congratulations to Lesley's niece. Sam bathed in the attention. This whole situation had seemed entirely wrong to Angela, who had excused herself after one glass, feigning a potential migraine coming on. Angela's departure went largely unnoticed by Sam, who waved to her friend with her spare hand whilst receiving a celebratory hug from a stranger whose white beard had yellowed around his nostrils.

Alone on her sofa, Angela wasn't sure what she should do. If Sheila was supporting this and Lesley was indifferent, who was there to look after Mollie's best interests? Her thoughts now turned to George. She had not heard from Sam as to how her father was taking this decision. George was a lovely man. He was kind and caring and nothing was too much trouble for his wife, daughter and granddaughter. She had known George for over fifteen years and on every occasion she could remember he had steadfastly maintained the view that his own happiness should come behind that of his family. He was helpful and thoughtful. He idolised them. Perhaps vitally, he doted on Mollie. But for all his kindness and attentiveness he was invisible to them. They never listened to him. They never enquired anything of him. It seemed that nobody had ever thought about what George needed. It was as though his kindness and selflessness were the only things that gave him any fragment of identity at home. But, because they expected him to display these traits, they would now have trouble separating these from who George actually was. They had simply moulded George's character into these few traits. As in the rest of his life, George had acquiesced and allowed them to do just this. Thus, on the very few occasions that he had offered his opinion on a given subject, he was simply disregarded. Over the years George had become gradually milder and gradually quieter. It was difficult to see how George would have any influence whatsoever in trying to help her persuade Sam that she was doing the wrong thing. In fact, although she was sure that locked deep inside George's mind was a voice that would stand up against the ludicrous engagement of his daughter, his speaking out would probably further confirm to Sam that she was doing the right thing. It was actually highly likely at this stage that George was not even aware of the engagement.

Angela decided to disregard George as a potential ally. This was something she would have to do alone.

George was absolutely, categorically, without question unaware of the engagement. Sheila had tried to mention it to him that morning when the alarm clock had sounded at half past five but he had leapt out of bed and excitedly headed straight for the bathroom. When he returned to the bedroom half an hour later, his hair perfectly groomed, dressed splendidly in his tuxedo and bowtie, Sheila had already returned to her sleep. She had the previous night's hangover to sleep off. George attempted to eat but the feeling of butterflies in his stomach had made him feel nauseated and he didn't feel confident he could keep his muesli down. Instead, he had a cup of peppermint tea in the conservatory and studied the map which that morning would take him into the city for the first time for as long as he could remember.

It had taken him weeks of clandestine telephone calls to all manner of people to finally source what he was after. It was only when he finally tracked down the supplier and placed his order that he had felt like he could truly relax. But over the weeks the relaxation had turned to frenzied excitement as he awaited news of his order. Each day would then conversely end with despondency over the lack of communication from the supplier. The waiting had begun to feel endless and each night the dejection increased. And then, one day, the telephone call to inform him that it had arrived and was ready for him to collect finally came. The call had come the afternoon before and he had hardly slept that night.

Now, he used a green highlighter pen to meticulously mark the route on the map and then (for safety) rewrote the directions on the back of an envelope. It was time to prepare himself properly for the hour-long journey. He returned to the kitchen and filled a flask to the brim with more peppermint tea. He collected the torch and travel rug from the top of the cellar stairs and laid them on the work surface. He opened the door of the kitchen cupboard under the sink and pulled out boxes of cling film and greaseproof paper until he lighted upon the kitchen foil. He studied the box, noting that it had not previously been opened and that it contained five metres of foil. He studied his body momentarily, roughly calculating whether five metres would be enough to cover all four limbs and his torso should he become unexpectedly marooned. Satisfied that he had sufficient foil, he collected his emergency bundle along with the radio and made his way to the car. He wasn't about to get stranded in his vehicle without this careful, yet necessary, advance preparation.

The journey into the city passed without incident and George was relieved to see familiar street names which he recognised from his map. He smiled, internally praising himself for his punctilious planning. A moment later he had reversed his car into an on-street parking space and purchased a ticket from the pay and display machine. He peeled the adhesive back and stuck it to the inside of his windscreen. An hour would easily be enough – by his calculations the shop he was visiting was only two hundred and thirty-nine yards away. George retrieved the city street map, which he had cut from the back of the road map, and unfolded it. Across the road he could make out the street sign of the road he was parked on and he marked a pencil cross on his map to indicate precisely where the car was parked. He had already marked the shop's location with an asterisk.

He set off walking briskly through the streets, turning the map from portrait to landscape each time he rounded a corner. The streets were fairly deserted, which pleased George – a busy street would have added a little extra pressure to his navigating. It was a drab and grey day but as he rounded his final corner and saw his destination right in front of him the sky seemed to become instantly brighter. The bold grey and gold copperplate sign shone out against the blackened stone buildings. To George, the sign seemed positively ablaze, the heat from it beckoning him into the shop. He had made it.

George returned the map to his pocket and pushed open the heavy black gloss door. Inside, the shop was clean but sparse. The little brass bell which hung above the door had alerted a gentleman who came out from a side room to greet his first customer of the day.

"Welcome to The Chancery Shop, sir. Can I help at all?" said the man in an extremely posh public school accent.

George stared in admiration at the man. He was dressed extremely smartly in a brown and black three-piece tweed suit. It was just possible to see the chain from his pocket watch crossing the front of his waistcoat. His shoes were shinier than any George had ever seen.

"Yes. I've come to collect my wig," said George proudly.

"Right away, sir – now if you'll just join me over here…" The man indicated towards the shop counter.

George and the man stepped half a pace forwards.

"Here we are," said the man.

"That's better," replied George.

The man lifted a large, well-worn, leather-bound book from a shelf below the counter and placed it down in front of them. He opened the book and began leafing through the pages slowly and precisely, ensuring he didn't crease any. George positively brimmed with excitement. The man continued to turn the pages in silence until he got to the correct day and looked up at George knowingly.

"You must be Mr Poppleton?"

"Yes!" gasped George, glancing down at the book and spotting his name.

"I have you down for a bench wig, sir."

"That's right!"

"In a size fifty-eight, sir."

"Yes, right again!" said George, grinning.

The man went back into the side room from which he had first originated, and emerged holding a large black box embossed with a gold lion. He slowly lifted the lid and George peered excitedly inside. The man enquired as to whether George would like to try the wig on before purchasing it. George readily agreed, and after both he and the man had put their white cotton gloves on George was given permission to reach into the box. He carefully lifted the wig with both hands as if cradling an injured bird, and brought it out into the light, his arms bent so the wig was inches from his face. He was speechless. It was perfect.

The man took him over to the mirror and helped George position the wig correctly. George kept his eyes closed throughout, savouring the experience. The man then instructed him that it was time, and he nervously opened his eyes. He could not believe the vision in front of him. He felt his heart pounding and knew that at this moment everything had fallen into place. It was just how he had imagined it to be. For a moment he was worried he may faint. The man stood proudly behind him with one hand on his right shoulder.

"One hundred percent Mongolian pony hair, sir. The finest horse hair in the world."

"It's wonderful," managed George, eyeing the two thin white ponytails which hung down from the back, "just wonderful."

The man beamed at George. "Only the best for our clients, sir."

"I think I may need a glass of water," said George, suddenly feeling unsteady.

"Right away!" said the man. He helped George into a high-backed brown leather chair and left for the water. George closed his eyes once again as the adrenalin pumped through his body. He had never felt so excited, so alive.

Fifty-five minutes later George's heart palpitations had slowed and he had composed himself enough to be able to stand again. He rose to his feet and returned to the till to complete the transaction.

"Feeling a little better now, sir?"

"Yes," said George, "much. Thank you."

The man was happy to accept a credit card and fully understood that George didn't feel comfortable carrying eight hundred pounds in cash with him. George carefully placed the receipt in his wallet and thanked the man before turning to leave.

"Sir," called the man after him, "sir, would you like me to package up the wig in its box?"

"No, thank you. I think I'll wear it to go home in."

"Very well. What about the box?" said the man.

"Oh, I won't be needing that. You can keep it. Thank you again."

"No, thank you, sir. I hope we'll see you again."

George didn't hear this; he was already through the heavy door and onto the street. Outside it was still grey and drizzle filled the air. George marched proudly through the streets. He didn't need his map for the return journey; he could remember the way he had come without it. From time to time he caught a glimpse of himself in a shop window and beamed widely. He felt somehow taller now and each stride he took seemed wider and more pronounced. One or two people stepped aside as he walked proudly on. He could sense them looking at him after he had passed by, which delighted him.

He strode confidently around the last corner and was horrified to see a police motorbike parked directly behind his car. The officer was standing at the front driver's side noting the car registration down. As he got closer, the officer seemed to be noting down details from the ticket on the windscreen. He glanced at his watch and realised that his ticket had indeed expired seventeen minutes earlier. This simply won't do, he said to himself.

"I'm so sorry, Officer. I'm, er, running a little late," George offered.

"I'm aware of that, sir," said the policeman, continuing to note down the ticket details without looking up.

"Yes, it's been, er, a rather busy morning, Officer."

"I'm sure it has, sir, I'm sure it has," replied the policeman in a weary monotone.

"Yes, I, er…"

"Save your excuses, sir," said the officer, bending down into a squatting position to check the front tyres.

"I'm sorry for, er, passing the expiry time, Officer."

"Yes, I'm sure," continued the officer before straightening his back and turning to face George.

The officer looked visibly shocked and immediately changed his tone. "I don't think we'll be needing this, Judge," he said, winking and tearing up the ticket in front of George's eyes.

"Oh," said George.

"I didn't realise who you were," said the officer. "We can't be handing out fines and tickets to fellow purveyors of justice, now, can we?"

"Er, no, thank you," said George.

"Sorry to have bothered you, Judge," said the policeman, patting George on the back as he unlocked the door and climbed into the car. George started the engine and indicated before pulling out of his space and onto the road. Through his wing mirror he could see the policeman standing alongside his motorbike raise his black leather glove to wave him off. To be mistaken for a judge, of all things, George chuckled to himself. The look he had been aiming for was more Vivaldi.

twenty-seven

It had been a whirlwind few days for Sam. There was just so much to organise now. The contact from Carl had come completely out of the blue. She had deleted his number from her telephone after the incident and hadn't expected to hear from him again. Of course, she wouldn't have recognised his number when he did text, because these days, after all, does anyone actually memorise anyone's telephone number? Of course not, everyone relies on their phone to tell them who is trying to get in contact. A few people had suggested to her that she knew from the moment she received the text that it was Carl, but she could honestly say that this wasn't the case.

At the hotel, Sam had ignored the texts for the best part of three hours before deciding that perhaps she had played a little hard to get for a little too long. It suddenly entered her mind that due to her lack of contact perhaps the communicator had now lost interest. Suddenly, the tables swung back in the mystery man's favour and Sam became immediately impatient, desperate to find out who this person was. She had waited until her mother had gone to the ladies and then retrieved her phone, powered it up and awaited the deluge of texts that had been sent during her period of abstinence. There was no immediate indication of any messages received and Sam waited a moment, staring at the phone as if waiting for it to catch up. This happened regularly when she switched on her phone. It was almost as if numerous messages were queuing patiently somewhere in the ether for a place to go. All the messages were eagerly staring down from some satellite mast in sky, willing the intended recipient to bring their phone to life so at last their waiting would be over and they could finally be delivered. Sam waited a few moments more, desperate for the phone to beep and at the very least the display to show "1 New Message Received".

Nothing.

"Mum!" Mollie interrupted.

Sam stared at the phone.

"Mum!"

"Not now, Mollie, can't you see I'm busy?"

"I'm hungry."

"You'll have to wait until your grandma gets back."

"But…"

"Just wait!" Sam said sharply.

Sheila returned from the toilets swaying slightly and crumpled back onto the sofa.

"Mollie's hungry," said Sam, still looking at her phone.

"Are you love?" said Sheila. "Do you want some chips?"

Mollie shrugged an "okay" to her grandma. Sheila decided that this was an opportune time for her to change for the evening and agreed to take Mollie up to the room for room service whilst she had a bath. She felt a little woozy and this strategy would surely bring her round a little and allow her to freshen up. Sam declined the invitation to go to the room, instead choosing to stay in the bar and finish her wine. Mollie and Sheila headed towards the lift, promising to be back in an hour.

When they were both safely out of view, Sam decided to refresh herself of the earlier exchanges, reading back through each text message to prepare herself for her next move. It wouldn't be fair to say that Sam panicked at this stage, because panic wasn't something that Sam ever did. She knew every decision she made was unquestionably right, so there was no need to panic. She did, however, feel slightly unnerved that if she was to renew the text communication it would have to be her who made the first move. She contemplated waiting until the morning to see whether any further messages arrived but quickly discounted this. She couldn't wait *that* long. Flicking back through her inbox she reread the final missive she had received:

txt me bak sam please x

It was beginning to make sense. The final text she had received was quite obviously the last message she would have expected. Of course there were no further messages; this was a message begging her to make contact. The wording was perfectly clear. This was a desperate attempt for her to respond. Realistically, she convinced herself, she would never have expected anything further! For her to respond now would not be admitting defeat or capitulating in any way. The tables swung firmly back in her favour. She was still in control of the situation; it was up to her when and if she responded. She would consider that.

Two seconds passed.

Tap, tap, tap.

ok, i'm txting bak

(Nonchalance was the name of this game.)

Beep.

nice 1 fancy a drink 2mora x

Tap, tap, tap.

depends

(Oh, and indifference.)

Beep.

on what?

Tap, tap, tap.

who u r and whether I want to

(Finished off nicely with control.)

Beep.

2mora sam at 3 al pik u up wear that d&g top I got u for xmas x

Once she had known it was Carl, it hadn't taken her long at all to decide that they should meet. Apart from a half dozen nights out (which could loosely be described as dates), she had been single for what seemed like forever and she had persuaded herself that her time with Carl hadn't been all bad. True, there had been the incident, but looking back it was probably as much her fault as his and he had only done it *just that one time.* No, she had concluded, she wouldn't let his one little slip up get in the way and she would meet him for a drink and a chat.

Tap, tap, tap

ok S

The next day, the train journey home was an extremely difficult occasion for both Sam and Sheila. The previous night had disintegrated into more and then more wine and neither had much of an idea how they had got to bed. It was even more of a mystery how Mollie had managed to have been in her pyjamas asleep on the sofa bed in the corner of the room. To the best of their recollection neither had unfolded the mattress and made the bed up. The most of the journey passed in silence. Sam deep in thought about her forthcoming liaison. Sheila deep in thought about how queasy she felt. Mollie deep in thought about how to finish her sketch of a burning goose.

George was at the station to meet them and as they got into the car he enquired after "the girls' trip away".

"Just drive, George," commanded Sheila. She suspected that she was going to be sick and was in no mood to make idle chatter.

"Can you have Mollie this afternoon, Dad?"

"Of course," George replied, winking in the rear-view mirror at Mollie. He had intended on tuning into the afternoon *Full Works* show, but with Sheila looking deathly green and obviously bed bound and with Sam otherwise engaged, some time with Mollie would be nice.

Mollie smiled back at her grandpa's eyes in the mirror, her freckled nose wrinkling up, before turning back to stare out of the window.

Carl had arrived at exactly three. It wasn't exactly perfect timing for Sam, who was still applying the final touches to her face. She had been preparing for the best part of two hours and wanted to ensure that Carl saw exactly how beautiful she was. It had taken a little more time than she had expected to fully cover the scar at the top of her nose. To ensure her ascendancy she had kept him waiting at the door for more than five minutes.

So as they could talk without interruption, he had driven them far into the countryside to a quiet pub. The journey had been mainly peppered with stilted comments about the escapades their shared acquaintances had been enjoying. Neither spoke about themselves or each other. At the pub, Carl insisted on buying the drinks and they sat down at a table near an open fire. The exposed stone walls were adorned with horse brasses.

"Nice top," said Carl, complimenting his own choice of Christmas present.

"Thanks," said Sam.

"You been okay?"

"Yeah, fine. You?"

"Yeah. Not bad."

"Good."

"Just been working."

"Busy?"

"Yeah."

"Oh."

"Mollie, okay?"

"Yeah, fine."

"Good."

"Your mum?"

"Yeah."

"Good. Another drink?"

Sam looked down and noticed that she had almost finished her pint of Stella.

"Please."

As Carl stood at the bar, Sam couldn't help but think he had changed. He had always dressed smartly but today he seemed to have gone to an extra effort. His cream Stone Island shirt was certainly a new addition to his wardrobe and it clung tightly to his arms, accentuating his huge biceps. Her eyes followed it down his broad back to where it was tucked neatly into his dark blue Henri Lloyd jeans. He also seemed more generous than before. She couldn't remember a time when they hadn't taken turns to collect drinks from the bar and previously this had annoyed her. After all, she was a girl and for her to stand queuing wasn't really acceptable. It was obvious now, though, that Carl had noticed this behaviour hadn't been acceptable to Sam and he was changing. For her. He was also more attentive to her. He had noticed that her drink was nearing its end and had immediately offered her another. She hadn't had to wait, or even ask – he had noticed and he was her bringing one. Thus she swiftly concluded that he had changed.

Carl returned to the table with another pint of lager.

"Thanks."

"You missed me?" he said directly.

Sam looked at Carl. His face looked different. Momentarily, she felt that she saw a glimmer of regret in his piercing blue eyes. She couldn't be sure of this because Carl's face was permanently expressionless, but she knew him better than anyone and trusted her own judgement.

"You missed me?" she replied. She wasn't about to give away control that easily.

"Yeah. A bit, you?"

He had conceded first.

"Yeah."

"How much?"

"A bit."

The "bit" that Sam had offered was enough for Carl to feel confident in his next line.

"Wanna try again?"

He is asking *me*, Sam thought. He has made contact, laid his heart out on the line and begged me to give him another chance. From the moment that he got back in contact *he* has asked *me* to make every decision. She could go with this on her terms, but she needed further clarification to make sure that his intentions were serious.

"Do you?"

"Yeah."

And with that word, Sam was sure that Carl was sorry for everything that had happened. Okay, so he had not said as much, but Carl was not a man to express his emotions. He hadn't apologised for attacking her, but he didn't need to. His actions and the way he had spoken had been enough for her to know he was truly sorry. There was no need to discuss it further. It was water under the bridge and the time had come to move on. To get life back on track.

"I do too," Sam confirmed.

Carl's face broke and a half-smile cracked open his thin lips, displaying his teeth for the first time that day.

"I was thinking, we ought to, like, get engaged. Make it proper and that?"

This was not what Sam had expected. *He* wants *me* to marry him. Be a family. Be together forever. To Sam, this outpouring of emotion was so unlike anything Carl had ever said before. She had usually felt like a hindrance when they had been out. She couldn't remember just how many times she had sat at the end of a table (smiling at the right times) whilst Carl and his mates had drunk pint after pint and whistled and howled comments to other girls in the pub. Carl had, of course, always insisted that his behaviour had just been a "laugh" and what "him and his mates" did. Sam would have to get used to it, he had told her. Today was different, Sam told herself; this was a different Carl who had lost her, had spent time thinking about his behaviour, endeavoured to change that and returned today to ask to spend his life with her. Excitement filled her body. One final check, Sam thought, to convince herself she was reading the situation correctly.

"Are you asking me to marry you?"

"Yeah."

"Yes, then."

She grabbed Carl's huge hand across the table. It was like squeezing a brick.

"Nice one," Carl said, breaking into his second half-smile of the day.

Sam gently rolled the engagement ring around her finger and smiled. Once she had taken care of the party arrangements she could relax. Now she had Carl back, everything was going to be okay.

twenty-eight

David collected his hire car and after checking the oil and screen wash (along with a brief perusal of the tyres and the vehicle's bodywork) he adjusted his mirrors and pulled out of the car park and onto the main road. Things hadn't entirely gone to plan and the journey he was about to make had never been even considered in his initial itinerary. He had, of course, factored in some time with his parents in the north of Scotland. After all, they had visited him annually since his move to Japan. But this sojourn was supposed to be two days overnight in Scotland and not, as it was now turning out, ten days. His parents had moved to Scotland shortly after his move to Japan and so the only people that he would know on arrival would be them. There was no doubt that David was looking forward to seeing them, but somehow he had envisaged things altogether differently.

He drove away through the city until the roads became no more than thin, twisting country lanes. The winter sun shone down brightly through the windscreen making it difficult to see the bends and curves in the road as he approached them. He allowed himself a quick glance around the car, torturing himself that there was indeed only him in there. His own kind of solitary confinement. He then allowed himself to revert back to his imagination, back to how the two (now ten) days were actually supposed to be in his original plan.

He would be driving the eight hour trip up various A roads and motorways to his parents' residence. He would glance over to his left and Sam, with her beautiful blonde hair pulled back into a ponytail, would smile widely at him, her right hand meeting his left on the gear stick. The perfect silence would be broken by a child's giggle coming from the back of the car. He would smile at her reflection in the rear-view mirror, watching as she devoured the joke book she was reading in the back. She would look up and return the smile, her face glowing in the sun. Sam would turn around and ask Mollie what the joke was and when Mollie repeated it all three would laugh long and hard together. Sam would know when he was thirsty and without him even asking she would offer a carton of pineapple juice in his direction. She would have prepared the straw to be facing in the exact position he needed so he could take a drink without taking his eyes off the road or removing his hands from the wheel. At times, he would become alone again. Sam would be outstretched, her naked feet on the dashboard and her head lolling to her right, eyes closed, asleep. He would allow himself another look in the mirror and he would see that, in complete synchronisation, Mollie was asleep in the back, imitating her mother. Then Sam would awake, rub her eyes wearily and ask him whether he was alright to keep driving or whether he needed a rest. He would smile and assure her he was just fine, and she would look at him in admiration before leaning over to kiss his cheek. The two of them would sing along to old songs, taking it in turns to sing each line and laughing when they got their words jumbled. At times of silence, Sam would lovingly stroke his forearm and from time to time pop sherbet lemons into his mouth. She would tell him that she had never been this happy and that she had never thought that this day would come. He would smile back, knowing that he had always steadfastly believed that this was meant to be.

Swerving heavily to his left to avoid a grouse before swinging to the right and narrowly missing a tractor abruptly broke David from his daydream. Undeniably alone in the car, he concluded that it was an understatement (to say the least) that things hadn't gone entirely to plan.

Sam had returned from her afternoon with Carl elated. Closing the door to her flat behind her, she immediately headed for the lounge, where she had made herself comfortable on the sofa and began calling her family and friends. Unfortunately, she explained to her mother, Carl had needed to go off and price up a job so she wouldn't see him again until later. Her mother had seemed excited on the telephone and had sworn that she would not breathe a word of the news. Sam had warned her in no uncertain terms that this was *her* news and she would be extremely unhappy if Sheila mentioned it to anyone. She had tried Ange but the only response was voicemail. There was no point in trying Auntie Lesley, who had still not successfully managed to make the leap into the mobile phone world and was more than likely in the pub. Sam had then settled down to go through her mobile and ring her wider friends to give them the good news. It was somewhat of a race against time, because despite her warnings, Sam knew that her mother's discreetness could in no way be relied upon. Twenty minutes later, she had made it through to Kayley, imparting the same news as before, each time to be met by girlie screams of delight and congratulations before then quickly ending the call to move on to the next person. She was loving this. Lisa went to voicemail, and as she dialled Louise, eager to impart the story again, the door buzzer sounded. She began her news but the buzzer didn't stop. It continued and continued and continued. Frustrated, she told Louise she would have to call her back and leapt up from the sofa and marched to the door.

Unlatching the chain, she flung the door open, ready to dismiss the person who was interrupting her news despatches. At that moment her face, gnarled with anger, quickly dropped to an expressionless blank.

"Hello, Sam."

As near to speechless as she could get, Sam stared blankly at the man who stood in her doorway. What was David doing here?

She looks beautiful, David thought, more beautiful than I'd ever remembered. The brown eyes that he had fallen in love with stared up at him. After all these years she hadn't aged at all; if anything, she looked younger and happier than before. Now, where were those gorgeous cheeky dimples which appeared around her mouth whenever she smiled? David looked more closely but they were not at all evident, which was when he realised that she wasn't smiling. No, she definitely wasn't smiling. She seemed to be pulling a more shocked face or, at best, a face of confusion. Perhaps, she didn't know who he was.

"Sam. It's David, David Cross," he repeated for clarification. Soon the hugs would begin.

"I know who you are, David," Sam said matter-of-factly. "You've still got the same fucking haircut."

Leaving the front door open, she turned down the hall and David followed, uninvited. She waited momentarily before David turned the corner into the open-plan kitchen. So she did do the conversion, thought David, admiring the island complete with three high-backed leather breakfast stools.

"What are you doing here, David?"

"Er, well," stammered David. "I, er, came to see you."

"Me? Why?"

"Well, er, it's been some time and, er..."

She always made him feel like this.

"Yes," Sam continued slowly and precisely. "It's been some time and what, David?"

"It's been some time and I wanted to see you, Sam and, er..."

This is like pulling fucking teeth, thought Sam, immediately enraged. Didn't he know that she had phone calls to make and time was slipping by? Mum could have told every man and his bloody dog by now.

"Well, you've seen me now, David – is there anything else?"

David considered turning and leaving at that exact moment. This was not going according to plan in any way. He had dreamed about this day for so many years and in none of his dreams had it turned out like this. It would have been so easy to walk out of the flat and never return. To leave now would at least soften the blow of the inevitable which was now about to arrive. No, he thought, he had travelled thousands of miles for this moment and he wasn't about to let Sam do what she always did. He would have his time and he would say what he had come to say and then he could leave, knowing that his mouth had spoken what his heart felt.

"Yes, Sam, as a matter of fact there is something else."

"Oh?" she replied, raising her eyebrows.

"Sam, I love you. I've never stopped loving you."

There was a pause. This was make or break. The next words were vital.

"I don't love you, David. I'm getting married. In fact, right now I'm trying to plan an engagement party for a week on Saturday."

"Oh," said David.

"So, if you don't mind," she said, shepherding him towards the door, "I'd really like you to go."

"Oh, er, okay," said David as Sam closed the door behind him.

Inside the flat, Sam shrugged and returned to the sofa. Later she would have to revert back to the beginning of the alphabet to fill everyone in with this latest bit of news. But far more pressing than that was to call back Louise and everyone else between M and Z before her mum got in first.

David lingered on the other side of the door. It hadn't gone well at all. Perhaps it was this morning's kippers, he pondered for a moment, before realising that he hadn't ordered them after all.

David awoke after a fitful night's sleep. It was now approaching lunchtime. After the near miss with the grouse and the tractor he had decided that his erratic driving was potentially dangerous to other road users and had decided to stay overnight in a hotel to break up the fifteen-hour journey. He dressed, and before leaving for the second half of the journey decided to telephone George to say his goodbyes. He liked George and felt that it was impolite not to update him of the events which had unfolded just thirty-six hours earlier. He dialled the number and sat upright on the bed, leaning back against the bed head.

George answered.

"Hello, Mr Poppl… er, George."

"Oh, hullo there," said George, sounding extremely excited about something.

"Hello, George, it's David."

"David?"

"David Cross, George."

"Oh, hullo! What a lovely day it is today!" George said enthusiastically.

"I went to see Sam," David continued glumly, "and I'm afraid it didn't work out."

"Oh dear," said George, trying to imitate David's tone.

"So, er, I suppose I'll be heading back home soon."

"Right, okay," said George cheerfully.

"I'm sure you'll know she's getting married soon. There's going to be a party."

"So I hear," said George, "that'll be nice."

"Hmm…" pondered David quietly. "So goodbye then, George. All the best to you."

"Yes. Thank you," said George, chuckling. "Do call again."

David hung up the receiver and lay outstretched on the bed. He wondered whether George was feeling alright.

George replaced the receiver in the kitchen. He was feeling better than he could ever remember. As Sheila pushed open the kitchen door he swiftly managed to hide the wig behind his back before she spotted it.

"I'll be a few hours, George. Who was on the phone?" she enquired whilst zipping up her coat.

"I've absolutely no idea," he beamed before cantering through to the conservatory.

twenty-nine

The bell rang and moments later the reinforced glass doors were pushed open from the inside. The children, lined up inside, were released one by one by the teacher as each spotted their parent or grandparent or family friend waiting to collect them. Screams and shouts of happiness were heard as the children lumbered those collecting them with lunchboxes, coats and pictures before excitedly chattering about their day. Towards the back of the queue of children was Mollie. One of the last children to leave, as usual, she trudged out of the door and across the playground. Her coat was unzipped but she had made the effort to button her red cardigan beneath (albeit buttons into the wrong holes). Mollie walked unenthusiastically in the general direction of where her mother waited without looking up. Her feet dragged across the tarmac playground, her scuffed shoes a testament to many previous such departures from school.

"Hi, sweetheart!" cried Sam excitedly.

Mollie jumped slightly and continued to look down. It had certainly sounded like her mother's voice.

"Mollie! Gorgeous! Have you had a good day?"

It was her mother's voice. Something was wrong. Mollie looked up at her mother, who was standing a few metres away, and smiled awkwardly.

Sam looked radiant. Her hair was straightened and she was fully made up. She was wearing a figure-hugging black Armani halter-neck top with some tight dark-blue jeans. To keep out the winter elements she wore a three-quarter length cream Burberry cashmere coat. Brown knee-length leather boots finished her outfit.

As Mollie reached her she stooped down and hugged her closely, making sure that her coat didn't drag along the floor. Mollie accepted the embrace wearily, offering her cheek to Sam's lips.

"How are you then, darling? I've missed you! Tell me all about your day."

This was confusing to Mollie, to say the least. The usual greeting was a complete contrast to this and Mollie was unsure how to react. In previous years Mollie, like any other child, would have rushed to her mother's arms from leaving school, excitedly telling her of the events that had taken place that day. She had learned, however, that her mother didn't really have time that day to listen to the stories of what she had learned in school. She was always much too busy with one thing or another. Previously, she would have loaded her mother's arms with lunchbox and coat, but Sam had always snapped back with "What do I want to carry those for?" or "Carry them yourself!". So now Mollie didn't even offer them to her mother – she simply carried them as asked.

Today was altogether different, though. Something was definitely wrong. Mollie noticed that her mum looked extremely pretty and wondered whether she would be dropped at her grandpa's straight from school. It looked to her like her mother was dressed to go out somewhere else.

"It's been okay," she offered wearily.

"Tell me what you've learned about today then, sweetheart."

Mollie shrugged, pulling away from what remained of their embrace, and headed for the school gates. As they approached the car Mollie reached for the door handle of the rear driver-side door.

"Not today," smiled Sam. "You can sit up front with me. I've moved your car seat to the front."

Sam climbed in alongside her daughter, still smiling.

"I thought we'd go out for tea tonight, gorgeous," she said as Mollie pulled her seatbelt across and clicked it in place.

Mollie looked blankly at her mother.

"Would that be nice? To Pizza Hut, maybe?"

Mollie shrugged. "Who's going?" she asked.

"I thought maybe just you and me," said Sam, beginning to feel like her smile was about to permanently expire.

"What for?" asked Mollie, unimpressed.

Sam could feel her patience starting to wane. She had made the effort to turn up at school and offer her daughter a nice treat and this was the way she was repaid.

"I thought it'd be nice."

"We never go out for tea, Mum. Can't we just go home or to Grandpa's?"

"Well, I just thought it'd make a nice change."

The look on Mollie's face was one of blank indifference. Sam was right. It would make a nice change from traipsing round clothes shops for hours on end after school. It would make a nice change from Mollie being sat in front of a television in one of Sam's friend's houses whilst the grown-ups had endless coffees in the kitchen. It would even make a nice change from listening to her mother talk on the telephone in the kitchen all afternoon whilst motioning to Mollie with her hands that she could get what she wanted from the fridge or the biscuit tin. As long as Mollie was quiet. Mollie weighed up the trip to Pizza Hut against going straight home, and quickly decided that she just wanted to go home.

Back at the flat, Mollie removed her coat and climbed on to one of the breakfast stools. Sam was disappointed that her planned surprise had not been as well received as she had anticipated. However, she knew that she must continue to focus on Mollie.

"Would you like a glass of Coke, sweetheart?"

Mollie nodded.

Sam delivered the Coke and a KitKat and went through to Mollie's bedroom. Mollie stared out of the French windows at the dark sky outside. Grey rain clouds loomed in the distance as she idly nibbled at her biscuit.

"Here's your paper and coloured pencils..." announced Sam on her return "... and something special for my amazing little girl."

Mollie looked up.

Sam pulled a large glossy-covered colouring book from behind her back and held it up.

"It's Tinkerbell and all her friends from Pixie Hollow," she said, desperately trying to inject enthusiasm whilst flicking through the black and white line drawings.

"Thanks," said Mollie, forcing a slight smile.

"Have a look through, sweetheart, see which one you want to colour first."

"Will you help me colour, Mum?" Mollie's large brown eyes made contact with her mother's for the first time that day.

"Not now. Maybe later on, love. I've got to get tea ready. Now, is there anything special you fancy?"

Mollie looked at her mum again, searching for signs of exactly what was happening.

"Oh God, I nearly forgot, sweetheart, I got you these today as well."

Reaching for a large red plastic bag on the floor, Sam retrieved a new life-size baby doll which could walk and talk and cry and placed it on the breakfast bar. It was swiftly followed by a bright pink woollen Burberry coat with matching gloves.

Mollie forced another smile.

"What do you say, sweetheart?"

"Thanks, Mum, thanks a lot," replied Mollie in a monotone pitch.

"Right, for tea, what do you fancy? I'll make you whatever you want," declared Sam excitedly.

"Mum?"

"Yes, sweetheart?"

"What's going on? Why are you acting, like, weird?"

"Weird? I'm not acting weird, sweetheart," Sam responded in a slightly patronising tone.

Mollie shrugged and selected a yellow pencil to begin colouring in Tinkerbell's hair.

Sam stared at her daughter momentarily before continuing, "I've got some big news for us, Mollie."

Mollie continued her colouring without looking up.

"Mollie!"

She jumped for the second time that afternoon and looked up.

"I said, I've got some big news for us."

"Carl's coming back, isn't he?" Mollie replied quietly.

"Er, yes. Yes, he is, but it's going to be different this…"

There was a scraping sound as Mollie edged the breakfast stool backwards and climbed down from it. She picked up her pencils and colouring book and left for her bedroom without a sound.

"She'll come round in time, don't worry, love," calmed Sheila from the other end of the phone.

The afternoon had been less than a success and Mollie had gone straight to bed following her fish finger sandwich. It had been her own choice and Sam had returned to her room half an hour later in order to continue the conversation they had almost had earlier. By this time, she was already asleep. Sam had pulled the covers over her sleeping daughter and switched off the light. Then, frustrated, she had telephoned her mother with an update.

"I know, Mum. She's too young to understand what Carl means to me right now. It's just bloody frustrating when I've bought her all that stuff and she just doesn't seem bothered."

"I understand how you feel, love."

"Well, she'll have to get bloody used to it. I mean, I was out shopping all afternoon looking for nice stuff for her. I had to cancel the special cake at Pizza Hut…"

"I know, love. I know."

The buzzer at the door rang.

"Anyway, Mum, I'll have to go, there's someone at the door."

It had not been an easy afternoon for Angela at all. She felt drained and exhausted from lack of sleep over the last week or so. Her thoughts were filled with the conversation she knew she needed to have with her friend. She was acutely aware that it wasn't going to be an easy conversation and was convinced that whatever she said wouldn't make one iota of difference to the forthcoming celebrations and her friend's chosen union. At times she had convinced herself that she should simply stay silent over the matter and let her friend make the mistake that Angela knew she was making. But the little palpitations had continued to arrive in the dead of the night, waking her. She knew that for the sake of Mollie at least she would have to say something. And so, as she pushed the buzzer to the flat, her hand trembling, she desperately tried to retain the short dialogue of advice that she had practised over the last twenty-four hours.

"Ange, it's not like you to be out of the house at night! Come in."

Angela followed Sam through to kitchen. Sam flopped down onto the sofa and kicked her boots off.

"Pop on the kettle, Ange. I'm knackered."

The two friends traded small talk until the drinks were made and Angela placed the two cups down on the coffee table before sitting in the armchair near to Sam's feet.

"So, what brings you over, Ange? A bit lonely?"

Angela smiled sheepishly. "Not lonely, no. I just needed to talk to you about something that's been bothering me, that's all." Jesus, this was going to be difficult.

Sam smiled in a mock caring fashion. "What's up, Ange, babe?" she asked.

Angela swallowed. She could feel her neck becoming red.

Sam noticed. God, she thought, this is going to be something pathetic like a boy at work has asked her on a date and she doesn't know what to say to him or the window cleaner winked at her and she doesn't dare speak to him now (and he collects his money the next day).

Sam smiled sweetly.

"Well, I have to say something because…"

"Because what, Ange?" Sam's tone was becoming increasingly patronising. Jesus, Ange, spit it out.

"Because I can't live with myself if I don't, okay?" Angela snapped.

Sam adjusted her position and sat upright. She hadn't heard this tone before from Ange and stayed silent, allowing Ange to continue.

"I think you're making a mistake, Sam. I don't think you should be marrying Carl…"

Sam was shocked; her mouth opened slightly.

"Don't interrupt me, please. You know how much I care about you. You're my best friend…"

Only, thought Sam.

"… but I don't think you are doing the right thing. He hit you, Sam, and he'll do it again. And what about Mollie?" Angela was in full flow, her voice firm yet calm. This wasn't exactly her planned script but the gist was nevertheless the same.

"Mollie?"

"Yes, Mollie. What about her? You don't want her to grow up with Carl around. She doesn't even like him."

"What do you mean?" Sam snapped back defensively. She wasn't taking this; how the bloody hell would Ange know?

"She doesn't like him. He's a bully. It'll end in a mess and you'll both end up getting hurt over this…"

"Yeah, like you'd know." Defensive had turned to aggressive.

"I do know, Sam. I'm only looking out for you both. I don't know why you can't see it. I just don't like him." Angela's voice had remained calm and composed throughout. Things were about to change.

"Well, it's a good job that you're not bloody marrying him, Ange, isn't it?"

Sam bolted forwards and swung her feet onto the floor in front of her. She stood over Angela, who remained in the chair, pointing her index finger towards her.

"Now you listen to me, Ange. I don't know who you think you are coming in here and giving me fucking advice. But, listen to me. I am getting married, Ange. You're just jealous because you've never had anyone. And you don't want me to be happy, do you? Admit it, Ange. Go on."

Angela paused. She knew there was more to come and decided to allow Sam to say everything she wanted to say before responding. The short burst of silence ended almost immediately as Sam continued her diatribe.

"You're jealous 'cause I get all the attention, Ange. Not you. You've been fucking jealous since school. And bringing Mollie into it. How the fuck would you know what Mollie thinks, Ange? Eh? You just want to ruin my chance at happiness, don't you? Just fucking admit it, Ange."

Angela rose from the chair. She had heard enough.

Sam stepped back slightly.

"Listen," said Angela quietly, "I'm only trying to help. I'm not jealous in any way at all. I just want the best for you. I'm going."

Angela walked calmly from the room and down the corridor. Sam remained where she was and watched as her friend reached the door.

"And one last thing, Sam," said Angela, turning. "It's Angela, not Ange. I must have told you a thousand times I hate being called Ange."

thirty

The last week or so had passed in the blink of an eye for George. There was just so much activity in the house. People were coming and going almost daily and the house was beginning to have the feel of a drop-in centre or a soup kitchen. George had spent his time quietly keeping himself to himself in the conservatory, whiling away the days listening intently to whatever classical choices of the day the radio presenters had hand-picked for him. Had it not have been the need for regular visits to the toilet (which due to George's age were a little more regular than he would have liked) he would have not moved from the comfortable wicker recliner but slept day and night in his haven. Unfortunately, though, his bladder had a knack of springing into action almost on the hour and he had no choice but to answer its calls. He did find that if he held it long enough he could probably make it to two hours, but it made the last half hour of listening an uncomfortable experience.

Each time he removed his headphones and headed through the kitchen there would be another gaggle of women in there making plans. "Hullo," he would say as he passed through. On occasion they would stop what they were doing to greet him but generally they were preoccupied, each one listening intently to Sam as ringleader who was revelling in the attention her forthcoming engagement was bringing.

"So, I was thinking, maybe a hog roast would be best?" said Sam.

"Mmm…" considered Sheila, "what about a barbeque?" (Obviously not considering that February and barbeques were somewhat of an odd couple.)

Sheila should, of course, have realised that none of the "questions" which Sam introduced to the conversation were in fact questions. Instead, they were statements which were made to sound like questions to keep the interest of those in attendance.

"No, a hog roast," Sam confirmed.

"I think a hog roast would be best," capitulated Sheila, nodding in agreement.

It was an interesting dynamic. The kitchen had been temporarily converted into a military headquarters for planning the party. Sam expertly played the role of field marshall, directing all those gathered to how she envisaged *her* party to be. Indeed, there was never any doubt whose party it was. Sheila, ever present at the daily assemblages, ably played the lieutenant general role. It was her role to feebly question the field marshall's decisions in a justification of her rank before quickly and unconditionally surrendering her view in favour of that of her superior. The other attendees, who varied from day to day and played a role no more than cadet or at best private, stroked the ego of both their superiors without any challenge to their views. Catalogue after catalogue was opened and perused for ideas as to how to make this a party befitting of someone of the field general's stature. Over the days, the agreements made at the meetings began to shape the forthcoming party.

"Ecru, lilac and champagne balloons, I think."

The battalion nodded in agreement.

"Presents for all the guests as well, you know, as a thank you for coming from me and Carl. I was thinking maybe perfume for the girls and I dunno, something for the men. Aftershave?"

Another nod of approval from the lower ranks. From time to time as the troops became weary the conferences would become heated.

"And, what about champagne for the guests?"

"Champagne? How about Cava instead?"

"Cava? I can't give my guests bloody Cava, can I? May I remind you, Mum, *I* am getting married soon. I don't want the people at my bloody engagement party going home afterwards and saying, bloody Sam and Carl, they didn't even give us fucking champagne."

"I like Cava," Lesley interjected, proving her statement by finishing the bottle in front of her.

Sam turned furiously. "Who asked you?"

"I'm just saying, Sam-an-tha, that I like Cava."

159

"Well, don't. It's not your fucking party, it's mine. And *my* guests are drinking champagne."

Sam flicked her hair back and sighed before looking to the ceiling for inspiration.

"Okay," Lesley replied apologetically before mouthing "Have you got any more Cava?" to Sheila.

Sheila brought another bottle over.

"We're sorry, Sam."

"You don't understand, Mum. Its a lot of pressure, all of this, and I don't need any negativity around me."

"I know, love, I know," Sheila said, stroking her daughter's hand. (This sudden physical display was perhaps pushing the boundaries of acceptable military behaviour.)

In the main, however, the discussions had gone well, and as time passed by Sam began to get the feeling that it would be the best party ever. George and Carl's absence from the meetings had been noticeable, but that didn't matter. After all, they were only providing the funds.

The week had frustrated George, not least because he hadn't had the opportunity to unveil his new purchase to the family.

It had long been accepted that George dressed in his tuxedo and bowtie each day and this had brought much derision. But gradually over the weeks his family had become used to his new apparel and Sheila had tired of telling him to remove it. In the early days, she would greet him with a "What the bloody hell are you wearing?" or a "Get that bloody suit off", but George had steadfastly refused to change. In truth, he hadn't actually argued his point with Sheila, he had simply spirited himself away in the conservatory. He would be met with a similar comment next time their paths crossed but again continued his business, almost as if the words hadn't even been heard. Now, nobody mentioned his chosen dress.

But he wasn't sure at this stage whether the wig would be the right move. And anyway, he wanted to enjoy it to himself first before introducing it to the family. It was not dissimilar to a child who wants to be the first to play with a toy before, over time, sharing it with his siblings. The activity in the house had made it impossible for George to spend any time alone with the wig, to try it out properly. Any normal week would have given George hours of time alone in the house, but unfortunately, this was not a normal week.

After three or four days, George could wait no longer and he took the wig and the radio to the tool shed. It was a cramped and dusty space and not really big enough for an orchestral performance, but he had little choice. He locked the door behind him and covered the window with a discarded piece of plywood he found under the workbench. The only lighting available was a small battery-operated pull-cord light above the workbench and an inspection light which he clipped to the side of the wooden shelving. It was by no means ideal. "This simply won't do," George sighed to himself. However, on this occasion it would have to.

He pulled on the wig and extended the headphones to accommodate the new addition. The radio clicked into action and George widened his arms into his initial pre-performance stance. The pose was similar to that of a proud fisherman displaying the size of a legendary fish he had once caught. From the moment the music came to life, George instantly recognised the opening of Strauss's *Also sprach Zarathustra*. He gently waved his hands to the BUM-bum-BUM-bum sound of the timpani and threw his arms out wide to allow the brass to burst in. Unfortunately, due to the limitation of space in the shed, his right hand made direct contact with a jar of paintbrushes which were bathing in paint stripper on the shelf by his side. The jar fell from the shelf and crashed to the floor, smashing and simultaneously dispersing its grey-white liquid upwards towards George. Horrified, George looked down to see that the liquid had splashed onto his right shoe and the front of his right trouser leg. He quickly reached for a rag and rubbed the stain, hoping to reduce whatever effect it may have on his costume.

He removed the radio and placed it on the workbench before sitting adjacent to it on the stool. It took him a few moments to catch his breath. He considered this an extremely close shave. Goodness only knows what would have happened if he had been closer to the jar when it impacted. The liquid could have gone in his eyes, or (a look of horror crossed his face) on to his wig.

He concluded that he had been somewhat fortunate and decided that the wig would not get another airing until the house returned to its usual peaceful state. Surely, whatever it was they were planning in there couldn't take much longer.

thirty-one

Sam stared at the phone on the coffee table. She had set it to silent mode, so instead of audibly distracting her its screen simply flashed from dark to light. She pondered for six or seven seconds and then picked it up. She had ignored it enough and this time would take the call.

"Hello?"

"Hi there."

"What do you want?"

"It's about the other night…"

"Yeah?"

"I just wanted to apologise. I didn't mean it to turn out that way. I just…"

"What?"

"I just wanted to speak to you about everything. But, well, you seem happy and…"

"I am."

"… and, well, if you are then I'll support you. You both mean a lot to me and I want you to be okay…"

"We will be. You still coming?"

"If I'm still invited."

"Course you are."

"Thanks. I'll be there. Let me know if you need any help preparing for it."

"I will."

"Okay, bye then. You take care."

"And you, Angela."

thirty-two

As was now his usual daily routine, George spent the morning of the party in the conservatory. The house was busier than any time in recent weeks and George suspected that whatever was going on was finally reaching its crescendo.

Sam breezed into the conservatory.

"Morning, Dad!"

Silence.

"I said, morning, Dad!"

George was staring out of the window. "Let's get these off," she said gently as she lifted his headphones from his ears. This startled George slightly.

"Good morning, Dad!" she repeated.

"Oh, you, er, made me jump, Samantha."

Sam beamed a large white smile and then hugged George.

"You're cheery today."

"I know," she said excitedly, "the day is finally here."

"Very good," said George smiling back. What day? he wondered.

"Still lots to do, Dad!"

Just then Sam was interrupted by a serious looking Sheila at the door. She told Sam that she had better come to the phone, there was a lady on the line who had said it was a call she must take. George replaced the headphones.

Sheila stood a safe distance away from Sam looking for a clue in her daughter's facial expression to what message the serious sounding voice was imparting.

As the voice at the other end of the phone continued, Sam's happy demeanour swiftly plunged to a frown. Something was wrong.

"And there's absolutely nothing you can do?" Sam said into the receiver. "But there must be someone else... But I'm getting married... " Sam's voice suddenly took on an aggressive tone. "I need him to be here. Today. Get it?"

Sheila watched. She didn't like how contorted her daughter's face had now become.

"I don't want a refund!" Sam screamed. "I want him fucking here. Today. To do what I am fucking paying him to do."

Sam replaced the receiver and turned to her mother. "It's all going wrong," she said as tears welled in her eyes. She wasn't sad. She was livid. Sheila sat her down and Sam explained what had happened.

The farmer who was to be responsible for the hog roast that night wouldn't be able to make it after all. He had been out the previous evening and butchered the pig for the party. Unfortunately, as the farmer's wife had explained, when he had returned to the pen that morning for the first feed of the day he had been ambushed. The remaining pigs – obviously put out by the brutal killing of one of their own – had laid in wait for the farmer, determined to reverse the injustice. They had been hell-bent on revenge, she explained, and as her husband had entered the pen they had come from all angles grunting and snorting and squealing. He had stood little chance. She heard the screams whilst washing the dishes and rushed to her husband's aid. The sight which had greeted her was horrific. Her husband was curled in a ball in the middle of the pen whilst eight or nine of the beasts jabbed and butted him with their snouts. She had managed to avert their attention by launching a bucket of swill at the ringleader. After this, she had helped her husband out of the pen and onto the grass outside. He had suffered a bite to his leg and was badly shaken.

"One bloody pig bite, that's all," Sam said.

"I know, love," consoled Sheila.

"One bloody pig bite and he can't be arsed to do my party."

"It's just not right, love," said Sheila sympathetically.

"Badly shaken. What the bloody hell does that mean? He'll be alright by tonight. He just can't be bothered to do it. Simple as."

Sam was furious. All this planning and effort and then some lazy pig farmer decided he'd just ruin it all. Over one lousy pig bite.

Sheila leapt into action. It was down to her to save the day.

"Don't worry, love, we'll sort it," she said confidently.

Sam looked inquisitively at her mother.

Sheila banged on the window between the kitchen and conservatory. "GEORGE, GAMMON!" she screamed at the top of her voice.

George jerked slightly. He thought he had heard someone shout his Christian name but the second word was certainly not his surname. Perhaps it was his imagination. He sat back and continued listening to his music.

"GEORGE, GAMMON!"

There it was again. Over the double bass and bassoon he had definitely heard his name. But he was Poppleton not Gammon. No, he swiftly concluded, the voice couldn't be calling him.

Sheila burst into the conservatory and ripped the headphones from George's head.

"For once in your bloody life can you stop listening to this thing and help. We have a crisis on our hands," Sheila cried.

"Oh," said George, startled, stowing the radio in his inside pocket.

"We need gammon now!"

"Do we?" asked George, perplexed.

"Go and get some gammon, now, George, NOW!"

It seemed a funny request to George. Personally, he didn't really want any gammon, but Sheila forcibly chivvied him into the kitchen. Before he could blink, she had put his coat on him, zipped it up and passed him a handful of notes.

"Go to the supermarket, George, and don't come back until you've spent all this money on gammon."

Confused, George acquiesced and left immediately.

There followed a period of Sheila somehow keeping the wheels on an extremely shaky cart. She quickly adapted her rank to replace her battle weary general and took control of the planning from there on.

Sam, for the most part defeated, wandered the kitchen bemoaning the pig disaster and questioning why everything in life seemed to go wrong for *her*. There were threats of cancelling the whole event followed by self-pitying comments of how the entire party would be a complete disaster and of how people would comment about how cheap it all was (I mean gammon, for Christ's sake!). Soon after, frustrated tears were accompanied by a glass of wine suggested by Sheila to assist Sam in numbing the horror of her perceived disaster.

After a few hours of mostly silent resolute exertion on Sheila's part, Sam slowly began to come round. The cycle of one gammon joint into the oven, the next one out, cover it in foil and into the hot trolley caught her attention. Sheila chopped lettuce and cucumber and tomatoes and carrots. She boiled bag after bag of new potatoes. She boiled eggs and let them cool. She chopped more lettuce and more cucumber. The eggs were sliced and cubed and mixed with mayonnaise. Chicken legs joined the gammon on the oven conveyor belt. Mushrooms were washed and peeled and boiled. Garlic was added. Sam began to look more interested. Peppers were washed and chopped. Baguette after baguette was sliced and filled with garlic butter. More lettuce. More tomatoes. Another gammon out. Another in. More new potatoes. Mayonnaise was mixed with lemon and pepper and a dash of mustard. Potatoes were added. More carrots were peeled. More peppers, red, green, yellow. More lettuce. Sam sat upright and watched intently. Another gammon out. Another in. More chicken legs. More tomatoes. More mushrooms. More garlic. Gammon out. In. Out. In. Sam could see the phoenix of her party rise in front of her. Maybe it wasn't going to be such a disaster after all. Maybe things were going to be okay.

Around four o'clock, at the exact moment Sheila collapsed down at the kitchen table, exhausted, Sam rose and declared that it was time for her to leave to get ready. Mollie had returned from her friend's and was to get changed with her grandparents. Sam had already explained that she wanted a bit of time to rest and to get ready in peace. As she put it, she wanted "Some '*me*' time". She decided against disturbing her father, who had been peacefully relaxing in the conservatory since his return from the supermarket, and headed outside.

"See you there!" she sang cheerfully as she opened her car door.

"Yes, see you there," agreed Sheila, busily loading food into the back of the car for what would be the first of many trips.

She had managed to persuade George to do the driving – back and forth – to the venue. George had reluctantly agreed after being told it was the least he could do for his daughter's engagement.

An engagement party, he thought to himself, so that's what all the fuss has been about.

thirty-three

Guests began to steadily arrive at the cricket pavilion, careful to not be a minute after the eight o'clock start. The invitations they had received had warned them not to be late and no one had any intention of testing the unknown consequences of doing so. As they drove up the long drive which swept around the side of the cricket field they were greeted by the huge ten-by-ten-foot banner which welcomed them to the "Sam's Getting Married!" party. It was attached to the side of the pavilion and expertly lit by a red laser which weaved its way across the vinyl, double underlining the word "Sam" as it crossed. Outside the main entrance guests were greeted by two exotically dressed girls who spun fire for entertainment. Two further girls dressed in huge white costumes in the shape of wedding cakes handed neatly wrapped blue and pink gifts to each attendee. Just inside the door, Sam, who was dressed exquisitely in a cream Burberry pleated sun dress, greeted each arrival, thanking them for coming. Carl towered alongside her, gripping her hand tightly and handing out glass upon glass of champagne.

George arrived with Mollie and Sheila and greeted the happy couple. Under some duress, he had followed Sheila's directions and made an effort to look smart for his daughter. His shoes gleamed following an extended polish and he had taken the time to expertly colour over the paint stripper splashes on his trousers with a permanent marker. He clutched an orange polythene bag tightly in his right hand. Mollie, herself sporting a more traditional Burberry dress, skipped passed her mum and Carl without a word and made for her great-grandpa in the corner of the room.

"You must be Dolly?" Walter joked.

"It's Mollie!"

"That's what I said, Dolly!" he teased.

"No! It's Mollie!" she laughed.

"Oh, I see... Polly!"

"No!" She was giggling now. "MOLLIE!"

"I'm a little deaf now, you know, I'm sorry, Holly."

"It's Mollie. M-O-L-L-I-E!"

Walter winked. "I see, hullo, Mollie!"

Mollie laughed, faking exhaustion, before collapsing into Walter's shoulder. She liked Walter; he reminded her of her grandpa.

The venue was the downstairs bar of the cricket pavilion. At the front of the room was a dance floor with the bar running the full length of the back wall. Running down one side of the room were huge glass windows which on a summer's afternoon gave spectators an excellent view of the pitch. Tables and chairs were lined up in rows filling most of the floor space. Meticulous care had been taken by Sam and Sheila. Each table had three ecru-coloured balloons floating above. The letters S, A and M were printed on them in bold black lettering. Each bunch was secured in the centre of the table with a weight which was beautifully decorated with champagne-coloured paper and ecru ribbons. Colour-coordinated banners and streamers adorned the walls and ceiling, giving an almost grotto-like effect.

At the present time many of the tables were unoccupied, the guests happier to stand and little by little edge their way to the already heaving bar. So as to keep the guests' interest whilst they waited to be served, Sam's main project was displayed above the bar. Over the previous few weeks she had carefully selected photographs of herself from baby to toddler to teenager to adult and converted them to a huge bunting display. She had stylishly scanned each photograph onto a triangular shaped card and then laminated them. Each was then attached to the next in chronological order. It was possible to scan Sam's entire life by simply following the bunting from left to right across the bar. A number of amused eyebrows were raised whilst people got ever closer to receiving their drink.

"Hullo, Dad," said George, who had followed Mollie to the corner of the room.

"Hullo, son," replied Walter, noticing George's attire. "You look extremely smart today."

"Thanks, Dad," George said contentedly.

"Reminds me of when you went to that Ball all those years ago," Walter continued wistfully, "you know, the one where you met Sheila."

George nodded in agreement.

"Where is Sheila by the way?"

George wasn't sure. They had separated from one another soon after arriving, George heading for Mollie and Sheila, well, somewhere else.

"Bloody hell, Lesley!"

Sheila had finally found her sister-in-law at a table by the window. She was surrounded by empty wine glasses and beer bottles. Sheila had spent an hour participating in short (and somewhat disinterested) catch-up chats with various distant family members and neighbours. She was ready to relax and more than ready for a drink.

"Heeey! Sheila!"

"How much have you had, Lesley?"

"One or two! It's a party," she slurred.

Pete rolled his eyes and stoically took a large gulp from his Guinness before clasping both hands around his glass and resting his elbows on the table.

Sheila tittered. "It's only half nine Lesley! You're gonna be on your back."

"I hope so!" she laughed, winking seductively at Pete. Receiving no response, she nudged Pete, causing him to spill his drink down the front of his shirt. "I said I hope so, Pete!" she repeated.

"Bloody hell fire, Lesley – watch what you're doing," he said, wiping at the Guinness with a napkin.

"Ooooooh! Sorry!" Lesley mocked.

Without speaking, Pete finished the small amount that remained in his glass and left for a replacement.

"I'll have a Babycham," Lesley called after him before turning to Sheila. "The grumpy bastard!"

The two laughed.

"So, have you been keeping well, Mr Poppleton?"

"Call me Walter, Norman. I think we've known each other long enough by now."

Norman smiled.

"I've been keeping very well thank you. I am nearly ninety, you know."

"I'm pleased to hear it," replied Norman.

"And, how are you and, er, Nora keeping?"

"Norma. We're very well indeed, thank you. Enjoying our retirement, you know."

"Ah. Good."

"Is George here? I haven't seen him as yet. I haven't seen him for a while actually."

"He is, yes. He'll be around somewhere. Do you know where your grandpa is, Mollie?"

There was no answer from Mollie. It was unlikely she had heard the question. The music wasn't particularly loud where they were seated at the back of the room, but Mollie was deep in concentration. She rifled through her pencil case trying to find the silver pencil. The pliers that were currently extracting the eye of a monkey in her drawing wouldn't look right unless they were coloured silver.

David wasn't entirely sure why he was walking up the dark perimeter of the cricket field at that precise time. He had returned from Scotland that afternoon and was due to fly back to Japan the following evening. He hadn't actually been invited to the party, but then again he hadn't expressly *not* been invited either. After a week of haggis, hot chocolate and early nights he couldn't contemplate his final night in the country of his birth alone in a hotel room. To spend a night, *this* night, alone would be akin to a death row inmate awaiting execution. The fact that his final meal would be room service was inconceivable. He hadn't left the train with the intention of attending the party, his feet had just somehow carried him there. He sat on the boundary staring across the field at the lights bursting warmly from the pavilion.

Lesley was going to be sick. She had felt it coming after her last Drambuie, and she was now locked in a race against time to get to the toilets before it came. Lights and voices blurred as she desperately swayed from side to side past the buffet table, clutching unsuccessfully at solid objects to keep herself upright. She reached the door frame of the inner entrance doors and swung herself spectacularly through two hundred and seventy degrees straight through a second door into the ladies' toilets. She was in luck. Both cubicles were free. She stumbled to the one nearest to her and vomited directly into the toilet. She had made it. And just in time. She collapsed to her knees and grabbed the porcelain in front of her with both hands, resting her forearms on the rim. The nausea rose again and she leaned forwards slightly to ensure the contents of her stomach were projected into the toilet, before rocking back again. Blurry eyed and hazy, she reached up and flushed the toilet in an attempt to remove the smell. Then she rested, her head lying on her right arm which still gripped the rim.

The door squeaked as more people entered the toilets. With an enormous effort, Lesley pushed herself up and locked her cubicle door before reverting back to her position of rest. Her eyes closed of their own volition.

"She does look nice, though," a voice said.

"Yeah, she does. I just can't believe she's got back with him."

"I know. After what he's been up to."

The lock of the cubicle next door was pulled across.

"Do you think she knows?"

"Are you daft? 'Course she dunt know. Sam's not stupid. She wouldn't get back with him if she knew."

Lesley's left eye opened slightly.

"I just cannot believe that he got Charlotte pregnant. She's only seventeen."

"I know. And then to have to pay for the abortion for her as well!"

"Tell you what, I'm surprised he didn't punch it out of her."

"I know. I mean it's not Charlotte's fault, she's only a nipper and she didn't know anything about Sam. She reckons, though, he gave her Chlamydia as well."

"You're joking!?"

"No, she's had tablets for it from the doctors. Cleared up now, though."

"Jesus Christ. I hope Sam knows what she's doing?"

"I know. Do you need a piss?"

"Nah, I'm alright."

Lesley heard the sound of the toilet flushing and clothing being reinstated before the lock clicked and the door was pushed open. After the brief sound of water followed by the air of the hand dryer the voices disappeared.

Lesley stared ahead, eventually focusing on the word "twat" which someone had artistically added to the wall of her cubicle. In her state, this was a quandary she could certainly do without.

Sam pulled Carl with her to the dance floor and called a halt to the music. She had an announcement to make and wanted quiet so that no one was distracted from her moment. She had waited until the food had been finished and cleared away. She didn't want this moment being spoiled by the sound of someone munching loudly on crisps or the scratching of cutlery on the pottery plates she had insisted on. As far as she knew, the food had been an absolute success. She hadn't heard any disparaging comment regarding the last minute substitution of gammon for hog. Yes, everyone seemed to be enjoying themselves at her party. She tapped the microphone to quieten the room further and, when satisfied that all eyes were on her, opened her mouth to speak.

"I've just got a few things to say tonight," she began before raising her eyebrows disapprovingly at two girls who were whispering.

Both stopped immediately and faced Sam.

"Firstly, on behalf of me and Carl, thanks for coming. I hope you're all having a good time. I can't say it's not been hard work for me to put this do on, at such short notice as well, but..." she grabbed Carl's brick hand, "... well, I didn't know this was gonna happen two weeks ago!"

Carl smiled awkwardly. He wasn't sure that he'd known either.

"And," she continued, "I'm just pleased you could all be here for me. And Carl..."

She noticed that a few of the heads down the window side of the room were not facing the right way and appeared to be looking instead onto the cricket pitch outside.

"Ahem," she coughed into the microphone.

The heads didn't turn and instead more heads followed suit, turning their attention away from her.

"Excuse me!" she said, her temper rising, "I am, you know, still talking."

Those sat at the tables not immediately adjacent to the window had risen slightly off their chairs and were now also looking down onto the cricket field outside.

"Excuse me!" Sam shouted, but by now she had lost the room. Almost everyone had now switched their attention outside and away from the dance floor. A large crowd was gathered, watching intently through the window.

"For fuck's sake," Sam exploded, throwing the microphone on the floor, "it's my fucking party."

She barged her way through the crowd until she reached the window to see what all the fuss was about.

The cricket field sat in complete darkness. The crease, however, was lit by a single spotlight which beamed into the night, casting long shadows of the stumps across the wicket. In the centre, between the two sets of stumps, was George. Drowned in light, he stood with his arms outstretched in a crucifix pose facing the pavilion. He had his eyes firmly closed and the expression on his face was that of pure concentration. He reached down into a small polythene bag which was at his feet and pulled what appeared to be a dead rodent from it. The faces inside the pavilion were transfixed. No one made a sound. George lifted the rodent out in front of him between cupped hands and held it aloft to the sky. Furrowed brows were exchanged. After a few moments he brought the rodent down from the sky and placed it on top of his head. A gasp was shared by the crowd. Slowly and calmly, he reached down into the bag again and pulled out a small black box. He then appeared to put something else on top of his head before his body went limp and he flopped forwards like a rag doll.

"I'm not watching this shit," muttered Sam, who barged back

through the crowd and sat at a table with her mother and a less-than-sprightly looking Auntie Lesley.

The guests continued to watch. George fumbled with the small black box before suddenly and dramatically coming to life. All of a sudden, he was frantically waving his arms from side to side with rigid meticulousness. His right foot tapped frantically on the newly mowed grass below him as his head shook violently from side to side. The crowd were completely shocked. They had no idea why George had decided to put on such a spectacle for Sam's party. Maybe it was something that Sam had asked him to do? This didn't seem to be the case, though; Sam's reaction had affirmed this. And anyway, who in their right mind would ask their father to put a dead creature on his head and perform a silent dance to entertain people? In fact, for those who knew George well, his shy and reserved nature would have made agreement to this type of spectacle an impossibility. Even if it was his daughter's engagement party.

George continued to conduct, his arms at times flapping and swaying before abruptly slowing down to barely any movement at all. The crowd looked on. But then, there was a build-up. It began in George's fingers and the rapid movement of his hands gathered momentum into his arms. The symphony was reaching its crescendo. His arms moved ever quicker. His foot tapped like the wings of a humming bird. His head jerked quickly from right to left with such force that you would not have been surprised if he had broken his neck. His arms began flailing wildly, faster and faster, faster and faster. Due to the distance from the pavilion to where George was standing, the crowd couldn't see that the veins in his neck had grown to the thickness of pencils. His face was entirely scarlet. Saliva dribbled down his chin and collected in little white puddles in the corners of his mouth. Sweat flew from his head as he jerked ever faster from side to side. His shirt and what remained of his hair were sodden. Still the movement continued. His arms, faster and faster. His foot, faster and faster. His head jerking, ever faster. And then, as the music that only George could hear stopped, so did George, who collapsed forwards into his original bending position. A sharp intake of breath was taken communally inside the pavilion. Nobody took their eyes off the pitch. Then George, his eyes still shut, calmly bowed and, using his body to form the shape of a star, fell rigidly backwards onto the grass.

The crowd didn't know how to react and more confused and puzzled glances were shared. Were they supposed to clap? Was George actually okay? What *was* that all about? But there was no time for the crowd to draw any conclusions. Their mutterings were swiftly broken by screaming, this time coming from the other side of the room.

"What the fuck have you been up to?" Sam shrieked at Carl.

Carl towered above Sam, a wide churlish grin covering his face.

This was certainly an entertaining night, and the crowd who had craned and arched from the back to see the performance outside now traded ringside seats with those by the window.

"Uh-oh..." said Walter.

"Looks like trouble at the mill," replied Norman.

Mollie looked up from her colouring for the first time that evening. She was pleased with her harpooned giraffe.

"I think we three better get outside," said Walter, gesturing his head towards Mollie whilst looking at Norman.

Outside, George still lay star-shaped on the grass. David had watched the entire performance from behind a small bush. As he saw the heads turn away in the pavilion windows he left the boundary to see whether George was alright. Quietly, he kneeled down beside him. George appeared to be asleep.

"Mr Poppleton, er, George," he said, gently shaking his shoulder.

"Are you alright, George?"

George muttered incoherently.

"George, are you alright? Do you want a glass of water?"

David wondered whether George had been drinking.

"I'm fine, thank you, Adam," said George, smiling sleepily, "and how are you, son?"

"George. It's David. David Cross."

"It's been a long time, Adam. I've missed you, son."

His words slurred slowly, as if an anaesthetic was about to take him over. The contented grin remained on his face.

David didn't speak. There didn't seem to be any possible words that would be appropriate right now. Instead, he removed the wig and headphones from George's head and replaced them in the plastic bag. He lifted George up from under his armpits and put his arm around his shoulders to guide him. Then, slowly, he escorted him across the cricket field to his car.

"Do you remember when you broke the fish tank?" George slurred. "And when you squirted the hose." He smiled fondly. "I never did use those charcoal briquettes that day…"

David managed to retrieve the car keys from George's pocket and bundled him into the passenger seat. He was greeted by Walter and Norman in the car park. They had left through the back door and were accompanied by Mollie, who looked extremely tired.

"Everything all right, son?" said Walter to David, oblivious to the events that had taken place a short while earlier. Walter had seen the people staring through the window, but from the side of the room where he was sitting, it had been impossible to make out anything that was happening. He was nearly ninety, you see.

"I think so," said David. "I'm going to take him home for some rest."

"This one needs some rest too," said Norman, nodding towards Mollie.

"Can I go with Grandpa?" said Mollie sleepily.

"Of course you can, Polly," said Walter, winking.

Mollie raised her eyebrows at Walter. She was too tired for this now. She climbed into the back of the car and closed her eyes.

"Can one of you let Sam know that I've taken Mollie and her dad home?" requested David.

"Of course," smiled Norman. "We're heading off now anyway. It's all getting a bit heated in there."

David reversed George's car out of the parking space and set off down the long winding drive to the main road at the bottom. As he pulled left onto the road he noticed flashing lights and sirens in his rear-view mirror which disappeared up the drive from where he had just come.

The police cars and riot van screeched to a halt metres from main entrance of the pavilion where Walter was standing. At that moment a chair shattered the window and landed on its side on the cricket pitch. Norman hurried out from the pavilion he had just re-entered with a look of panic on his face.

"I think we'll go right away, Walter. I'm not minded to make my way back into there."

The police officers tore past the two men and into the pavilion.

There had certainly been an interesting turn of events and the room which had previously been filled with celebrating revellers was now all but empty. Following Auntie Lesley's torrent of unbelievable truth, Sam had reacted in the only way she knew and confronted Carl, demanding to know the truth regarding the revelations. Carl had not expected this information to come out quite so early and when Sam had unleashed her wrath on him he had only managed an awkward smile (with his limited intelligence he could not have been expected to come up with a cover story on demand). Sam had screamed for the truth and when this was not forthcoming she had put her face within an inch of Carl's. Carl had reacted in the only way *he* knew, which was to grab Sam by the throat and shove her backwards against the dance floor wall.

"Who the fuck do you think you are?"

"I want to know the fucking truth, Carl."

Carl grabbed Sam, lurching her forwards towards him before slamming her back against the wall.

"Don't. Fucking. Get. In. My. Face," he had snarled.

Fear had crossed Sam's eyes. He was hurting her.

"Is it true?" Sam had asked again with artificial assertion. She was desperately trying to remain in control. She was also shaking slightly.

Carl glared at her. His eyes seemed to pierce hatred through hers. He didn't answer. Sam summoned her rapidly depleting strength and screamed again.

"IS IT FUCKING TRUE?"

She already knew the answer.

Carl's grip on her neck tightened as his left hand formed a fist and rose high into the air. As the fist was beginning its descent Carl was hit squarely on the side of the head by a garlic baguette which disintegrated into ten or more pieces and scattered across the mixing desk. No one (not least Carl) had expected this and Carl spun around swinging both fists. Angela – the aggressor – had the foresight to move as soon as she administered the blow and Carl's fist hit Uncle Pete squarely on the jaw. Pete, distracted by the events regarding his brother-in-law, had been heading across the dance floor to break the melee up.

This is when the trouble had really begun. Within minutes, punches were being thrown from all angles. Friends and family of the betrothed couple were forced to quickly select a side and then go all out to destroy the other. The room quickly became a bear garden. Girls jumped onto the backs of men, scratching and pulling hair. Men swung around trying to dislodge the girls whilst dodging punches from other men in the room. Everything became a blur but for the sound of bones making contact with skin and the tearing of various designer-label fabrics. Chairs were lifted and swung around violently to ward off would-be attackers. Those who didn't really have the courage for hand-to-hand combat instead set about pushing over tables and smashing glasses. That would be the legacy they would brag about the next day.

And then, as the distant sound of sirens was heard, the fighting quickly ceased. People stopped and stood rigidly holding the same pose, their heads cocked, listening to the increasing nee-naws outside. It was as if the sirens had brought on an impromptu game of musical statues. A few more cowardly punches were thrown. A final chair made its way through the window. And then, when the consensus was that the arrival of the police was imminent, the room emptied in seconds. Excluding the extremely dangerous-looking broken window, there were only two real exits from the pavilion. Those who ran through the back could escape across the cricket pitch or over the sprawling recreational fields which stretched behind. Those who made their way to the front ran straight into the arms of the police.

The police, without asking any questions, simply dragged anyone they believed to be involved into the back of the riot van. It wasn't hard to identify potential suspects and the police selected those who looked most like they had been mauled by lions. The police would ask questions and bring charges later that night in the safety of the custody suite. The priority at this stage was to restore the peace. After ten or so protagonists were safely in the van, the police entered the now quiet venue to investigate further.

A police radio crackled. "No, nothing happening in here, over."

"Okay. Over."

"You can take the van back to the station."

The officer outside banged on the side of the van and its engine started and slowly pulled away. Carl, with blood and garlic still stuck to his face, kicked the cage inside the van with frustration.

"Hello?" called the officer. "Anyone here? Hello?"

Sheila, Sam and Angela emerged warily from behind the mixing desk.

"Good party, ladies?" the officer asked smugly.

"There's another over here, Mick," said an officer, checking behind the bar.

Lesley emerged slowly from the back of the bar with a freshly opened bottle of Reef in her hand.

"You okay, love?"

"Fine, sweetheart," she slurred, smiling.

After checking the remainder of the room, the two officers sat the four women down at a table which seemingly had been spared from destruction.

"We'll need you all to make a statement," said Mick slowly. "One by one."

He knew that this was pointless. What type of information were four drunken women going to be able to provide? It appeared that three of them had hidden during the fracas; the other had helped herself to supplies from behind the bar. He could imagine the defence lawyer in the case.

"And where were you, madam, when the assault took place?"

"Behind the bar."

"Had you been drinking?"

"Yeah! I'd had a few."

"And what did you see?"

"Bacardi. Martini. Pernod…"

No, there was no prospect whatsoever that the statements of these women would stand up in any way. There wouldn't even be a court case. Not one of those arrested had seemed particularly badly injured. A bit of blood, a couple of bruises. He had seen it all before: they were looking at a couple of charges of drunk and disorderly followed by a few cautions. Everyone involved would be home by the following lunchtime. But this didn't matter. He would take the statements and meticulously go over each fact, being careful to question everything they stated. He glanced at his watch. Only a couple of hours until his shift finished. Yes, he thought to himself, the questioning would take about that length of time. He would certainly be too tied up with the four women tonight to respond to any other emergency call.

"Okay, ladies, this may take some time," said Mick, glancing at his colleague. The colleague smiled back, understanding fully.

Mick began the interview, asking basic details of the names of the attendees, the purpose of the event, the time the event started and a whole host of seemingly irrelevant information. Each interruption or protestation from the ladies was greeted with a stern "It's procedure, madam" before running through the information again.

"So, you say that your husband was here?" asked the officer, nodding at Sheila.

"Yes, George was here."

"And where is he now?"

"I haven't got a bloody clue."

"He was out on the cricket pitch earlier," slurred Lesley.

"Fighting, madam?"

"No, conducting."

Mick shot his colleague a confused glance. Jesus, these people were pissed.

"I saw him after that," interjected Angela.

All eyes turned to her. She felt a little uncomfortable.

"Yeah, I saw him being helped across the cricket pitch."

"Was he injured, madam?"

"No. This was before all the fighting started. He was being helped across the pitch by David. I think they…"

"David who?" snapped Sam.

"David. Your David, Sam."

"Slow down, ladies, who's David?"

"My David, Ange? I haven't got a David."

Mick was struggling to keep up.

"I haven't got a David, have I, Mum?" Sam reaffirmed.

"No, Ange. She hasn't got a David," confirmed Sheila.

"David Cross, Sam."

"David Cross?! He wasn't even here, Ange."

Angela resolutely confirmed that she had *definitely* seen him through the window as she had come out of the toilets before all the trouble began.

"What the hell was he doing here?" said Sam to no one in particular.

Lesley stood and left the table. She had finished her Reef and fancied another.

"Madam, can you please sit back down."

"In a sec, love," she said over her shoulder, heading for the bar. It did appear to be a free bar now after all. She didn't notice the bar staff (who had quickly locked themselves in the storage room behind the bar when the trouble started) re-emerge. Mick smiled to himself – a few more to interview. Lesley reached down into the fridge and pulled out a bottle of Smirnoff Ice. She opened it and casually asked whether anyone else wanted anything. Everyone declined and she made her way back to the table.

"You seen my husband anywhere?" she asked the policeman sitting next to her.

"Er…"

"That's a point," said Sheila. "Where's our Pete?"

The unnamed policeman radioed through to the station and confirmed that Pete was currently assisting the police with their enquiries. No one batted an eyelid.

"Least he's safe," slurred Lesley, apparently appeased.

The interview continued on in its own ramshackle way. Sam and Sheila corrected one another on who had hit whom, with what and when. Angela sat quietly, wishing that the evening would end, worrying that her garlic bread assault would come to light. She wasn't sure whether garlic bread was classed as a lethal weapon? She cursed herself for too many nights alone watching *CSI*. Sam and Sheila embraced the spotlight and encouraged one another in fabricating wild accusations about the incident. Didn't Carl have a knife? Yes, I think he did, Sam. This was not strictly untrue – most of the guests had knives (they had, after all, been eating from the buffet). Lesley, for the most part, smiled at the mirror ball above her head whilst sipping on her drink. Mick listened intently and scribbled furiously in his notebook for effect. He glanced at his watch. Fifteen minutes to go.

"Well," he announced, "thank you for such a thorough analysis of the evening. You've been a great help."

"Will you want to speak to us next?" asked one of the bar staff from the back of the room. Damn, thought Mick. He'd forgotten they were there.

"No, that won't be necessary," he said dismissively.

"I think we've got enough," said the second officer, noticing the time. "After all, you won't have seen much locked in that room, will you?"

"I think we all ought to get home," said Mick, rising from the table.

Everyone stood to leave. The slightly deflated bar staff began switching off the lights and putting down the metal shutters which covered the wall of glass to their right. The broken window would have to wait until the morning.

"Well, thanks, ladies," said Mick. Three minutes.

"No problem, officer," said Sam, touching his forearm. "If you need anything else just let us know."

"I will," smiled Mick, knowing he wouldn't.

Angela propped up Lesley as they made their way to the door.

"Sam?" asked Angela in a questioning tone.

"Yeah, Ange?" said Sam, feeling quite deflated that her limelight for tonight had come to an end.

"Where's Mollie?"

"That's a point, where *is* Mollie?" said Sheila.

"Jesus!" said Sam, spinning away from Mick and towards Angela. "I haven't seen her!"

Mick checked his watch again. Two minutes.

Sam spun back towards Mick. "My daughter! She's only eight. Where is she?!"

"Where the bloody hell is Mollie?" Sheila joined in.

Sam stopped dead. She stared into the black night sky and spoke as if reading the words from the stars up above. "David."

Angela glanced at her questioningly.

"Sorry, love?" said Sheila.

"David," she repeated, suddenly overtaken by hysteria. "He's bloody kidnapped her!"

Kidnap, thought Mick. He knew that the very utterance of child and kidnap was not something he could ignore. He had been within a minute of finishing a nice uncomplicated Saturday evening. An evening interviewing four drunken women in the warmth of a cricket club pavilion was far more preferable than the usual nights patrolling around the city centre being abused, punched and spat on. And, he noted, the young blonde one was pretty good looking. The accusation of a kidnap was all he needed.

Sam's imagination was running away with her. "Why else would he bloody turn up at my engagement party? He's taken her 'cause I turned him down. The bastard. He's come here and taken her away. I mean it's obvious, isn't it? Why else would he be here?"

"Oh my God!" said Sheila.

Mick clicked the button on the small black radio on his lapel.

"PC-one-four-five-six, we've got a possible kidnap of a child, over."

Overtime beckoned.

thirty-four

As soon as the possibility of a missing child was announced, the thoughts of a quick and quiet end to the shift disappeared. The police followed procedure, asking when Mollie had been seen last, what she was wearing, who she was with. In all honesty none of the women had any clue as to her whereabouts. Sam confirmed that when they arrived she had seen her daughter skip in the direction of her great-grandpa but that was the last time she had seen her. The police were incredulous that she hadn't seen her daughter for more than five hours. They also found it mysterious that the daughter hadn't come looking for her mother in this time. They publicly wondered whether she could have been missing for all that time. All the women confirmed that it was possible to the best of their knowledge. The group were separated and bundled into two police cars and driven at speed towards the Poppleton home. Mother and daughter went with Mick, auntie and friend with his colleague.

On the journey, the police attempted to build up a better picture of the events of the evening and asked about David's background whilst making further checks over the radio to the station. Angela confirmed that from what she knew David had always been a nice, gentle type – it would be out of character for him to be embroiled in a kidnap. She did concede, however, that his *raison d'être* had received an almighty setback and his emotional state may be fragile to say the very least. Lesley sat alongside, desperately trying to keep her eyes open and to look alert. The alcohol was now taking its toll and the motion of the car wasn't helping her battle against somnolence at all. From time to time, she would slur into action and answer a question from a few sentences earlier before her eyes began to drift shut again.

In the second car, a much more resolute story was beginning to take shape. Sam and Sheila were absolutely sure that David was behind this. Well, who else could it be? Mick tried to remain impartial as he listened to daughter coercing mother into embroidering an ever more far-fetched tale. David had returned to be with Sam, she told Mick. He had been away for more than seven years, following the previous breakdown in their relationship. He had never got over it and when the time had seemed right he had returned from Japan to recapture her. But she had rebuffed him and told him in no uncertain terms that she was neither interested nor available. David's romantic scheme had been an utter failure. Yes, Sam confirmed, he had seemed different this time. When she had summarily dismissed him there *had* been a certain look in his eye. What type of look? Mick asked. Sinister, Sam replied, he had looked sinister. Sheila agreed with Sam's statements as if she had been a first-hand participator in the events that Sam described.

A desperate telephone call was made to Walter's property, her great-grandpa being the last person Mollie had been seen with. Walter, tucked up warmly in his blue and white striped pyjamas, slept soundly, his hearing aids on the bedside table next to him. The unanswered call further heightened the hysteria and cemented the definitive truth that David was behind this. Theatrically, Sam began to sob in the back of the car, wailing for the return of her "baby". Subconsciously noticing how effective her daughter's tears were, Sheila followed suit and resolutely stated that "she could be halfway to bloody Japan by now" (her geographic knowledge of the distance between England and Japan was obviously somewhat lacking). The women wailed and sobbed whilst Mick desperately tried to regain order.

The increasing hysteria that engulfed the inside of the police car was in stark contrast to the quietness that enveloped the Poppleton household.

David had enjoyed an almost silent journey home from the party. Mollie had fallen asleep instantly in her car seat, snoring lightly behind him. George, himself in a state of semi-unconsciousness, had lolled from side to side in the passenger seat. From time to time his eyes would open widely and stare directly ahead. He would then mutter his thanks to Adam for the lift home and state how proud he was of him.

Outside the house, David had left them both in the car whilst he fiddled to find the right key to fit the front door. Once inside, he had switched on every light in the house to illuminate the safe passage of his sleeping passengers and returned to the car to retrieve them. He carried Mollie up the two flights of stairs to her room, being careful not to catch her trailing legs against the walls. Once in the attic he delicately laid her on the bed. He looked around the room, amazed that anyone could rest in such a garish gold and pink colour scheme. Mollie was deeply asleep and looked perfect. Her long dark hair was still tied back neatly and she wore a contented half smile. He thought about changing her out of her expensive looking dress and into something more comfortable but decided against it, instead covering her in a purple fleece blanket. She would be much too hot under the duvet. He removed her shoes and socks and pulled the fleece down to cover her feet. She wriggled slightly as he kissed her on the forehead. "Goodnight, princess," he whispered before turning off the light and slowly making his way down the stairs. He knew that this would be the last time he saw her.

In the car outside George had managed to fall completely to his right and was now laying with his head on the driver's seat. David sighed; this trip wasn't going to be as easy as Mollie's had been. He stood outside the passenger door pulling and dragging and fighting to move him. After six or seven minutes of manoeuvring he finally managed to get George back in his own seat. It hadn't helped that the handbrake had become inextricably lodged in the inner pocket of George's dinner jacket and David was sure he had heard a tearing sound when he finally got him upright. Once vertical the momentum had continued and George had swung like a pendulum towards David before sliding out of the car and onto the road. David was amazed that throughout this George had somehow managed to stay asleep. Even as he thudded onto the tarmac he had not given an indication that he was aware of the position he was in.

David had then reverted back to the same arrangement which had worked so well across the cricket pitch and helped George into the house. It had been an incredible struggle and once inside David sat George on the bottom step of the stairs so he could regain his composure. After several seconds of panting and gasping he crouched down onto one knee to be at eye level with George.

"Would you like a nice cup of tea, Mr, er, George?"

No answer.

"George, would you like a drink?"

George's head lolled to one side then the other. It was as if the right side of his brain was slowly filling up with liquid before getting too heavy and causing his right ear to sharply make contact with his right shoulder. Then, the left side would slowly begin to fill as the right drained, sharply snapping his neck the opposite way. Something was not right. After watching this occur four or five times, David cupped George's head in his hands to stop the motion.

"George! George!" he implored. "GEORGE!"

George's eyes flashed open. It wasn't possible to see his irides and instead David was greeted with just a grey-white.

"George, can I get you a drink? Some water or something?"

Slowly, the circles of blue colour made their way down from the inside of George's eyelids and settled on David's face. David got the impression that although George's eyes had returned to normal, they couldn't see him and were instead focusing on something directly through his head and behind him.

"George?" said David, waving his fingers slowly across George's line of vision. "George? Would you like a drink?"

George smiled broadly in a slightly ominous, inane way. The look deeply troubled David.

"No, thank you, Adam," he said fastidiously. "I think I'm ready for bed now, son."

David was forced to make a decision as what to do next. George was quite obviously unwell. If the events on the cricket pitch weren't enough then the unnerving conversation he now found himself in was certainly testament to the fragility of George's mind. Since he had rescued him from the centre of the crease, George had continually referred to him as his long deceased son. David considered whether George was perhaps just a little drunk – never before had he seen anyone behave in this way. He appeared exceptionally tired and perhaps bed *was* the best place for him. Jesus, what did he know? He had only seen George twice in seven

189

years, perhaps this was how he always behaved? George's eyes snapped shut again. David looked down at his watch; it was coming up to midnight. Surely the rest of the family would be coming back soon? He could leave George in their hands then.

"Bed, Adam," George murmured.

David made his decision. He couldn't leave George sitting here until whatever time Sheila and Sam rolled in. He would follow his wishes and take him up to bed. Hauling him up again for the third time that evening, they began their ascent of the stairs. Although George didn't appear to have any concept of what was happening the journey to the top was surprisingly uncomplicated. George continued his mumblings about how helpful his son was being and David, rather than correct him, cajoled him up the stairs with the promise of a bed. At the top of the stairs David calmly took George's hips from behind and rotated him ninety degrees to the right into his bedroom. David had remembered the route following his pre-chess clothing change just a couple of weeks earlier. At the door, however, George suddenly became rigid and threw both his arms out wide, clutching the door frame on either side. David gently pushed the middle of his back to nudge him through but George was not moving.

"Bedtime, George," he coaxed in the way a parent does to a toddler, "nearly there."

George stood rigid.

"Come on, George, just a few more steps."

No movement.

The conundrum at the top of the stairs was more complicated than one that David had overcome at the bottom a few moments earlier. At least at the bottom George was seated. Now at the top he was standing rigid, his entire energy focused on apparently holding up a door frame, and there was no doubt he was not about to enter his bedroom. He was also perilously close to the top of the stairs. David was now faced with the possibility that he may have to stand behind George at the top of the stairs until the family arrived home. And that could be hours. He sighed heavily again, cursing his decision to move George up a floor. It appeared David's sigh registered with George, who turned, his eyes tightly shut, and grinned again.

"I'd like to stay in your room tonight, please."

"My room?" This was confusing to say the least. There was no way that David was going to get George back downstairs, into the car and to his hotel. And for what purpose? Why would George wish to stay at the hotel with him? This was beginning to get very disconcerting. In fact, David felt frightened. He wished he had never turned up at the party now. Before he had the chance to question George's sleeping intentions, George spoke again.

"Yes, son. It would be nice to sleep in your room."

Aaah! thought David. Not *my* room, Adam's room.

"Okay, that's fine."

He rotated George again and helped him across the landing, reaching around his hip to open the door.

"Here we are, George."

Although his eyes were still firmly shut, George seemed to sense that he was in the right place and walked straight across the room and collapsed on the bed. Adam's room was now no more than a place for storage. Only someone with a very keen eye would have noticed that there was even a bed in there. It was obscured behind various boxes of bric-a-brac piled up high near the window. A clothes airer covered with recently washed clothes stood immediately inside the door. Kurt Cobain's forehead could be seen poking up above a dismantled wardrobe which leaned against the wall. David was amazed that George had managed not to collide with anything en route to the bed. He waited for a few moments, watching George as he hugged a pillow tightly under his right arm, his head resting on the top of it. David concluded that George would be warm enough in his tuxedo without a blanket and switched off the light.

Downstairs, he tidied around a little. He moved George's plastic carrier bag which he had brought in from the car onto the kitchen worktop. Then he made himself a coffee and sat down. It had been an extremely long night already and he wasn't exactly sure what to do next. Whilst Mollie and George slept he contemplated the past few weeks. It had been an utter failure from start to finish and he knew that the dreams that he had brought with him would not be making the return journey. Sam was engaged and would no doubt arrive back later that evening full of excitement over her party and her forthcoming marriage. He had been a fool to even think that something had changed which required his return. He should never have made the journey. It was now past midnight and he would be flying back to Japan later that day. He had fully expected that his time in England would be spent day and night with Sam and Mollie. There would, of course, have been time spent with Mr and Mrs Poppleton when the five of them would plan the future together. There would be a great deal to sort out as well. Where would he, Sam and Mollie live? He had already tentatively sorted out employment in England, having the foresight to subtly enquire about transfers from Japan before he left. He had even typed his letter of resignation from his employment in Japan, citing destiny as his sole reason. Thank goodness he had not submitted it.

He flicked on the kettle for a second time and wondered out loud why he was still there. He could just leave right this moment before anyone returned and go back to the hotel. He could have a few hours' sleep before packing (and repacking for completeness) and making his way to the airport in good time. It wasn't as though anyone was expecting him to be at the house or indeed anyone would be remotely interested that he was. But he felt compelled to stay. It was obvious that George was not exactly well, *sane*, right now and it wouldn't be safe to leave Mollie in his "care". There was a possibility that Sheila and Sam and even Carl would return to the house that evening. The prospect of this was very unsettling and he felt a rush of palpitations at the thought. However, despite what he may have to endure it was more important that the two people he was watching over were safe. Pouring the milk into his coffee, he pledged to stay until they returned.

Sam and Sheila were beginning to annoy Mick. It wasn't as if he didn't care – he was taking this matter extremely seriously – but neither were being helpful in finding a way to provide a solution. They had already concluded that Mollie had been spirited away across land and sea to the east. Although he had tried to divert the conversation to something more helpful to his enquiries, the two witches in the back seat of his car had taken their own path. There was no way of stopping them as each statement caused the other one to make a similarly ridiculous statement in response. Each return comment was multiplied up by an exaggeration factor of two. Mick had tried to point out that David would have needed a passport to take Mollie away. This was rebuffed by Sam, who stated that David wasn't stupid and that he would probably have been planning this for the last six years. "I think he'll have remembered a bloody passport for her," she had stated patronisingly.

The other police car had radioed through for permission to drop the now completely useless Lesley off at her home and asked Mick for further advice regarding Angela. Mick had agreed that they both could return home until the morning, but had asked Angela to telephone anybody who was at the party to see whether they had any further information about the whereabouts of Mollie which may assist them. Angela had agreed and arrived home moments later.

Mick glanced into his rear-view mirror. The blonde one didn't seem as pretty anymore.

"Next right, love," Sheila said suddenly, shouting to make herself heard over the sirens.

Mick swung the car off to the right.

"Oh my God, I hope she's okay."

"How do you think I feel, Mum? She's my bloody daughter."

"I know, love." Sheila leaned forwards again. "It's next left and we're here."

Thank fuck, thought Mick.

David heard the sound of a high speed vehicle pulling into the road outside and listened as almost immediately the car outside screeched to a halt. He heard three car doors open and then thump shut. They were back. He hesitated a moment longer to make completely sure it was them and heard the key enter the lock of the door. He then exited through the back door simultaneously to them entering through the front.

His job was done.

thirty-five

Sadly for Sam and Sheila the ensuing melodrama that both had expected to extend through the night did not occur. They had arrived back home to an illuminated house which suggested that someone was back. Mick had asked them both to stay outside whilst he and his colleague stealthily worked their way through the house. They were informed that this was potentially an extremely dangerous situation that should be handled by trained officers. Outside, as they waited patiently they could only imagine the search that was taking place inside.

Ten minutes later the officers arrived back downstairs and informed them that they could now enter the premises. There was no sign of an intruder and they believed that the missing girl was in fact asleep in the attic at the top of the house. Sam made her way upstairs and moments later confirmed that the little girl was, in fact, Mollie. Of course, Sam was extremely pleased that Mollie was safe and well and there was a happy ending to the story. She was, on the other hand, slightly put out by the fact that the events of the last few hours didn't really equate to anything much in particular. She had imagined the telephone calls to her friends about the desperate kidnap and the race to the airport to apprehend David just as he boarded the flight with Mollie. How *she* had spotted them both heavily disguised, handing their passports and tickets to the flight attendant at the gate. The way *she* had to be held back by the police officers as she had tried to attack David. The warm embrace that *she* received from Mollie, her eyes gleaming with admiration for her mother. In Sam's story, no harm had come to Mollie but at least there was a little more to talk about. The real story – that she had thought Mollie had been kidnapped and then it turned out she hadn't – was too anodyne to relate to anyone. If anything, retelling such a story was likely to make her a look a little stupid. All in all, it was a bit of a disappointment.

The officers contacted Angela to relay the good news and to ask her to call off the search. Mick then dismissed his colleague before turning to Sam.

"Right, we're all done here."

Sam sobbed tears of mock relief.

"Thank you, Officer. Thank you for everything. You don't know how much this means to me."

"Or me," piped up Sheila.

"It's alright, not a problem," said Mick, pleased that his extended night shift had been swiftly curtailed.

"Well, goodnight, ladies."

He closed the front door behind him and headed for the police car.

Sam's brain whirred. *This* was the end of her engagement night? *This?*

As Mick pulled the handle on the car door he heard a shout from behind him.

"Officer!"

"Jesus wept," he muttered to himself.

"Officer! What about my dad? Where's my dad?"

"Yes, Officer," parroted Sheila, "my husband. Where's my husband?"

"Room next to the bathroom, love," he said without turning.

Sam slept fitfully that night. Due to the events of the night before she and her mother had climbed into the marital bed and slept side by side. Sam spent a good proportion of the night pushing her mother back over the imaginary border which ran down the centre of the bed. Sheila's legs crossed over numerous times, wrapping themselves around Sam's, immediately waking her up. When Sam managed to get her mother back into position on her side, she loudly snored appreciation to Sam for her efforts. After the building of a fortress wall between them with pillows failed, Sam gave up. Unable to take any more of this torture she made her way downstairs and on to the sofa.

After just a few hours' sleep, the morning sun woke her, bursting brightly through the lounge window. She lay staring at the ceiling, contemplating whether she would get back to sleep. After ten minutes she concluded that she wouldn't and therefore the rest of the house should be awake as well. She made her way into the kitchen, the clock on the wall confirming that it was seven o'clock. She filled the kettle and retrieved a mug and the coffee from a cupboard overhead, making sure that the door slammed shut. A spoon was taken from the cutlery drawer, which she closed firmly enough to make the rest of the cutlery jump and clatter inside. The near silent whoosh of the fridge door was a disappointing end to the plan. But then she heard footsteps above and immediately knew that her strategy had been effective. Moments later a sleepy looking Sheila made her way through the kitchen door.

"Morning, Mum," said Sam cheerfully. A faultless plan.

"Morning, Sam, how are you, love?" asked Sheila, a concerned look on her face.

"Best I can be, I suppose," replied Sam, quickly remembering that she was supposed to be heartbroken that her forthcoming marriage was now off.

"I'm sorry, love. I really am. Anything I can do?"

"Coffee would be nice, Mum," she replied, putting down the spoon and walking mournfully to a seat at the table.

The two talked for hours about the events of the evening before.

They concluded that Ange was most definitely mistaken about the appearance of David at the party. She had quite obviously been drunk and for some reason had tried to take some of the spotlight. On another day Sam would have made a mental note to berate her friend for this indiscretion. Today was different, though: at her time of need Ange had stepped up and defended Sam. If it hadn't been for her garlic-bread-wielding friend, Sam may have spent another night in the Accident and Emergency department of the local hospital. She decided this once to let Ange's attention-seeking fabrications go without comment.

When Sheila and Sam first sat down for coffee Sam had expertly played the role of the heartbroken maiden who had been cast aside by her betrothed. It took all of an hour for her to announce (confidentially, of course) that she was over Carl and that she had known it was never going to work. Sheila listened and agreed with her daughter, swearing her pledge to secrecy over the discussions they were having. Sam forced her to do this so she, and only she, could retell the events at a later date to anyone who would listen (she had her whole mobile phone contact list to go through).

At around half past nine, an excited Auntie Lesley arrived at the house with a tale of her own to tell. Pete had been released without charge at six that morning and had come back to find her asleep in the front garden. He had managed to untangle her from the rose bush and get her inside and up to bed. Then he had told her about George's performance on the cricket pitch the previous night. She delighted in her descriptions of George conducting and the entertainment he had provided for the audience inside the pavilion. Of course, Sam was aware of the performance, having seen the opening. This was the first time Sheila had heard about this though, and her brow furrowed as she took in the details. She wondered whether George was all right.

"So where is George now?" asked Lesley.

As far as Sam and Sheila knew he was upstairs in Adam's room, but neither had bothered to check the previous night. Sheila knew that George had certainly not been himself over the past few months and Lesley's story worried her. It was true that her husband had developed somewhat of an obsession with the radio, but for such a shy, quiet man to perform so publicly? It didn't make sense. Pete had seen George lying star-shaped on the field, but before he could assist his attention had shifted to the other side of the room. Sheila wondered how, if George had been in the state that Lesley was describing, he had managed to drive Mollie back to the house.

"He's in bed upstairs," said Sam, keen to begin her story. She was hopeful that her auntie's memory of the night before was vague due to her stupor. She hadn't asked about Mollie, which suggested that certainly the latter part of the evening was a blank. With a bit of luck, she could tell the story right from the garlic bread incident.

"Well, we think he is," Sheila said, concern flashing across her face. "In fact, I'm going up to check."

At the exact moment she reached the bottom of the stairs she saw George (wearing just his white underpants) cross the top in the direction of the bathroom. She called up to him but he continued on his path and she heard the bathroom door lock behind him.

"He's here…" she said, relieved, "…just gone in the bathroom."

Sam shot a look of annoyance at her mother before recapturing her auntie's full attention.

George stood in the shower, the water crashing down on him from above. He felt a little bit muddled today. He wasn't sure why he felt that way but the fact that he did made him feel muddled all the more. He couldn't remember anything at all about the last twelve hours. Everything was a complete haze. Everything seemed so very unclear. And now as he stood in the shower things felt all the more hazy. He wasn't sure what he was doing in there. He concluded that he must have got in the shower to clean himself (after all, that's what he usually did), but instead he stood just staring. His eyes met those of a small yellow duck which sat on an olive-coloured flannel on the corner of the bath. He looked at it hard, trying to understand what exactly it was and what it, too, was doing there. The duck offered no clues. It wasn't as if his brain was even processing thoughts, it was simply fixed into one long, monotonous, silent haze. He continued to stand in the shower, slightly hunched forwards so the water crashed into the back of his neck.

The water continued to pour down until George momentarily snapped out of his trance when the warmth of the water transformed into ice cold. Subconsciously, he felt that the sudden change of temperature must have signified something, and he climbed from the shower and collected a towel. He stared into the mirror on the bathroom cupboard, trying to work out who the man was that stared back at him. One of the sliding mirror doors was open and George reached inside for an ear bud. He felt extremely off balance. The only sound he could hear was the sound of the blood whooshing and flowing inside his head. The world seemed extremely distorted. Without thinking he had reached for the ear bud in the hope that his ears were simply filled with water. A quick clean may remove the muffled feeling he was experiencing. He inserted the ear bud into his right ear and began to slowly move it around. He suddenly felt cold and looked down to see that his towel had become unfastened and was now lying in a horseshoe shape around his feet. He reached down and retrieved it before tying it firmly around his waist. Something told him that the next stage of the morning routine was to get dressed and he exited the bathroom to get changed.

In his bedroom he was startled to see that his favourite clothing had been laid out for him on the bed. Yes, he thought in a fleeting moment of clarity, I recognise those clothes. The tuxedo lay neatly on the bed (just where he had left it before his shower). Whoever had been so kind as to leave the clothes out for him had left them very neatly. The trousers were stretched out at the bottom of the bed, with the shirt neatly inside the jacket and the bowtie placed perfectly around the collar of the neck.

George dried himself off and chuckled when he noticed that he was still wearing his sodden underpants. "Someone must have accidentally put them in my drawer wet," he said to himself, laughing. He removed them and replaced them with an identical dry pair. He was disappointed to discover that there seemed to be pieces of grass and tiny leaves on the back of his trousers and dinner jacket. He wasn't at all sure where they had come from. Obviously, whoever had left the suit there for him hadn't noticed either. He put the trousers on anyway and buttoned his shirt. Then he discovered a second disappointment. The inner pocket of his dinner jacket appeared to be torn. He held the jacket open and stared at the shiny silk fabric which hung down. What remained of the pocket had folded back on itself and was now being held in place by a sole purple button. He stood with the jacket aloft, gazing at the pocket.

Four or five minutes passed.

Then he heard a sound that for the first time that day broke through the whooshing inside his head. He spun around and noticed the ringing was coming from the bedside table. It was the telephone! Yes, he recognised that noise. He remembered what the telephone was for. Perhaps it was the hospital? Perhaps they had some news about Adam? He had to answer it. He marched over and picked up the phone, bringing it quickly up to his right ear.

The sheer volume of the high pitched ear-piercing scream from the bedroom above made all three women simultaneously bolt upright. Sam's dramatic story immediately ceased.

George stumbled backwards, dropping the telephone receiver as he fell. The ear-piercing scream had been exactly that: a scream from a person whose ear had just been pierced. The entire length of the ear bud was lodged deep inside George's ear. Blood poured out and George instinctively held his hand over his ear to stop the flow. The blood forced its way between his fingers and dripped onto the white duvet below. George fell to his knees as Sheila arrived at the door, quickly followed by Sam and Lesley.

"My God, George, what have you done?" she asked.

George stared blankly at Sheila. He vaguely recognised her.

"George? George? Are you alright?"

Sheila was alarmed by the amount of blood which was already pooled on the duvet. She kneeled alongside George, putting her arm around him.

"For God's sake, phone a bloody ambulance!" she screamed at Sam. "You'll be fine, darling," she repeated over and over in a whispered tone. "You'll be fine."

George stared at the carpet. He wasn't sure whether he had seen it before.

thirty-six

George opened his eyes and then quickly closed them again. Goodness, it was bright in here. He tried again, opening them slowly and meticulously allowing an ever growing amount of light to enter his pupil. He surveyed his surroundings. He was lying on his back with a light green blanket over him. His eyes adjusted a little more as he stared directly above him. He appeared to be inside a brightly lit white box. He glanced forwards and noticed that the box had some kind of tinted windows at the far end. Above him and to his left he noticed further tinted windows which ran along the side of the box. These had strange hieroglyphics on them which seemed to be from another language. He read them slowly and carefully: E-C-N-A-L-U-B-M-A. Ecnalubma, what on earth was ecnalubma? George had always considered himself quite the wordsmith but even after years with *The Times* crossword this was a word that meant absolutely nothing to him. Most important at the present time was trying to establish where he was. He would consider the mysterious word later.

There was also a strange feeling in his right ear. It felt, well, a little full. A little odd. He lifted his hand from beneath the blankets and sheepishly touched his ear. The first thing he noticed was that around his ear lobe it was slightly sticky. He pushed his finger further into his ear and was confused by the fact that it felt like something was protruding from it. He pulled his finger away sharply. And then, like a moth which cannot resist a light bulb, he returned his finger back to his ear. Yes, there was something sticking from his ear, something soft to touch. It stood about a centimetre from where his ear canal finished. He touched it again. This was most unusual, he thought.

It was at that moment that he noticed the white box appeared to be moving. Broken sunlight flashed through the tinted windows. Yes, he was certainly moving and at some speed. And that noise, what was that noise? It resonated loudly through the box in a seemingly never-ending repetitive two-note tune. The craft on which he was travelling seemed to slow down quickly before thrusting forwards again at an alarming speed.

George had no idea where he was. He began to put the pieces together in his mind to try to make sense of the situation. The clinical whiteness of the craft, the strange writing on the window, the strange protrusion coming from somewhere inside his head, the tortuous noise. There was only one answer. He had somehow been spirited away by some extraterrestrial force. He was on his way to Ecnalubma.

"Bloody hell!" Lesley said, sitting back down at the kitchen table. "There's never a dull moment in this house recently."

"I know," Sam agreed.

She sighed. Her father had looked in a pretty bad way when the paramedics arrived. She had watched them help him onto the stretcher and then gently carry him down the stairs and through the lounge. She had insisted that her mother accompany him to the hospital. Sam's story could wait until another time. She had watched as the doors of the ambulance had slammed shut with her parents stowed inside. Then the siren began its screeching monotonous wail and the vehicle pulled away from the house and quickly off to the end of the street.

"So, what happened then last night?" Lesley asked eagerly.

Sam shrugged, "Oh, you know, we had a bit of trouble."

"Trouble, eh?" coaxed Lesley, desperate to be brought up to date with any gossip which the previous night's alcohol intake may have caused her to forget.

Sam didn't respond and just stared into the distance.

"You alright, Sam, love? What's the matter?"

"Oh, nothing," Sam said distantly. She didn't like the hospital. She didn't like the thought of one of her family members in the back of an ambulance. She didn't like the idea that her father wasn't at home. Safe. She knew what happened when people in *her* family were taken to hospital. Tears welled in her eyes.

"Sam? Sam, what's up love?"

Sam stood and made her way to the kettle, discreetly wiping

her eyes as she did so. "Another coffee, Auntie Lesley?"

"Er, yeah, alright I will. Are you okay, Sam?"

Sam didn't want Lesley to see the tears that had escaped her eyes and were making their way down her cheek. "I'm fine," she said, trying her hardest to block the frog in her throat and sound like herself. She remained where she was, facing the kitchen cupboards, busying herself by moving jars and tins around as if looking for something.

"Well, good morning, Miss Lazy Bones!"

Mollie lolled against the door frame to the kitchen, as if deciding whether to fully enter the room or not. She smiled, unconvinced, at Auntie Lesley through her thumb which was pushed deeply inside her mouth.

"And still in your party dress as well," continued Lesley, unperturbed. "The walk of shame, eh, Sam?"

"Morning sweetheart," said Sam, composing herself. "I'm just going to the loo."

Sam strode past Mollie to the stairs. "Get our Mollie some milk," she shouted on her way up.

"Will do," called Lesley behind her. "Come on you," she said to Mollie, opening her arms for a cuddle. Mollie unenthusiastically stepped forwards.

Sam locked the bathroom door behind her and pulled down the toilet seat. Sitting down, she allowed the tears to flow. She was in no doubt that her dad would be fine, but something deep inside her had opened up and that something was forcing out tears that she had held in for perhaps too long.

The panic which eclipsed George's thoughts for a matter of moments was broken swiftly when he heard another sound coming from his right-hand side. Just audible above the nee-naw coming from above he heard a voice which appeared to be whispering his name. Up until that moment, he had not looked over to his right. The pain from the brutal alien "ear experiment" had made it uncomfortable and for now he had enough to consider with the riddles which had been presented from looking to his left and straight ahead.

"George," the voice said.

He slowly turned to the right and was shocked to see a female human-like face just a few feet from his.

"George," the human whispered, "are you okay?"

He closed his eyes tightly – to blink away any trick his mind might be playing – and reopened them. The human face rapidly came back into focus.

"George, it's me. Are you okay?"

He vaguely recognised the face but couldn't quite place it. He continued to stare blankly.

"Do you think he can hear me?" the human said, turning to its right.

It was then that George noticed another human in the white craft. This one appeared to be the surgeon. He was dressed all in white and sat on a black bench alongside the one that was speaking to him.

"I'm not sure, love. His ear's taken a pretty nasty injury there. He's probably in a bit of shock as well. We'll get him checked out any second now."

"Oh dear," said the female, returning her eyes to George.

"You'll be alright, George" she promised, stroking what was left of his hair.

George stared again at the face. She looked very much like the person who had been with him in his bedroom earlier that day.

Suddenly, the craft came to an abrupt halt and the male human leapt to his feet. He pushed the end of the box open and bright sunlight poured through, causing George to close his eyes once again. Then, without any warning, his bed slid out of the craft and down onto the surface below. The female followed behind him. George didn't notice this; he kept his eyes closed, afraid of what may happen next.

Sam had composed herself and returned to the kitchen to prepare Mollie's breakfast. Lesley was on her hands and knees picking up Coco Pops from the stone floor. Mollie was already tucking into a bowl at the table, her upper lip displaying an impressive chocolate-coloured milk moustache.

"I won't ask…" said Sam.

"Auntie Lesley knocked the box off!" Mollie shouted excitedly.

"I can see that," replied Sam.

"Bloody Coco Pops everywhere," said Lesley, looking up from the floor. She was beginning to feel slightly queasy. The previous night was obviously catching up on her.

Mollie's spoon clattered down as she jumped up from the table. "She knocked the whole box on the floor, Mum," she repeated, skipping excitedly.

"Okay, Mollie, sit down. Finish your breakfast." Sam wasn't in the mood for this type of excitement right now (not that she was particularly at any other time).

"All of them," Mollie continued, "she just knocked the box and it fell off…"

"Finish your breakfast…"

"… and it was on its side…" Mollie danced from side to side, recounting the hilarious tale.

"Mollie!"

Lesley continued to retrieve the Coco Pops, for the first time that morning concluding that the Hoover may be an easier option.

"… and they were all pouring…"

"MOLLIE! For God's sake. Sit down and…"

It was at that point that Mollie's excitable jig to her left coincided with Lesley adjusting herself forwards to get at some Coco Pops which were particularly difficult to reach. Mollie's left knee caught Lesley squarely in the face and Mollie flew forwards towards the work top. Desperately trying to remain upright, Mollie's natural reaction was to grab the first thing she could. This turned out to be a polythene bag which until then lay undiscovered on the worktop. Giving no resistance, Mollie, simultaneously followed by the distinctly unhelpful polythene bag, fell backwards. Fortunately, Lesley was there to break her fall. The bag continued a little further across the room and a shattering sound was heard as it made contact with the stone floor.

There was a lot of commotion in the place where George's moving bed had come to rest. George had seen human after human pass by him. He noticed some were bleeding, some were shouting, others wore uniforms. He wasn't at all sure what was going on or where he was. He wondered whether he had now arrived in Ecnalubma? It was certainly busy enough to be some kind of processing area for new arrivals. He decided that, for now, keeping quiet was perhaps the best option. He couldn't help notice that the female human he had seen earlier in the bedroom and had recognised in the white craft was still following him everywhere.

"How are you feeling, George?"

He still wasn't quite sure how she knew his name.

"You'll be just fine soon, don't worry."

George smiled politely. Until he got his bearings, he certainly didn't want to ruffle any feathers.

"Aargh!" screamed Sam.

Mollie and Lesley both looked up from their position on the floor. The scream had sounded bloodcurdlingly real and both were shocked at the volume. Sam pointed towards the bag. It appeared that some kind of small creature was trying to escape and had become caught in the handles. All three eyed the creature.

"What is it?" asked Sam.

"I don't know, love," said Lesley, edging away from the bag into a sitting position against the kitchen cupboards. Mollie hung onto her like a baby koala.

The three continued to watch the static creature.

"It doesn't seem to be moving much, Sam," said Auntie Lesley.

"Do you think it's dead?"

"I don't know."

"What is it?"

"I don't know. Looks like a racoon or a possum, or something."

Mollie laughed. "They don't have possums in England, Auntie Lesley," she giggled. "It was on TV; they live in Australia!"

"Well, I don't care," snapped Lesley, "I'm not going near it."

"I'll have a look at it," said Mollie.

(At this stage Sam, as a mother, should perhaps have warned her young daughter against going near the mysterious creature, but she was curious to know what it was and was too nervous to find out herself.)

"Okay then, Mollie," Sam encouraged, "but be careful."

Mollie gingerly crept across the floor and prodded the creature with her finger. Sam jumped back in expected mock shock. Nothing happened. Mollie got a little closer and poked again, this time harder. Again there was no response from the creature.

"Mollie, be careful, sweetheart," echoed Auntie Lesley, who had now managed to strategically slide up the kitchen cupboards and get fully to her feet. (If the creature lurched at her she could now rely on both hand and foot combat.)

Mollie crept closer, then put both hands on the creature and held it aloft. Both Sam and Lesley screamed simultaneously.

"What the..."

"It's a bloody wig," said Sam through the fingers of her hand which was spread openly across her eyes.

Mollie giggled before throwing the wig down onto the stone floor.

"Bloody hell!" said Lesley, breathing a lengthy sigh of relief before laughing.

"Jesus Christ Almighty," said Sam.

"God, I was so scared then," said Lesley, continuing the theme of religious expletives.

Mollie continued peering into the bag. There was something else in there. Something black. And whatever it was seemed to be in a number of pieces.

Since arriving at Ecnalubma, George had decided not to utter a word. There was so much activity and it seemed that the female human had strict orders to chaperone him wherever he went. After less than twenty minutes, his bed had once again been wheeled to a different place. In this location, a dark-skinned bald male (again dressed all in white) had arrived, drawing a light green curtain around the bed as he entered. The female human then began to answer numerous questions about George's past. She knew his full name, his age, his previous medical conditions, even the name of his doctor (on earth). It was incredible. George concluded that she had obviously been studying him as a potential abductee for some time. What was most confusing was why he, out of all the humans on earth, had been selected. Whilst the female human continued to answer questions, George surreptitiously reached his arm out from under his blanket to touch his right ear again. It was now beginning to hurt.

"Er, Mr Poppleton, I don't think that's a good idea," the bald human said.

George jumped. He was about to say that he didn't think it was a good idea to carry out an unrequested ear probe on him, but thought better of it. He had no idea to what lengths these people would go should he upset them.

"Is it hurting you, Mr Poppleton?"

No answer.

"Mr Poppleton, is your ear hurting you?"

George couldn't decide how to respond. He didn't want to show weakness to his abductors, but then, in truth, it was hurting. He groaned softly.

"Oh, George," said Sheila.

"I'll get him some painkillers," said the nurse helpfully.

Mollie turned away from the bag and faced Sam. She grinned. She had found something. For extra importance, she knelt up to make herself taller. In her right hand she held a small black box which was connected by a wire to some orange headphones in her left hand.

"It's grandpa's radio," she beamed.

She put the radio down on the floor and using both her hands she untangled the earphones. The chrome bracket which joined the two orange sponge-clad speakers had become slightly twisted in the fall from the worktop. Mollie corrected them as much as she could before placing them on her head.

"Just like grandpa!" she exclaimed.

It wasn't quite. One orange headphone covered her left ear, the other her right eye. Sam and Lesley laughed.

"Can I have some music on?" said Mollie.

"Why not?" replied Sam, still laughing. She approached Mollie and bent down to the floor, picking up the radio for the first time.

Up until this point her father had guarded his prized possession twenty-four hours a day. There had been times when her mother had become so exasperated with his endless listening that she had confided in Sam her dreams of confiscating the radio and disposing of it. But during his waking hours, George always seemed to have it on his person, and whilst he slept it was squirreled away somewhere she couldn't find it. Sam noticed that there was a cracked space where the dial to switch on the radio had previously been. She reached into the polythene bag with her left hand and located the dial, along with a bowtie and another oblong piece of broken plastic. This must have come from the radio as well. She turned over the radio and found the space where the oblong piece would fit. It was the battery compartment. Looking more closely, she noticed that both inside and surrounding the outside of the battery compartment was a burnt orange-coloured stain. The same stain covered one side of the oblong piece as well.

"Bloody hell!" she exclaimed.

"What?" said Lesley.

"These bloody batteries. They're ancient."

"Let's have a look."

Lesley moved away from the kitchen cupboards towards Sam. She peered at the radio from above where Sam knelt. It was true, the batteries were ancient. Such was the corrosion that it wasn't even possible to make out the manufacturer of the batteries. All they could see were two rust-coloured cylinders which had quite obviously not served as batteries for well over a decade.

Lesley looked at Sam. "Jesus Christ," she said.

Sam, suddenly realising what her discovery meant, looked up at Lesley. Her mouth fell open.

"Can I listen to some music, then?" asked Mollie.

No one spoke.

"Can I? Pleeaaasssse," Mollie begged.

"Er, no sweetheart," said Sam, stunned. "It's, er, broken."

"I'm afraid he's going to need an operation."

Sheila looked down at George who lay on his bed still wrapped in the green blanket. His eyes remained tightly shut.

"You're going to have to stay in, George; they'll have to operate."

George could hear the words but again chose not to respond. It was all too confusing. And furthermore, the injection which the bald man had administered moments earlier had made him feel extremely light-headed.

"Will he be alright?" asked Sheila.

"He'll be just fine," said the nurse comfortingly. "Just a short operation to remove it and then we can see whether he's done any long-term damage to his hearing."

"Okay."

"We'll operate as soon as we can and keep him overnight. He should be home later tomorrow."

The nurse arranged for George to be taken up to a ward and Sheila rose to leave for home. She would return later with some essentials for his overnight stay. She kissed his forehead lightly.

"I won't be long, George."

Again, George didn't respond. He was now beginning to feel extremely drowsy.

"Well, he's going to be okay," announced Sheila loudly as she slammed the front door behind her. "They're keeping him in overnight, but…"

She had reached the kitchen.

"… they say he'll…"

Her voice trailed off.

It was quiet in the kitchen. Eerily quiet. Sam, Lesley and Mollie were sitting at the kitchen table. Sam smiled awkwardly as Sheila entered the room. Mollie didn't look up from her colouring; she was still upset about the radio. To make herself feel better, she was finalising a drawing of what appeared to be a fox nailed to a tree.

"What's the matter?" said Sheila, instantly noticing the atmosphere.

"Mum…" said Sam.

"He'll be alright, you know, a short operation, that's all…"

"Mum," Sam interrupted sharply.

Sheila immediately stopped talking. She could see that Sam was holding up George's radio. She reached forwards and took the radio from her. At last she could destroy it.

"Look at the batteries in the back, Mum," Sam instructed.

Sheila followed her daughter's order and turned the radio around. Her mouth dropped open.

"It's never worked, Mum, it's never worked."

Sheila suddenly felt unsteady and sat heavily on the chair next to Lesley.

"I think I'm going to need a glass of wine," she said.

The room that George shared was mostly light greys and whites. In it he could see five other beds. Three on one side, three on the other. The ends of the beds met a small aisle, which ran down the middle of the room. All but one of the beds were occupied. Some of the beds had strange machines clicking and whirring alongside them. George couldn't quite make out the faces of the other residents so he was unsure whether they were human or not. From time to time, a human dressed in white would approach a bed for a short while, making notes, asking questions, fiddling with the machines. Then they would leave though the doors at the far end of the room. George stared straight ahead. He had absolutely no idea where he was. He had absolutely no idea how long he had been there. He had absolutely no recollection of how he had got there. All he did know was that the protrusion was missing from his ear.

Suddenly, the double doors at the end of the long room burst open, which startled him. Looking down the room past the other beds, he could vaguely make out a small human running towards him. He shielded his face as the human got closer.

"Grandpa!" it shouted as it threw itself onto his stomach.

He pulled his knees up towards his chest to protect himself.

"Grandpa!" it said again.

He didn't recognise it or the noise that it made.

In the distance, he could see another human coming towards him. This one walked more directly with firm, measured steps. He recognised this one. This was the one who had kindly chaperoned him earlier that day. But something was different now. The face that had smiled earlier was now twisted and contorted. It looked extremely angry.

Its slow strides continued, getting ever closer to him. When it was within a few feet, it lifted its right hand, holding aloft a small black box.

Overcome by sheer terror, George pulled the green blanket over his head, squeezing his eyes shut.

He hoped that, soon, all this would stop.

About the Author

M. Jonathan Lee was born 1974. He lives and works in Yorkshire, England and has three children.

The Radio was shortlisted for The Novel Prize 2012 and is his first novel.

www.jonathanleeauthor.com